FACT

In 2003 a collection of manuscripts, written by Sir Isaac Newton—predicting that the end of the world would commence in the year 2060—was discovered in a library in Jerusalem.

FICTION

Ever since witnessing an avalanche devour his parents at age twelve, Michael DiBianco has had an odd obsession with the divine. Today, a renowned physicist, Harvard Divinity professor, and bestselling author of *The Newton Theories* and *The Book*, DiBianco has devoted his life to uncovering the secrets of the Bible.

A prophetic collection of Newton papers have been stolen from a library in Jerusalem. DiBianco is escorted from his classroom and questioned by the FBI. He's shown a fistful of Polaroids displaying several assassinations along with several unclear xeroxes of mysterious clues left behind on the bodies... Newton Papers.

An earth shattering explosion, nearly leveling Harvard Divinity school, propels Michael DiBianco on a perilous mission to clear his name; a quest that swiftly escalates into a life and death race to save the world from a terrorist plot over fifty years in the making.

THE NEWTON
PROPHECIES

The Newton Prophecies

Published by TopShelf Publishing
Imprint of TopShelf Indie Authors & Books, LLC

Book design by Keith Katsikas
Cover design by Keith Katsikas
Cover Photography by Creative Commons
Book set in 12 pt Garamond

Trade Paperback Revised 2nd Edition © 2016

ISBN: 0-9817619-5-X
ISBN 13: 978-0-9817619-5-4

www.KeithKatsikas.com
www.TopShelfPub.com

Retailers my order additional copies from:

Baker & Taylor
Ingram

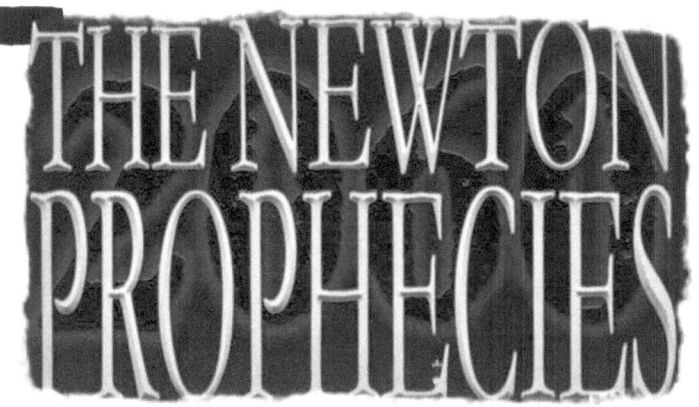

KEITH KATSIKAS

www.KeithKatsikas.com
www.TopShelfPub.com

For my wife,
who never leaves
no matter how many
threats fling my way.

I Love You!

ACKNOWLEDGEMENTS

There are so many people who have inspired me, taught me, and who have kept me writing, even when I was determined to stop. First and foremost, my wife, Rebecca, who hates to love my passion; my uncle Donald, who has been excited about this story since its conception and whose help has benefitted me in ways he may never fully understand; my dear friend, Andrew, who has read every version of this story since day one and who has never let me stop until it was done; God, for giving me this wonderful talent; and last but not least, Isaac Newton, for inspiring this really fun story.

Thank You.

PROLOGUE

In a church slated for demolition three months prior, Father Driscoll prepared to unveil the darkest secret he had ever known. Media from all over New England—gathered in by the renegade priest—infested the cathedral like cockroaches. They had been told to expect the story of the millennium and were ready for it, or so they thought.

The sun's rays beamed through the many rows of stained glass—scenes of the Lord's birth, ministry, and death—casting a warm, yet haunting array of color over the congregation. The aroma of incense filled the cathedral. Father Driscoll, in full robe, held a chalice to the heavens, mumbling, his heart in profound prayer. The congregation bowed as he lowered the cup and drank from it.

Lurking in the bowels of one of the oldest churches in North America, unseen by the worshipers and the growing masses of blood thirsty media, a lone dark figure shifted through the blackness toward the bustling chapel.

The congregation rose in song, dressed in their Sunday best, hymnals tight against their breasts. To the media they were like spirits; their voices like angels singing to their God. The cathedral ran thick with the spirit of the Lord.

Father Driscoll watched his faithful sing while the media readied their equipment. The events that would soon transpire played through his mind like a late night horror show. It was not a secret he could simply sweep under the rug like so many before. This was too dire; and was happening right before his very eyes; not just some rumor floating about cyberspace, no, his brother had unwittingly confessed to that.

He had no choice but to stop it.

Something struck the back of his neck. It stung for a moment, then went numb. His hands instinctively rose to feel what it was. A warm liquid spilled across his fingers. His knees grew weak. Dizziness. The room spun.

Then darkness.

No one noticed Father Driscoll fall, but when the singing ceased and the congregation lowered back into their pews it became clear. Something was wrong.

"My God!" a voice fired from the altar.

The media hustled toward the priest, cameras in hand, tapes running, microphones listening, flashbulbs sparking.

Members of the congregation were shoved aside. Some got close enough to see, most fell to their knees and cried.

The priest lay face down on the altar floor, a pool of blood haloing his head. A long black dart protruded from the back of his swollen neck, as his body lay lifeless.

"He's dead!" a man shouted.

As the congregation grew hysterical, a woman dressed in black pulled a piece of paper from the priest's robe. Brittle, yellow, it crumpled slightly in her fingers.

"What is this?" she cried.

Every camera focused on the tiny piece of parchment; most of it had been blacked out with what appeared to be magic-marker; the writing that remained was hardly legible— very old. It would become the first of many clues in a murderous case the media would dub, *The Newton Prophecies*.

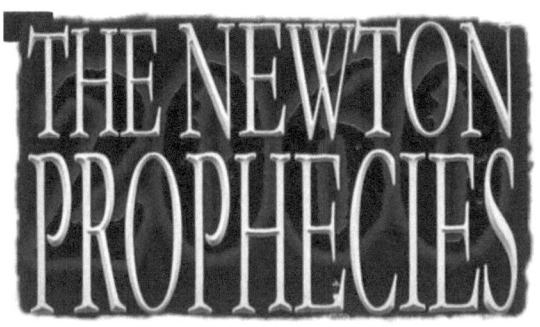

PART ONE

THE NEWTON PAPERS

1

"What's the difference between the end of the world and the date Isaac Newton predicted?" Michael DiBianco had a strong chin and raised it slightly when he spoke. It wasn't arrogance so much as confidence, confidence in what he said, and in what he knew. "It is a reasonable question—"

DiBianco spread his hands in front of him and paced circles around the mahogany conference table. His was a small class, one of the smallest at Divinity. Only those elite few, having shown unique interest in scientific divinity, ever came to know DiBianco in such an intimate setting. "—and a simple one, when you allow your mind to open the way Newton's did."

Caressing the stubble on his chin, DiBianco gazed out a tall window into a spacious courtyard. Divinity was an amazing place. A world far removed—spiritually and mentally—from Harvard, the main university, though physically, mere blocks separated them.

The sun shown with a brilliance the week prior had missed, and for a moment DiBianco imagined himself sprawled amidst the freshly trimmed grasses, gazing up at the countless mammals, birds, insects, and organisms woven into the very brick of the structures surrounding him; the craftsmanship was absolutely amazing, *stunning* actually. The warmth of the sun penetrated his skin, filling his soul with renewed strength and wisdom.

Part of him wasn't sure if he should be sharing what he was about to map out with his class; the other—the part grounded in the world of science and reason—was positive;

this was the best place to start.

His latest book, *God Science,* was days from landing on the cluttered desks of his scientific peers, who were always eager to slam his hypotheses and theories into oblivion. He longed to test his latest batch—before the entire world had their say—on those closest and dearest.

His students.

"He wasn't predicting the end," a female voice pierced from behind.

DiBianco spun on his heals at the wise voice. "*Yes,*" he declared. "That's precisely right." DiBianco looked upon his student with impressed eyes.

She was an attractive woman, fairly new to his class; young too, couldn't have been older than nineteen. Her crystal blue eyes beamed with purity—nearly made his heart flutter. He imagined it was for that very reason her parents had named her Crystal.

Such a wonderful name.

"Isaac Newton was not predicting the end..." DiBianco unlocked his gaze from hers and glanced about the class. "He was predicting the beginning."

"I don't understand," a young man said, his eyes deeply inquisitive. "How... Why?" His eyes narrowed. "We're already here, Professor."

"Fair enough." DiBianco's arms crossed at his chest. He circled the class with his index finger. "I bet you all, to some degree, have similar thoughts. Lord knows I did."

"You're losing us, Professor," another woman said.

"Don't think of it in terms of beginning and end. God is eternal. Remember. In Heaven there is no beginning or end." DiBianco clamped his hands together like he was about to pray, spun them inward and stretched them out in front of him. A long, loud series of crackles reverberated through the small space, sending shivers through his students.

He continued undaunted. "In 2003 it was made public that Sir Isaac Newton had predicted that the year 2060 would bring about the end of the world. That message was not only unfair, but untrue, and has since touched nearly everybody in earshot of the world's media. It astonishes me that Dan Brown hasn't written a book about it.

"But I digress. The point to be made is that—as usual—the media is wrong. Newton was a profound thinker, a spiritual man whose beliefs in the divine differed from that of the great and powerful church; beliefs he knew would have driven The Church to imprison him, possibly until death."

DiBianco noticed his students perk up at the word. Death. It was an intriguing subject.

"Isaac Newton studied the verses of *Daniel* immensely. Knowing the Hebrew language and having impeccable skills in the art of translation, Newton translated the book from its original writings. In fact, for over fifty years he pondered the Bible's many hidden messages and secrets—"

"Secrets?" Crystal's blue eyes lit ablaze.

"Absolutely." DiBianco's excitement over the subject was impossible to misinterpret. He was fanatical. "The Bible flows with hidden secrets; messages, codes, clues; answers to questions we haven't even begun to *think* about."

"Come on, Crystal," a young man injected, "everyone's heard of *The Bible Code*." The boy's tone was excessively sarcastic. "Have you been living under a rock?"

"That's enough," DiBianco said with a slight chuckle. "Isaac Newton knew secrets existed—not *The Bible Code, real* hidden messages. He studied the Bible in great depth over the course of his life, hand writing thousands of pages, journalizing his findings."

"What exactly *did* he find, Professor?"

"Patience. I intend to explain." DiBianco strode toward the end of the table, grabbed a large leather Bible and flipped through the gold-leafed pages to a section marked by ribbon placeholders. "As many of you know—hopefully by listening to my lessons on the factual matters behind the lure, though likely through Brown's fictional ranting—Isaac Newton is believed by many to have been one of the *Prieuré de Sion's most grandeur masters,*" he said in his best French accent.

It wasn't difficult to spot the sudden mystification flood his student's gazes. They were a brilliant bunch, and DiBianco knew it; yet somehow his words often got lost in his philosophical tangents. "The Priory of Sion," he explained. All at once, looks of recognition fluttered off their youthful façades like spring rain.

"I thought the Priory has been proven a hoax?" a young woman said.

"That's precisely what they want you to believe, my dear." DiBianco fingered through a few more pages, looking for the right place to start. "Do you really believe that if the Priory of Sion was a real organization, they would allow some *fictional scribe* to expose their most dire secrets?"

"I suppose not," she replied, somewhat sheepishly.

"It was Newton's pure brilliance in science, combined with a nearly inconceivable connection with the Church's most heavily guarded secrets, that compelled me to finish my latest book." Somewhere midway through the latter-half of the sixteen-hundred page volume, DiBianco planted his finger on the page and read.

"How long shall it be to the end of these wonders?" DiBianco glanced at the twelve youthful souls hovering about the conference table, their faces impressed by his every word. "Who can explain the *'Wonders'* referred to in this passage?"

The room was silent.

"Come on," he said in a serious, yet somewhat playful tone, "we discussed this *just* last week."

"The apostasy?" a young woman said, uncertain.

"That fairly well sums it up," he said. "*Daniel* is such a short book, one of the shortest in the Bible, and yet it encapsulates so many amazing and powerful—"

"I don't believe it," a young man interrupted. Sam was a good kid, a little rough around the edges, but good. DiBianco liked the challenges he often represented.

"Believe what, Sam?" said DiBianco.

"How can we be expected to believe half the stuff in here?" Sam said, waving his pocket Bible in the air.

DiBianco wasn't sure what to say.

Sam gazed at DiBianco with a raw blend of intrigue and doubt. "Don't get me wrong, Professor, I love Christ, God, my Church, but I think we all know how much Constantine screwed things up when he gathered the first council of Nicaea in the year 325; you know, to recreate God's Church to meet his own selfish needs..."

DiBianco cringed. This was where things could get ugly. His class was different from the rest at Divinity—DiBianco often got away with teaching things the rest of the school wouldn't dream of—yet, he was still just a professor at a school of divinity; a school—though officially nonsectarian—run primarily by deeply rooted Christians. He and the Dean were close. She wouldn't stand for half the stuff he believed in, and would likely despise him had she a clue. He could *not* allow this to go much farther.

"...There are countless books missing from the Bible," Sam continued, "and the books that *are* here have been doctored by the early Church, and by Constantine, himself."

"That's where you're mistaken," DiBianco declared, sensing a way out of the mess. "The Church did not doctor scripture to conform to their needs, nor to the needs of the empire." DiBianco paused. He knew what he was about to say next would cause a firestorm of controversy. But this was his controversy; controversy only he could get away with. It was classic DiBianco. A strategy he enjoyed and employed often. No other Divinity Professor could stimulate the attention of young souls like Michael DiBianco.

"The gospel authors themselves—even Matthew, Mark, Luke, and John—doctored their *own* accounts of Jesus's life in an attempt to conceal the greatest secret ever known to man."

2

Senator Roberto Rodriguez should have been grinning ear to ear, he had won what had been deemed an unwinnable battle and was now coasting into his forth month as the junior senator of the great Commonwealth of Massachusetts. But instead, fear and panic filled his veins.

Rodriguez stood upon a podium constructed just outside the Massachusetts State House, in the Beacon Hill district of Boston—mounds of snow cluttered the cityscape, evidence of the record snowfalls from months prior—his face now flooded with flashbulbs, floodlights, and the searing heat of a midday sun. The media had been swarming since early morning; now, all eyes were on him.

Rodriguez had slaved away two years of his life, campaigning against the Massachusetts senior senator. Most called him crazy for trying; but he was an honest family man and had worked his tail to the bone, spreading the word about his belief in Deity and in the strength of *true* family values. Roberto Rodriguez knew, if anyone could beat the odds, it would be him; and much to everyone's surprise, he had dethroned a political icon.

Soon he would speak to the media.

This was a very unexpected event.

The media—not just from Massachusetts, but New Hampshire, Maine, Connecticut, Rhode Island, Vermont, even New York—were called in. They had been told to expect an announcement so grand, it would assure front page coverage for as far as their media tentacles could reach.

They couldn't imagine what the recently elected senator

could have to say. What could possibly be so important as to call such an unexpected press conference? Rumors spread with haste. Everything from, *he's going to step down,* to *he lied about Kennedy's affair,* to *he has a gay lover who he intends to marry at Boston's Trinity Church.* It's amazing the rumors that surface the moment the actions of a conservative come into question.

But what Senator Rodriguez was about to tell the world would truly send the media into a frenzy, and would likely get him killed. Yet he had no choice. It was not a secret he could simply hide away; shove off into the dark recesses of his confused mind. The unthinkable was happening; and the people needed to know—they *must* know.

Every eye, every camera, was plastered on the senator. Without a single word said, this was proving to be headline material. Every television network, every radio station, and every newspaper within two-hundred miles were present.

Senator Rodriguez faced the crowd; his hands extended wide; his wife, sixteen-year-old daughter, and twelve-year-old twin boys crowded in around him. Everyone had been so comfortable with the decision to make *him* their voice. But the unorthodox nature of this event had suddenly peaked everyone's uncertainty.

Through the thick of heads, hands, and colorful banners, raised a single silver microphone.

Without hesitation the senator grabbed hold.

SNAP!

SIZZLE!

An arc of light ripped through the sky like a blade of lightening, carving deep into the crowd; it was a miracle no one was struck. The reek of burning flesh filled the air; followed by a high pitch squeal—the type air makes as it speeds through the stem of an over-inflated balloon.

Screams fired from the podium—a woman, crying for the life of her husband.

Few in the crowd could see what was happening, just those standing in the front rows, who instantly broke into sobs. They had just witnessed Senator Rodriguez virtually disintegrate before their eyes. A few began to vomit, others tried to run but were held back by the crowd.

With a thud Senator Rodriguez fell to the podium floor. His wife reeled in horror, tears gushing from her mascara smeared eyes. She crouched down beside her husband and retrieved a half-charred piece of paper. Lifting it into the bright camera lights she unfurled it for the world to see.

"What the hell's going on?" she cried.

Rodriguez had been right; the media went crazy.

It was yet another Newton Paper.

3

"But please," DiBianco said, "let us return attention to our friend, Isaac Newton."

"Professor, *really*," Crystal cried, "you cannot leave us hanging like that ... that's just, well, *evil!*"

"I know," he said with a smirk. "Don't fret, I'll not leave you hanging for *very* long."

DiBianco found his place in his Bible and continued. "*Daniel 12, verse 6* quotes a question voiced by a man who stood on the bank of a river within Daniel's vision. That man spoke to the Lord—also in the vision—asking, *How long shall it be to the end of these wonders?* And the Lord, who stood upon the surface of the river, rose his hands to the heavens and spoke, swearing by the Almighty who liveth forever, that *it shall be for a time, times, and a half of time.*

"What does *that* mean?" DiBianco asked the class. "*A time, times, and a half of time?*" But they remained speechless. Not even a whisper could be heard. The tiny lightbulbs DiBianco often imagined hovering above their heads while pondering topics of the day, suddenly dimmed...

"No one?" he asked again.

...then flickered out completely.

"Well," DiBianco said, slamming the massive Bible shut, "Newton believed he had discovered the answer."

"How could he?" A young man said. "The phrase clearly makes no sense."

"Newton's genius went far beyond science. His Biblical research shows compelling evidences contrary to mainstream belief; a few of his findings were so profound, that some religious sects might even kill to avoid awareness of them."

Crystal gazed at DiBianco, her eyes beaming, her youthful rose-like visage perplexed. "How can you know this?" Her voice was confident.

"Sorry?"

"If The Church would *kill* to keep these things secret, then how could anyone possibly know? The Church is very—"

"First off," he interrupted, shaken by the direction of the question. "I never said *The Church*, which most of us would concur is referring to the Roman Catholic Church. I said, *some* sects might kill to avoid awareness.

"Honestly, the majority of Newton's work only serves to support claims of divine intervention. Newton believed that science and God could not be separated; he believed the more we learn about science, the closer we become to God.

"In these last few years, since the media announced Newton's prediction of the end of days, a floodlight has been shed on him—not the scientist, but the man, and the spirit driving him. I've always been, shall I say, a bit of a fan—"

The class chuckled. They knew when it came to Isaac Newton, Professor DiBianco was on the brink of obsession.

"When I first heard about the writings he had scribbled on the topic of God, and his lifelong studies of the Bible, I became intrigued.

"I had just begun work on *God Science* and the prospect

of Isaac Newton predicting the end of days was simply more than I could resist. It was an exciting time. I traveled to Jerusalem, to the *Jewish National and University Library* where they keep those particular Newton Papers..." He paused, savoring the memory. "It was wonderful."

"Professor?"

"Oh my ... forgive me. There is so much to cover; so little time." DiBianco took a deep breath and retraced his thoughts. "Newton believed that he had figured out the actual..."

Just then the classroom door opened. Three individuals entered and stood politely just inside, allowing the door to close softly behind them.

"...date the end of days would begin." DiBianco placed the Bible on the conference table, grabbed a piece of chalk from the tray and wrote, large and wide on the blackboard.

He recognized two of the people standing by the door and winked: Sheila MacDougle, the Dean of Divinity; and longtime acquaintance, agent Camillin, from the FBI's Boston Field Office.

DiBianco had worked with Agent Camillin a few years back on a case involving an exhibit of historical paintings that had mysteriously disappeared from the Boston Museum of Fine Arts. It turned out to be an inside job.

DiBianco fought a nauseating contortion in his stomach. He would have much rather been thinking, *how wonderful it is to see you again, old friend,* but one look at the dark-skinned, foreigner—tall, wide, shaped like a brick—glaring at what he had just written on the blackboard, had any feelings of peace fluttering off with sudden butterflies.

"It would seem we have visitors." DiBianco gave a nod to the Dean and dropped the chalk in the tray. "What can we do for our lovely Dean?"

MacDougle waved DiBianco over. She obviously had nothing she wished to say in front of the class.

DiBianco gazed at his students and pointed at the four simple numbers written on the blackboard.

"Think about how Newton came up with this date." He rubbed the chalk from his hands and started toward the door, "It's all right there, in *Daniel*."

DiBianco watched the eager faces on the two men blossom as he approached. They obviously had something pressing on their minds—something that suddenly had him fighting off a bout of anxiety. A panic attack now, would certainly be an embarrassment, not only for him, but the university. He had never had a panic attack at work before, and did not intend to have one now. He focused on the dean's eyes and said with a nervous smile, "So, how's the new Mustang?" But the Dean didn't answer.

A sense of urgency filled his bosom when she pushed open the door and hustled them into the hallway, closing the door tightly behind.

DiBianco extended a hand, forcing another smile. "To what do I owe the pleasure, gentlemen?"

Agent Camillin grabbed hold with a solid shake and a stern nod, then tapped the foreign man on the shoulder.

In a thick middle-eastern accent, the man said, "Agent Afridi." His grip was massive; his skin, callused and cold, like his strong, yet drawn face.

"This is a highly sensitive matter, Mike. I trust you'll understand." Camillin's look was very matter of fact.

"Okay," DiBianco said. "Lay it on me, chief."

"We can't discuss this here, my friend." Camillin placed his hand on DiBianco's shoulder. "Please, come with us."

DiBianco's knocked Camillin's hand away. "Have I done something wrong?"

"I don't know, Mike." Camillin shrugged. "Have you?"

"We need your help, Mr. DiBianco." Agent Afridi said. "It is vital you come with us."

DiBianco's gaze turned toward the Dean. Her eyes were understanding. Clearly they had already informed her of their plans.

"Go, Mike," she said. "We knew damn well what we were getting into when hiring you. Your expertise may interfere at times, but that's the price we pay for excellence."

DiBianco's chin lifted at the compliment and a wink and a smile returned the thanks. "What about my class?"

"Don't worry..." The Dean waved at someone behind him. "It's covered."

Before DiBianco had the chance to see whose echoing footsteps trotted up the hall, the soft flowering scent gave her away.

"Savanna Campbell." A wide grin filled his face as he turned to lay eyes upon his dear friend. A stunning woman, tall, slender, wavy black hair professionally trimmed just above the shoulders. Savanna was a very matter-of-fact woman, yet somehow she managed to send paralyzing chills down DiBianco's spine whenever she neared. She was the only woman able to deaden the painful memories of his wife's death, eight months earlier when her private jet crashed into a small mountainside just minutes after takeoff from the Caribbean Islands. "How was Paris?"

"Splendid, of course." Savanna's gaze brushed the agents and she smiled. "Hello Boys." The Agents nodded.

"Sure wish you had been there," she said, returning her gaze to DiBianco.

"You and me both."

"You wouldn't believe how many beautiful men there—"

"Just take good care of my kids, ya hear?"

Savanna laughed. "Have I ever steered you wrong?"

DiBianco shook his head and smiled.

"What's the topic?"

"Twenty-Sixty"

"I should have guessed."

4

Traffic on Cambridge Street was typical for a Monday morning. The polished black, government issue Expedition jetted across the Longfellow Bridge with zero regard for the law.

Eleven massive steel arches helped span this medieval looking structure across the Charles River, connecting Cambridge Massachusetts with its behemoth mother, Boston.

Two Red Line trains raced head to head across the bridge's center rails, on what appeared to be a catastrophic collision course, both nearly as long as the bridge itself.

"...but the papers are public," DiBianco said, looking perplexed. The stench of hazelnut coffee accosted his senses; DiBianco hated coffee, especially hazelnut. He gazed to his left at Afridi who sat straight up in the SUV's stiff leather seat, their thighs close enough to touch.

Afridi's eyes were fixated on something off in the distance; something over DiBianco's shoulder. DiBianco imagined it was the John Hancock Plaza; but whatever it was, awe is what he identified in the foreign man's eyes.

"The original manuscripts are not public," Afridi said, still gazing over DiBianco's shoulder.

"I was granted access—"

"You," Camillin interrupted, his voice spitting from DiBianco's other side, "are a renowned physicist, a famous author."

DiBianco had a hard time accepting the term, famous. He cringed every time he heard it and had been hearing it more and more often since the success of *The Newton Theories* and the announcement of his newest book, *God Science*. DiBianco despised famous people, wanted nothing—or very little—to do with them. *He* wrote because he *had* to. It was part of his essence. He could no less stop writing than he could stop his heart from beating, or willfully cease his lungs from taking in air.

"I'm not the only one," DiBianco said. "The BBC—"

"The BBC had inside help." Afridi's face was bold.

DiBianco's was perplexed. "Why would anyone want to steal those papers?" DiBianco had seen them first hand. Skilled at the art of translation, DiBianco had found that much of what Newton wrote was still very much a mystery, even to him. "The translations available online are far easier to read and comprehend."

"So why would you want them?" Camillin's gaze was ominous.

DiBianco knew there was a great deal of Newton's work not yet adapted for the online catalogue. Many of his papers were of little importance to the mainstream world, very low on *The Project's* priority list. To DiBianco, however, these writings were at the very core of Newton's work, they helped forge every thought he ever put to paper.

"DiBianco?" The voice was nearly lost in his thickening thoughts.

It was then that it occurred to him. He had just spent a half-hour preparing his class for the revelation of this very topic, only to be cutoff, just before the meat was to be served.

Some religious sects might kill to avoid awareness of the matter. The thought flooded his mind and struck a cord deep in the pit of his stomach. He didn't understand why, but he knew he was a suspect. And the only thing certain about the road ahead was that it was uncertain; and he would have to somehow solve this thickening mystery, and quickly, for he knew then, that his life depended on it.

"Money," DiBianco finally said. "Those papers must be worth a hefty price."

"I'm sure," Afridi agreed. His eyes shifted from DiBianco

to Camillin. "You have a nice city."

"First time in Boston?" Camillin asked.

"First time in America," he replied.

DiBianco turned his head away from Afridi, away from the stench of roasted garlic suddenly infiltrating the car. "I thought the FBI only worked in The States," DiBianco said.

Camillin's face reeled in disgust. "We have offices around the world," he declared, "handling everything from terrorism and drug trafficking, to contraband smuggling and murder ... even cyber crime." He lowered the window, allowing the scent of the Charles River and the greasy stench of train exhaust work into the cab. It was a welcoming scent. "It pisses me off how few people understand the magnitude of our work."

"So, where're you from?" DiBianco said, returning his gaze to Afridi.

"Jordan," he replied, coldly, "but I work out of the US Embassy in Tel Aviv." Afridi pointed ahead, toward four towers topping the central supports of the bridge. "Are those watchtowers?"

"Perhaps a hundred years ago," Camillin said, "when this baby was built, certainly not today."

"Interesting enough, many call this *The Salt-n-Pepper Bridge*," DiBianco inserted, attempting to dislodge the knot of fear in his throat. "The towers look a hell of a lot like salt and pepper shakers, don't you think?"

Camillin snickered. "I've always thought they look like medieval watchtowers myself—"

"Yes," Afridi agreed.

The blinding reflection of sunlight beaming off the Hancock Plaza's towering wall of reflective glass, flickered as the monumental *salt-n-pepper shakers* streaked by, one encapsulated in scaffolding and blue tarps—a long overdue cleaning.

Afridi's face was stern, like an ox. "Perhaps you need a new yacht, maybe a new sporty car, Mr. DiBianco?"

"Excuse me?" DiBianco glared at Camillin. "I don't like his tone. I'm not on trial."

"Calm down, Mike, nobody's accusing you of anything." Camillin's face was understanding, his tone, friendly. "As I said, this is a very sensitive matter for the Israeli government. Agent Afridi is here because I informed him that you were the man to talk to. We need your help, Mike."

"I'm not a detective, I'm a teacher, an author. What help could I possibly be?"

Afridi turned his head toward DiBianco, his eyes still focused on something in the distance, possibly still the Hancock Plaza; finally, their eye met. "You studied those papers. You have a book about to be published that puts a great deal of focus on them. You're the closest thing we have to an expert. You *must* help!" It was the first time Afridi's voice shown any sign of emotion.

Camillin looked lost. Almost uncertain of what to say. "Mike, I've never seen the original manuscripts. Few have."

"I don't believe that. They were available to me for Christ's sake, and there's certainly nothing special about Michael DiBianco of Cambridge Massachusetts.

"All I did was schedule some time, and for the most part just showed up at the Jewish National and University Library—I practically moved in for Christ's sake. That place became my home for three weeks."

"Come on." Camillin's tone was thick with sarcasm. "How many of *us* do you think can just visit Jerusalem for a month?"

"I don't know where you're going with this; I'm not a rich man." His face shown a real disliking for the sentiment. "I blew my entire savings on that trip and there's never any guarantee I'll make a dime back with book sales. The publisher's petty advance didn't even cover half of it."

Afridi smirked.

Not far ahead, blocks beyond the river's edge, nestled a cluster of large buildings, the heart of downtown; the financial district; the home of the Boston Stock Exchange; and the headquarters to many of the nation's most successful corporations: Fidelity Investments, Putnam, and Bank of America, to name a few. Not counting the booming local businesses: restaurants, hotels, and the countless hordes of bloodsucking lawyers who have perched their offices amongst the mayhem. However, therein also hid the home of Boston's field office for the Federal Bureau of Investigation.

Veering off Cambridge Street onto a small side road beside the Center Plaza, the SUV caught a curb and tossed DiBianco and the agents about the back of the vehicle.

Camillin's coffee leapt from its holder. In an attempt to catch the cup, Camillin instead caught a fistful of coffee. *"Son-of-a-bitch!"* It splashed onto the floor soaking Camillin and DiBianco's pant legs in steaming hot sludge.

Camillin kicked the empty cup—it landed under the driver's feet—and slammed his burning fist into the back of the seat.

DiBianco yanked off his shoes and socks and swiftly dried his ankles with his jacket sleeves.

The driver glanced over his shoulder, swerving erratically, his sunglasses nearly blacked out. DiBianco could sense the man's displeasure excrete from his every pore. As swiftly as he turned to gaze at the mayhem, the driver returned his attention to the road and yanked the wheel, barely avoiding an oncoming bus.

Afridi showed no emotion. His face, like a rock.

The SUV careened into the Center Plaza parking garage. Darkness flooded the cabin.

A tunnel? Not the entrance DiBianco was familiar with.

The driver hit a small button on the dash. A buzzer sounded and a yellow gate lifted. DiBianco's head whipped against the back of the seat as the SUV sped down a long ramp, spilling into a small lot.

The SUV squealed to a stop.

Camillin stormed out of the car huffing, swearing, kicking his soaked pant leg and shaking coffee from his fingers.

The smell of burnt tires combined with the stench of hazelnut coffee turned DiBianco's stomach. He quickly scurried out of the vehicle into the fresher air of the garage.

Afridi slammed the door and stormed toward DiBianco. His face was strong. Determined. "There is a much darker side to this investigation, Mr. DiBianco."

"Save it, Uluba." Camillin's eyes shot at Afridi like gunfire. "Not here."

DiBianco felt those butterflies again, fluttering even harder now, trying with fury to exit his stomach, instead lifting it toward his throat.

Afridi's body stiffened. His shoulders reeled back. It reminded DiBianco of a drill sergeant he had in boot-camp.

Afridi snapped his head from side to side, his chin sticking out in an ape-like grunt, sending pops into the air— painful snaps that made DiBianco cringe.

"Let's get inside," Camillin said, wiping his hands on his slacks. "*Goddamn it.* I gotta quit coffee."

5

"Move your goddamn asses!" DiBianco's father shouted.

They tucked in close to their knees and rode the monstrous wave of snow and ice down the mountainside. It roared like a mighty beast longing to devour them in one solemn gulp. The sound was deafening. The ground shifted and quaked.

Time seemed to stop and suddenly DiBianco felt something grab him from behind, pulling him to safety. Though he wasn't safe. Not even close. He watched his mother and father tumble head over foot through the raging avalanche; skis twirling through the air, poles spearing the sky like deadly javelins.

Ding.

The elevator doors opened. A rush of cool air flooded the small space and sent a chill up DiBianco's spine, breaking him of his sudden anxiety attack. He took in a deep breath, wiped his sweaty palms on his pants, and gazed at the brass letters spanning the wall in front of him.

FEDERAL BUREAU
of
INVESTIGATION

The feeling of panic slowly lifted as they entered the FBI lobby, but the sweating did not. Without a word the agents led DiBianco down a corridor, through a set of double doors—gold Department of Justice seals etched into the glass—bypassing security, and entered the heart of the bureau's offices.

DiBianco knew nothing good could possibly result of this. His heart raced. He tried to concentrate on what he knew about the Newton Papers, on the theories he had whipped up. Who was behind their disappearance?

"Hi Artie," an attractive, yet overly made-up brunette said, cruising past a large restaurant-style coffee maker, then veering off into a brightly lit room just beyond.

"Uluba. Room B. I'll be there in a moment."

Afridi guided DiBianco through an old steel door—an opaque window with a black "B" stuck at its center rattled as it opened—into a small room with a square table barely large enough for two, perhaps four, if they didn't mind kissing, and a huge pane of glass, a massive window overlooking Cambridge Street. "Have a seat, Mr. DiBianco."

But DiBianco didn't sit.

The room was bright. The immense heat beaming in from outside made the room more like a sauna. His hair grew wet, like he had just stepped out of a shower, however the stench in the room did nothing to reinforce that sensation.

Afridi stood by the door, legs parted slightly, arms crossed, gazing at DiBianco with eyes that screamed, *I know what you did and you're going to pay.*

DiBianco gazed down at the street: people walking, jogging, living their lives, eating their sandwiches, drinking their Cokes. He didn't know why, but watching them seemed surreal. He felt his life dangling in the balance. He knew, if he didn't figure out this mystery, and soon, he would likely never walk those streets again.

I've got to get out of here, he thought.

The door opened and Camillin entered with a large manilla folder. "Have a seat."

Afridi closed the door.

Camillin tossed several photographs on the table and DiBianco's eyes reeled in terror. Some of the world's most influential people: priests, scientists, historians, politicians— *Dead... Murdered!*

"What is this?" DiBianco cried. "Why, how could this not be flooding the news already?"

"It is, Mike," Camillin was calm, but DiBianco had little doubt, it would not remain so for long. "Only, until now we've been able to cover up the details. Mike, This is one of the most serious problems we've ever faced. Frankly, until we have some answers, we keep this from the public."

"That's crazy! How in the world hasn't the media figured this out? You cannot keep this secret forever!" DiBianco's eyes bugged. "Jesus! That's Senator MacDonald! How is it possible that the press hasn't realized their prized presidential candidate is MIA?"

"As you can see," Camillin started, his voice losing its patience. "We haven't much time. All eight of these assassinations have taken place in just the last hour. This is a very organized attack. News of it will surely be plastered across every major news network in a matter of minutes."

"Holy Christ!"

"There is more," Agent Afridi said, dropping several black and white photocopies on the table.

DiBianco's eyes lit ablaze. "Are those—"

"Indeed," Camillin said. "They are xeroxes of evidence left behind at each one of the crime scenes. Each victim had a different page hidden somewhere on them."

"Original pages?"

"They appear to be."

"What the hell's going on?"

"Why don't you tell us, Mr. DiBianco?"

DiBianco was silent. He gawked at the photocopies, trying to make sense of it, trying hard to make out Newton's writing. All but one small paragraph had been blacked out. It was like someone had taken a magic-marker and had crossed out every line of Newton's writing except for one small area ... *a clue.* "I can't read this." DiBianco looked at the agents. "I need the originals."

"I'm afraid you can't."

"Why? They're obviously clues."

The agents looked coldly at each other.

"What is it?"

Just then the attractive brunette who had spoken to Camillin upon their arrival, stormed the tiny interrogation room. "Artie!" she cried. Her breathing was heavy.

"Jesus Christ!" he said, startled. "What is it?"

"Harvard Divinity," she gasped. "There's been an explosion!"

6

Harvard Divinity was a war zone.

The entrance to Divinity Avenue was sealed off. Agent Camillin flashed his ID and was swiftly waved through.

An unholy blackness choked the muggy air; billowing clouds of soot and pulverized concrete made navigation through ground-zero arduous.

Fire trucks, rescue vehicles, police cruisers, the entire Cambridge force and many others from Boston, were on scene, franticly trying to make sense of the situation and help those who had fallen in one of the worst tragedies to have hit Cambridge Massachusetts in recent history.

Camillin pulled the SUV as close to Divinity Hall as possible, which wasn't very, and veered to the side of the road, yanked the hand-break, and leapt from the vehicle.

DiBianco gazed out the window at the remnants of his school. Where his class had once been, now gaped a massive hole—a crater the size of the volleyball court in the Divinity Courtyard, now in the side of Divinity Hall.

A sinking weight filled his stomach. His students. Savanna. *God, let them be okay.* But he knew they weren't. How could they be?

No flames were visible, yet two fire trucks had been propped in front of the hall, releasing a steady belt of water onto the crumbling roof and into the gaping bowels of the 182 year old historic structure.

People gathered about the complex, sprawled out on lawns, sitting on stone walls, everyone in shock. Many held wet towels to their mouths. Some received attention from EMTs and nurses.

Afridi opened the back door and yanked DiBianco from the SUV. Out of a thick black haze which hovered low in the pathway between Divinity Hall and the BIO-Center ran Dean Sheila MacDougle. Her face blackened with soot, bright pink circles enveloped her eyes, her hair clotted with gray powder and debris.

DiBianco could tell she'd been crying—and not long ago. But now she had her Dean face on and was storming the agents with fire in her soul.

"What is this *bullshit?*" Her veins popped from her neck like the cables of the Zakim Bridge.

The agents froze in place, instinctively resting their hands on the butt of their guns, unsnapping the straps on their holsters.

"I know you're upset," Camillin said, "but you must calm down. I assure you we're here to help."

"You show up at my school telling me my staff is involved in some international crime, less than two hours later my school blows up, and you're telling me you're here to help!"

"Mrs MacDoug—"

"You listen to me." Her voice lowered, eyes tearing. "Thirty-six of my students are dead. Many more, missing. I have mothers lining up, crying for me to help them find their children. What the hell is going on here?"

The agents looked at each other briefly, then back at the Dean. "We're sorry," Camillin said. "We don't have answers."

"But I feel your Professor may." Afridi's face was stone cold, like a serial killer.

"Michael?" she cried.

DiBianco's eyes shimmered, glossed over in tears they looked like oil slicks. His thoughts grew distant. Sure, he had theories, estranged clues; nothing real, nothing that made any sense, at least not yet. Who could have done this, and why?

"Michael!" she yelled, her eyes like poison darts ready to pierce the hearts of anyone involved. "Do you know what happened here?"

His face chilled. Goose-pimples brushed his entire body,

sending shivers down his spine. Suddenly, he knew.

"Someone's trying to kill me."

The Dean's eyes glossed over. She was crying. "Michael," she started, her voice cracking. "Your class. They..." She could barely speak. "They're gone."

DiBianco's stomach squelched. His heart ached—his entire body ached. Tears streamed his face, burning his cheeks, before tumbling off his quivering chin.

"Why would someone want you dead?" Camillin said.

Choking back tears, throat sore, DiBianco spoke softly, *"God Science."*

"What?" MacDougle cried.

DiBianco knew whoever did this had to have gotten an advance copy of his latest book, *God Science* and didn't much like what he had to say in it.

"Whoever did this," DiBianco cried, "knows what I know and wants me dead for it."

"What exactly do you know, Mr. DiBia—"

Just then, another explosion rocked Divinity Hall; a massive rumble rocked the earth; and with a deafening crash a cloud of debris cascaded over them.

Everyone scattered.

Within seconds DiBianco found himself running down a dark, cloud-filled alleyway.

He was alone.

Debris and soot cluttered his way.

Still he ran. Nothing was going to stop him.

7

A teacher at Divinity for nearly a decade, DiBianco knew every route in and out of the complex by heart. He hauled ass for the most obscure of them—a labyrinth of tiny, little known passageways used primarily by students.

He could feel the agents closing on him. He weaved in and out of the many alleyways and passages. His palms sweating. His breathing heavy. His pulse racing. He couldn't see them, but he knew they were there—right on his heals.

He ran as fast as he could, running from the agents, running from ground-zero, spilling out onto Francis Avenue.

DiBianco stood in the middle of the street, panting, his hands propped on bent knees. Everywhere he looked, police: setting up base, taping off the area surrounding Harvard Divinity School. He was surrounded.

8

MacDougle's brand new, jet-black Mustang convertible razzed DiBianco from the Dean's residence, almost directly across the street from where the police were setting base.

DiBianco looked for a place to duck out of sight.

A brown truck. *UPS.*

He looked inside.

No driver. Must be delivering a package.

He stepped inside, watching the police run lines of yellow tape around the entire complex.

I've gotta get out of here.

DiBianco sat in the drivers seat and reached for the keys.

"SHIT!" They weren't there.

What the hell am I going to do? The driver would certainly return soon. He must move, fast.

Mind throbbing bass thumped out a heavy drone rap beat, causing everything in the UPS truck to buzz and hum. DiBianco's eyes squinted as the throbbing pain hit his temples. A bright red Mustang, host of the nauseating sound, crept by at a snail's pace. The police glanced at the vibrating muscle car but paid no further attention.

Then it struck him.

The Dean's new convertible.

DiBianco knew from experience that auto dealers often times hide a key under the vehicle—somewhere on the chassis. That way in the event they need to send the dreaded RepoMan, they needn't pry the keys from a distraught delinquent's hands.

DiBianco peered out the window at the police, glanced around for the UPS driver, then gazed at the Dean's residence, two houses away.

How the hell am I going to do this?

When it finally occurred to him, he had to think hard about it. It almost seemed too easy.

On the floor by the steps leading to the sidewalk was a brown ball-cap with the letters UPS on the front, and draped over the back of the driver's seat was a brown jacket.

I know what Brown's gonna do for me, he thought. *He's getting me the hell out of here!*

Slipping the jacket over his shoulders and capping his sweat sodden head with the UPS cap, DiBianco glanced around, grabbed a package from behind the seat, and walked from the truck.

Jogging across the street, making strides toward the Dean's residence, he felt his pulse rise. Sweat dripped off his brow, stinging his eyes. He wiped it away with the sleeve of the UPS jacket and found himself fighting off another wave of panic.

Be calm! Walk normal, damn it! Don't look at them!

A row of bushes lined the walkway in front of the Dean's residence. Half concealing the driveway and the Mustang which sat begging for someone, *anyone* to feed it attention.

DiBianco disappeared behind the bushes, dropped the package and swiftly patted the underside of the car for a key.

9

Agent Camillin mindlessly hoisted a large wooden beam off Dean MacDougle's chest and heaved her limp body over his shoulder and ran for help. Nearly tripping over a chunk of fallen debris, he caught sight of his partner, Afridi, laying face down in a pile of rubble. His arm twisted, obviously broken. He wasn't moving.

"*Christ,*" he hollered, struggling to find an EMT or anything at all for that matter in the thick chalky haze. His lungs hurt from sucking in the milky clouds of dust and soot. "DiBianco!" he yelled. "Where are ya, you son-of-a-bitch!"

Flaring through the gassy death-cloud flickered the pulsing strobe of red and white.

A fire truck.

Mist hit his face. They were still soaking the building.

"*Hey,*" he shouted at the four firefighters. "One of you, give me a hand ... *now!*"

A fireman immediately leapt from his station and grabbed the Dean, laid her on the ground, and began CPR.

Camillin ran back to where he had seen his partner. He barely knew him, but was sworn to serve and protect his fellow men. The cloud was blinding. Nothing looked familiar.

"Uluba!" Breathing hurt. He began to hack. His sinuses burned like fire, and his tongue and throat were parched.

"Uluba, where are you?"

Camillin felt his right ankle pop. His knee gave way and he fell, striking his head on a slab of concrete and steel.

His vision blurred, then turned black.

10

DiBianco searched under the bumper, the wheel-wells, even the rocker panels. The key wasn't anywhere. His heart raced like pure madness. He searched the front bumper. Nothing.

He plopped on the pavement in front of the car and laid his face in his hands. *I can't believe this is happening,* he thought.

For years he had suspected his theories—one in particular anyway—would generate tension, even hatred among biblical scholars and Catholic leaders, however he never dreamt it would come to this ... an attempt on his life.

As for the stolen manuscripts and the seemingly related assassinations, he hadn't a damn clue. And now it seemed he'd have no chance to clear his name. The gig was up. It was over. They would find him and would have no doubt about his guilt. After all, he ran, and that proves guilt, does it not?

Then he saw it.

Tucked deep inside the grill of the Mustang was a tiny black box with a golden key printed on the cover.

BINGO!

He frantically fished the box out of the Mustang's snout and removed the key from inside.

Throwing the UPS cap and jacket to the ground DiBianco hopped into the drivers seat and cranked the wild beast to life. The rush of the engine made the hair on his neck jump to attention.

"I've got to get me one of these!"

But just as the excitement flooded his senses, the harsh reality lashed back at him. *This is going to give me away.* If the

Dean was anywhere near there, it was over.

Throwing the shifter into reverse and releasing the clutch, DiBianco and the shiny black convertible screeched on to the open road, just feet from police, who gazed up at him.

There's no way this is going to work.

Throwing the shifter into first gear, DiBianco romped the gas sending the Mustang rocketing down Francis Ave.

"Shit!"

Looking in the rearview, DiBianco saw the officers shake their heads and continue stringing tape.

Without hesitation, DiBianco turned onto a side street and raced toward the only place that came to mind. Home.

11

DiBianco needed his laptop. It was where he kept his contacts, his research, writings, thoughts, memories. He was lost—empty—without it. He was suddenly thankful he had forgotten it at home that morning, otherwise, he knew it would have likely been lost in the explosion.

Dropping the shifter into second gear, DiBianco gunned it, sending the beast banking sharply onto Kirkland Street, nearly hitting a pedestrian while she mindlessly crossed the intersection.

DiBianco slammed on the breaks sending the Mustang into a brief tailspin, then stared at the young woman who was crossing the street in astonishment. "Crystal?" He yanked the E-break and stormed out of the car, his eyes fixed on his young student. Her eyes were unnaturally blue, her smile, bright, yet her body was bruised, beaten ... scourged. It was evident she had wondered off from ground-zero.

"Are you okay?"

She said nothing. She just smiled.

He grabbed her by her middle and carried her to the car, laying her inside. She had tried to walk, but her feet did more dragging than walking.

"We need to find help." He buckled her in the passenger's seat, ran around to the drivers side, released the break, and threw the shifter into first gear. The Mustang lit a smoking flame in its path and they catapulted down Cambridge Street with little time wasted.

"They have her," she said, finally.

"Sorry?"

"Your girlfriend. She's with them."

12

The roads surrounding Kendall Square were deadlocked. The Longfellow Bridge was sealed off to all traffic, even trains, going to and from Boston.

The mustang sat idle in a long line of impatient drivers, waiting for the opportunity to cross into Boston, or at least move beyond the mayhem of the Divinity Hall explosion.

The sweltering afternoon heat radiated off the sticky asphalt creating a thick haze that filled the muggy air with the stench of car exhaust and tar.

Up ahead, through the mishmash of cars, trucks, and SUVs, a long line of army-green military trucks made their way down Main Street from the Longfellow bridge.

Crystal sat quietly in the passenger's seat, her eyes closed, a soft smile caressing her chapped lips. Her clothes were badly torn and thick with filth. A large chunk of fabric had torn away from her pink blouse exposing the left cup of her lacy bra.

DiBianco struggled not to stare.

Her soft hands were cupped together, lying on her lap,

her fingers gently brushing the inner thighs of her tight denim jeans. Even through the heavy stench of exhaust and asphalt her sweet aroma filled his senses. DiBianco caught himself staring again and pulled his gaze away; when he did, he noticed a small piece of paper in her hands. His eyes locked on the yellowed parchment, but then, before it registered what it was he was looking at, his attention was yanked toward a new problem.

At the intersection, ten or twelve car lengths ahead, military officers were pulling people from their cars and perusing their belongings. He had to get out of there. *Now!*

Getting caught would mean the end of everything. It meant losing Savanna, and likely his life. Yet what troubled him more—even more than death—was that he saw his theories coming to life. He prayed he could live long enough to stop it.

The officers made quick time of their search. There were many of them, a dozen at least. DiBianco could feel them staring. His pulse raced. An old man in a neighboring car shouted—

"Move your goddamn asses, now!"

Michael watched in horror while his mother got sucked under the monstrous wave of snow and ice, loosing her for a moment, then spotting her again as she was spit back. Then his father took on the beast. Michael struggled to follow them both; they tumbled down the mountain, both sucked in, then spit back, only to be sucked in again and again and again and—

HONK!

His forehead dripped of sweat. His palms were slick. His heart raced with a ferociousness that sent panic through his veins. His mouth was parched from breathing too hard, too fast.

Calm down, you fool!

He glanced around the cab, searching for something, he wasn't sure what, but knew he needed something. He searched the glove-box.

Nothing.

He slammed the glovebox panel closed and searched for anything that might inspire him—tell him what to do next.

The paper, he thought.

Crystal appeared to be asleep. Her chest rose slightly with each breath, then fell. DiBianco glanced at the paper in her hands, and then at her face. Her eyes shifted from side to side under pinkish-blue eyelids. Her mouth moved minutely, shaping subtle words, but no sound escaped her peach lips.

DiBianco leaned over Crystal's youthful body. Her radiant warmth absorbing into his soul and reached down. With breathless care he removed the paper from her hands, her fingers gripping a second longer, then falling softly to her lap.

DiBianco's eyes sprung wide with amazement. A breath caught up with him and he sucked it in deeply. He couldn't believe his eyes. His skin crawled to life with goose-flesh.

He was holding one of the stolen Newton Papers.

13

"Arthur." The voice was faint ... distant. *"Arthur,"* it said again, almost sounding like it was under water. He couldn't breathe. *"Arthur!"* The voice was more excited now, yet still far away.

Agent Camillin felt something nudge his shoulder. Pain shot through his body. His lungs filled with mind-numbing agony instead of air with each attempted breath. His eyes opened slightly; the skin on his face was tight, his eyelids puffy and sore. The instant light hit his eyes he felt a sinking sensation.

Afridi wrapped Camillin's right arm around his shoulders and without a word, dragged his limp body out of the mound of suffocating dust and debris. Afridi brushed the sticky grey mess from Camillin's face and pulled a plastic mask over his head.

Camillin hacked and groaned, then gasped as the clean air finally found his lungs. His body was being dragged across what felt like broken glass or steel blades. He tried to find his step. He wanted to walk, but pain shot up his leg into the small of his back the moment his foot touched the ground.

Camillin watched with foggy disbelief. Afridi's right arm dangled at his side. He was bleeding badly. The bone in his forearm had broke in such a way that created an *S* pattern between his elbow and wrist. A splintered chunk of bone protruded from a bend in the *S*, coagulated blood clung to it like tacky red paste.

Camillin looked away. "Thank you." His voice was raspy.

Afridi remained silent.

14

DiBianco shoved the Newton Paper into his shirt pocket and glanced at the mass of cars surrounding them. He had to get out of there. But how? He couldn't drive. They were packed in like sardines. His head filled with dozens of possible escapes. He followed each to conclusion. They all ended in capture, or worse.

"Crystal." DiBianco nudged her shoulder.

She didn't awaken. Didn't even move.

"Please..." He nudged harder. "Wake up!"

She opened her eyes and gazed around a moment, then

glanced down and jolted upright, covering her exposed bra with her trembling hands. "What's going on?"

"We need to get out of here." His voice was stern, but soft—almost a whisper. The officers were getting close, wasting no time in their search.

"What are you doing?" Crystal's voice was almost panicked. She acted like she had no recollection of what had happened to her, or even that she knew this man who had picked her up off the street.

"It's not how it looks." DiBianco's voice was defensive, yet quiet. "You survived an explosion. I found you wandering the streets. I helped you."

Her striking blue eyes went wide with terror; slicking over with moisture, they released a river of fear and uncertainty down her trembling blush-streaked cheeks. "You!" Her voiced carried far beyond the interior of the idling mustang. "You had me tied up! You tried to kill me!"

DiBianco couldn't believe his ears; the people in the car next to them couldn't believe it either.

Shhhh.

He lifted a finger to her lips. "Quiet, please. I beg you... *Shut up!*"

She screamed. She screamed bloody murder. DiBianco knew then, she had to be in shock. And her high pitch squeals of terror had suddenly turned all attention on them.

Two officers, just yards away, glared at them with sudden recognition. DiBianco watched the men stare at each other; one shouted a few words into his walky-talky, then ran. Yet, oddly, not toward the mustang.

DiBianco could no longer see the officers. His gut wrenched with fear. Panic sank in his heart and drove molten spikes through his nerves. Sweat poured from his forehead. His hands shook. He tried to hold them steady, but could not. Suddenly Michael DiBianco was in a battle over his own body with possible the worst anxiety attack he had ever felt.

After the avalanche settled and the ground hardened over in a solid white blinding wasteland, Michael ran, tears flooding his eyes, heart racing a mile a second; he ran toward the spot where he last saw his father get devoured by the beast.

Plopping down on the calm icy surface, Michael franticly heaved fistfuls of the heavy ice and snow, knowing all along that every second he fought to save his father's life, was a second his mother had to suffer.

He followed them the best he could, but somewhere, somehow, along the way, he had lost sight of his mother.

Michael heaved massive chunks of snow from the hole with his arms—scraping, digging, pulling with all his might. The hole grew bigger and bigger. Then he felt something. He dug more. There was a hand. Rejuvenated, Michael dug faster, harder. Thoughts of his mother filled his mind and his heart.

"I'm sorry mom," he cried. "I love you." He dug and dug. His father's hair stuck up out of the snow. He wasn't moving, he wasn't making any noise. "God, I'm too late!" Tears streamed his face. "God help me. I'm so sorry!"

Both mustang doors shot open. Crystal and DiBianco were yanked from the vehicle.

DiBianco didn't fight. He couldn't.

Darkness swiftly took over.

15

"The lights," he cried, attempting to raise his hands over his head. But he couldn't. His hands were bound at his sides. His mind was groggy. When the room finally came into focus he knew with a sinking heart that it had not been a dream.

A tall, fit blond in flowery pink scrubs stuck a long needle in his left arm, then attached a glass vile at the end of the tube. The vile swiftly filled with blood. She wasted no time and replaced the vile with another, it too filling with haste.

At the same time a short stub of a man, with salt and pepper hair sporting a grey and white stripped shirt and a bright red Windsor-knotted necktie, held a cold stethoscope to his chest and counted seconds on his Rolex.

"Good to see you finally awake, Mr. DiBianco." The man's voice was gentle, with just a touch of an English accent. He had a name badge clipped to his shirt pocket:

Cliff Byron, MD.

"Where am I?" The restraints on his wrists fell loose and immediately he shook feeling back into his hands and crossed his arms over his chest, shivering.

"You're at Saint Mary's," Dr. Byron said.

"What happened? What's going on?"

"Why don't you tell me, Mr. DiBianco?" Dr. Byron said, slinging the stethoscope around his neck and sitting on a rolling chair beside the gurney.

"I don't understand."

"Two young men were kind enough to bring you here. They thought you had passed out from heat exhaustion, but they hadn't known for sure." He paused. "How do you feel, Mr. DiBianco?"

"Are they still here?" DiBianco said nervously, fighting hard to avoid another panic attack. "What about Crystal?"

"Crystal?"

"She's one of my students. She's hurt. She was with me in the car when they—" A bright light, swung into his face, sent stabbing pains through his head.

"I'm sorry Mr. DiBianco, there's no one by that name at this hospital." He frowned. "We really need to talk about you for a moment, okay?" Dr. Byron's face was serious. "We found large amounts of Methaqualone in your system."

"What?" DiBianco said, squinting into the light.

"It's one of the reasons why the light's bothering you so badly. Methaqualone is quite dangerous. Popular in the 60s as a recreational drug—at the time many medical experts thought it was safe, many even used it. Today, however, it's often used for far more devious purposes. You may have heard it called by one of its many common street names: Quaalude? ... Sopor? ... Parest?"

"Are you kidding? I've never taken drugs in my life."

"I feel compelled to believe you," he said, slapping his hands on his knees and rising to his feet. Dr. Byron grabbed a sheet of paper from the counter, pointed at a series of pills and capsules, and continued. "This drug is taken in one of these forms, giving its user a peaceful, often surreal feeling." Dr. Byron returned the paper to the counter and took DiBianco's right arm, a huge black and blue welt stood tall on his biceps. "Somebody injected the bloody stuff into your arm. To put it bluntly, you shouldn't be here. You ought to be dead."

"But I feel fine." DiBianco was lying, but he couldn't stay in a hospital bed, he had to find who stole the Newton Papers and clear his name. "I have to go."

"I don't believe you understand. You're in no condition to *go* anywhere. You *must* rest."

"But I must—"

"Mr. DiBianco!" Dr. Byron raised his voice for the first time since DiBianco's awakening. "You've been in a bloody coma for a week. You can't go anywhere!"

DiBianco couldn't believe his ears. *This can't be.* Sudden horror ransacked his thoughts. "I must get back to Boston!"

Dr. Byron's face was perplexed. "Boston?" He cocked his head. "Boston Massachusetts?"

"You don't understand. It's urgent!"

"Mr. DiBianco." The doctor's face was sympathetic, yet very matter of fact. "Do you have any idea where you are?"

All of a sudden it occurred to him. *Saint Mary's?* He'd

never been to a Saint Mary's Hospital. Never heard of one, quite frankly. DiBianco looked baffled at the doctor who gazed back with concern.

"You're in London, my friend. London England."

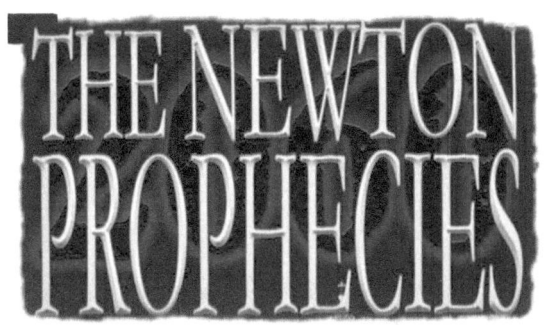

PART TWO

A FOILED PLAN

16

When the District Line Train arrived at Victoria Station, Peter Clinton tried to remember life before wallowing in the darkness of earth's mysterious underworld.

London's elaborate subway system carried an official nickname, *The Tube*. Clinton wasn't much for nicknames but adapted and often called it *The Tube*, even if it did sound ridiculous.

The Tube from Victoria Station to South Kensington was a short one.

Small LCDs played the early news—

> *"...Prime Minister Blair is prepared to give his fair-well speech this evening, christening Brown as his successor in the House of Parliament. It's expected to be a warm welcome for the new Prime Minister. After a decade of war and misrepresentation, England's people are ready for a new voice..."*

Clinton was one of the few who still appreciated Blair; not only did he think the war was justified, but vital to national security.

Clinton glanced back at the LCD.

The news anchor pulled at his ear. A disheartening gaze swept his face—

> *"This just in... The Pope has died. The ninety-seven-year-old Supreme Pontiff, who has struggled with Parkinson's Disease for most of his fifteen years at the*

*helm, died last night in his papal apartment. Again ...
Pope Seises XVI, has died at age ninety-seven."*

The camera panned to a young woman, blond, heavy makeup; her eyes glazed over, choking back tears.

"It's a sad day for the billions who loved him, a man who helped so many throughout his life."
"That's right Kim," the male anchor said. *"Now the waiting begins."*
"Our very own Frank Thompson is en-route to Vatican City. He'll be our eyes and ears while we await—"

Pope Seises ... dead, Clinton thought. He had just seen the Pope give a blessing from his papal apartment window on the news the night before ... the night he died. *How frighteningly unpredictable life can be.*
The train squealed to a halt.
The doors slid open.
An announcement crackled the loudspeakers.
Now Arriving, South Kensington Station.
This was his stop.
South Kensington Station was one brief stop Clinton had to make while taking the London Underground to and from school—It connected Victoria Station, across the street from his tiny basement apartment in Westminster, with Russell Square, just two blocks from Birkbeck University—but on this day Clinton's life was about to change ... forever.
On the brink of 21, Peter Clinton was sharp-as-a-tack, majoring in computer science, world history, and world religion, he was one busy kid. When not at school—mesmerizing his teachers with questions Einstein would have gotten lost in, or doing one-and-a-half reverse somersaults with quadruple twists, off a concrete slab over 30 feet above the surface of a mere 15 feet of icy pool water—he was

barricading himself in his apartment, searching the internet for dark secret societies, mythical cults, and crime and corruption of all types, in an attempt to unveil their existence to the world—shed light on the darkness.

Clinton was a spiritual man, didn't belong to any creed per se, but believed in God and served the best he knew how. With that said, he struggled to pull his attention away from the occult. It fascinated him. Filled his life with mystery and puzzles, more than he could ever dream of solving. Yet he understood the danger, and fought to stay clear of it.

Clinton laid his laptop bag on the concrete bench and pulled out a pristine hardcover edition of his favorite book and read silently while the Piccadilly train, heading to Russell Square, returned from Heathrow Airport—typically a ten to fifteen minute layover.

The title of the book, ironically, was *The Book*. He had read it three times since receiving it six months prior from his science teacher, a treasured birthday gift. He couldn't get enough of it. Written by Michael DiBianco—simply the best author of all time—*The Book* was chocked with complex and mesmerizing puzzles and dark mysteries. He couldn't resist a good mystery. Unsolved puzzles drove him mad.

In it were translations of masterpieces by some of the world's most influential people: Einstein, Galileo, Newton, Plato, amongst others. Clinton imagined that DiBianco's mind worked quite similar to his own, which made him a genius.

Clinton's knee began to bounce. It was his body screaming at him. *Find a restroom, fast!*

The train would arrive in less than five minutes. However, the ride to Russell Square was another fifteen; the buildup in his bladder was intense, and it wasn't easing.

Shoving the book into his bag and slinging it back over his shoulder, Clinton made strides toward the men's room, praying he didn't spring a leak in his jeans on the way. But the men's room was closed. Spans of crisscrossed caution tape barred off both entrances.

He had to go. It simply could not wait.

It was dark. Clinton flicked on the light switches. Nothing happened. Fortunately, he'd used this restroom before and knew right where to go. There were no doors blocking the entrances, light penetrated the series of passageways within the horseshoe restroom at both ends.

He tracked his way toward the urinals, slid his bag around to his back, unzipped his fly, and let the buildup of pressure gush out.

It was orgasmic.

When he first heard the female voice he swore it came from within the men's room.

He slowed the hot stream with a solid pinch of his right hand and tried to silence himself.

A man's voice replied. It was quiet; Clinton couldn't be sure where the voices came from.

"...room 326." The female said.

"Are you sure?"

"Positive."

"Make sure you keep your headset on."

"Of course."

"When you hear the signal—"

"—I know." She paused. "Is it truly necessary?"

"Savanna, you're in no situation to argue."

"I know."

"I'll take care of everything else."

"Are you sure he won't recognize you?"

"Absolutely."

"Can I see him?"

"Not yet."

"I love him."

"I know."

"Don't you dare hurt him."

"That's not part of the plan. You know that."

"I also know you follow orders like I do."

"This came from Fuller. Don't worry."

There was a long silence. The sound of piss striking the inside wall of the urinal rushed back into Clinton's head.

"He *is* the one, you know."

"Are you ready?" The man said.

Sounds of zippers and button-snaps echoed through the darkness. It was coming from the men's room, of this he now knew for sure.

Shaking himself dry, Clinton zipped his jeans and left the restroom without even a squeak of his sneakers on the tile. He ducked out of sight and watched a sharp dressed couple leave the opposite entrance to the restroom and make a swift B-line toward the Circle Line pad.

It was a dark unsolved mystery, taunting him to follow, and without a second thought, that's just what he did.

17

FBI, Boston Field Office. The evening before.

"Son-of-a-bitch!" Camillin's face ripped through every curse-word known to man and slammed the office copy of *USA Today* on his desk. Filling the front page was a picture of renowned author, Michael DiBianco, in a hospital bed.

"Rachel!" he shouted.

Rachel's newly permed hair bounced as she peeked around the corner into Camillin's office, her lengthy fingers decorated in sparkling rings, swept wisps of hair away from her excessively made up eyes. "Yes?"

"Book me the next flight to London. Heathrow Airport. *Stat!*"

18

Clinton sat at the back of the train, watching the couple stare blankly in his direction from the front. He tried not to stare. He looked at the many ads for Apple iPods and half naked women, supposedly smelling of Chanel No5, plastered along the walls above the windows.

His stomach twisted. His skin crawled. They were staring right at him. He felt it in his gut. They didn't say a word. No notable expression on their faces.

At one point he sensed fear. However that was gone before he realized it was there. Whatever devious event they had planned. It was huge, and he had to figure it out.

The train squealed to a halt. The doors slid open.

The couple didn't move. Neither did Clinton.

The entire train unloaded. No other passengers came aboard. When the doors closed and the train sped off toward High Street, Bayswater, and Paddington Stations, Clinton grabbed his favorite book and started to read.

They have to know I'm following them.

He didn't look up when the train stopped the second time, or the third. He saw them in his peripheral vision, sitting. He read, trying to be casual. Trying not to reveal how shaky his hands were, how much sweat pored from his forehead.

As the train slowed the fourth time, he saw the couple shift in their seats. *This is it. They're getting off.*

He looked up. Crammed his book into his bag and waited for the train to stop.

The doors opened.

The couple didn't move.

Crap, he thought. He had already shown he was getting off. If he sat back down now, they'd know for sure; who knows what they'd do.

Clinton stepped off the train and gaped at the sign overhead.

Paddington Station

Damn it!

The doors slid closed and the train squealed away. They *had* suspected him. They were testing him, and he failed— miserably. The only question was: Had he foiled their plan? *Or*, did they never intend to get off at Paddington Station.

Clinton shook his head in disgust and sat on a bench. Gazing at a large decorative clock mounted on a cast-iron post, it occurred to him. He missed diving competition. He practiced for months for that competition; it was all he thought about when not tackling the occult; yet he had gotten so caught up in the pursuit, he forgot about school and the swim team.

Damn it!

Just then a sharp dressed couple carrying black bags caught the corner of his eye.

They got off!

They walked hastily down South Wharf Road into the heart of Saint Mary's campus.

The room number struck him like brick to the head. *326.*

My God, he thought. *Can it be?*

The irony was incredible. The year before, his mother had spent a month at Saint Mary's struggling to recover from a life ending case of pneumonia. Clinton had stuck by her the entire time, often wishing she would die so he could carry on with his life. When she finally did, he hated himself for wishing it. Now he was going back.

All thoughts of school vanished. He was a staunch believer in fate, and this was fate ... times twenty.

Without a wavering thought he clutched his bag in his arms and raced to catch up with the sharp dressed couple.

19

Clinton watched the couple from the north side of South Wharf Road. They passed under Saint Mary's arch and made a B-line for the hospital's main entrance.

It was clear where they were heading; and while they strode up to a glass smoking area in front of the hospital and placed their bags on the ground, Clinton set his own plan into motion.

He had no intention of using the main entrance. He knew another way; he had discovered an employee stairwell in the rear of the building back when his mother was ill. Staffers never hesitated to let him use it to go out for a smoke. They enjoyed his company. They loved how he kept them thinking.

Things were different now. Not only did he no longer smoke, but he had no business being there. He had to be sneaky. He would get to the third floor and warn whomever was in room 326 before the couple even got to the elevator.

He ran across the street and down the sidewalk behind the historic hospital. He had learned so much about Saint Mary's while consoling his mother: C.R. Alder Wright first synthesized heroin there in 1874. Alexander Fleming went to school there in 1906. He was elected Professor of Bacteriology in 1928, and accidentally discovered penicillin while investigating the properties of staphylococci during that same year. Arguably however, the most fascinating discovery was that Elvis Costello, Kiefer Sutherland, Prince Harry and Prince William were all born there. That's what most interested his mother. She couldn't have cared less about science or chemistry.

Clinton ran to the door.

Employees were smoking at the picnic table not twenty feet from the building.

The door was propped open with an empty Coke can. Clinton quietly entered the building. Once inside he made strides up the staircase, two, sometimes three at a time.

Standing a moment, facing a large steel door with a big black 3 painted on it, Clinton took in a deep breath and counted back from—

Five. His heart pounded.

Four. His skin broke out in gooseflesh.

Three. His breathing made his head spin.

Two. His hand gripped the doorknob.

One. He opened the door.

20

The recovery floor was quiet. The corridors lit just enough to see where you were walking. It was quiet time. Clinton realized how ingenious the couple had been. They had picked the ideal time to execute their plan—whatever plan that was.

The floor was empty.

Only a single nurse on duty. She sat at a cluttered desk in the slightly brighter nurse's station, several yards from where Clinton entered, punching at a computer keyboard. She didn't look up. She didn't seem to notice him at all.

No sign of the couple either.

Clinton tiptoed toward room 326. It hid around the corner, out of sight of the nurse's station.

What am I doing? he thought. *What if I get killed? What if it's all in my head? My God, what if I'm going crazy!*

There it was. Room 326.

Clinton sprinted toward the door, grabbed the jamb, and stopped himself inside, out of sight of whoever laid in the hospital bed beyond the curtain.

He took a deep breath and entered the room, peeking behind the curtain. The patient laid in a fetal position, facing the draped window.

Clinton made his way toward the foot of the bed, careful not to make a sound, looked at the name on the chart and felt his heart stop.

Michael DiBianco

21

The sun was high in the clear midday sky. A gentle breeze caressed the grounds. Very pleasant. Very serene.

No one paid attention to the sharp dressed couple when they entered the hospital's main entrance, leaving their bags in the bus stop shelter.

22

It was fate and Clinton knew it, and it had led him right to the bedside of the greatest author the world had ever known.

He stood in silence a long moment, staring at his face, trying to be sure he wasn't hallucinating. He wasn't. It was him. Michael DiBianco was really there, and so was Peter Clinton, and in the same room even. DiBianco's eyes were closed. An IV strung from the bed frame was all that connected him to Saint Mary's Hospital.

He knew he had to wake him. Warn him of the impending danger. But something was stopping him. Something he had never felt before. Sure, he recalled being afraid a few times when he was young, but this was paralyzing. He could operate perfectly fine in the face of possible death; but standing in the same room with Michael DiBianco, had him unable to remember his own name.

Footsteps rang through the hall. Pins and needles attacked his flesh. He had to act, and he had to act now.

He scoped the room, trying to devise a plan. He needed to get DiBianco out of there, or at least make it appear that way.

The footsteps grew louder.

He glanced out the window. Spied the ceiling tiles. The closet. What was he to do?

They were right outside the door.

Damn it man, think!

23

"Doctor?" A female voice echoed through the dim corridor.

A dark man in a white coat, his right arm in a sling, did an about-face. "What is it Nurse?" His voice was thick with a middle eastern accent.

"A young woman is here to see Michael DiBianco."

"What?"

"I told her he's not accepting visitors, but she—"

"—Escort her out."

"But—"

"Just do it."

"I can't leave the floor."

"I'll watch over things ... go."

"All right," she said reluctantly.

"Just be sure to come back, sometime today please."

"Of course," she said, then disappeared around the corner in a huff.

The man stepped up to room 326, stood straight, shoulders back, chin up, and grinned widely.

He stepped inside.

"Hello Mr. DiBi—"

The man froze in his step. Stoned cold rage swept his ridged face. *"DiBianco!"*

The room was empty.

24

"Okay, you've got my attention. But, there'd better be a damn good reason why I'm scaling down a rickety old ladder affixed to the side of a building in nothing but hospital garments."

"Mr. DiBianco—"

"Mike." DiBianco tried to calm his nerves. He clutched onto the shaky rungs—chunks of brick and mortar falling away while he went—swiftly descending, trying hard to keep up with Clinton who made a B-line for the walkway below.

"I know this sounds crazy Mr. DiBianco, but this couple—"

"Right kid, I heard that part, and I told you, call me Mike. My enemies call me Mr. DiBianco. You're not an enemy ... right?"

"N-no. Of course not," Clinton stammered. "I don't know what this couple's planning, but they *are* after you, and not just to say hello."

"I have to admit, I've been looking for an opportunity to

leave this place ever since I woke up yesterday. I suppose, if for nothing else, I should thank you for that."

A window slid open pulling DiBianco's gaze skyward. A dark-faced man peered down.

"Mr. DiBianco!" The voice spit with anger.

DiBianco didn't recognize the man, but felt panic attack him. His heart palpitated. His hands grew slick. His vision blurred, then went black. An image of a skyscraper filled his head; it exploded; glass shattering, flames bursting out every window, people plummeting to their deaths. The world spun out of control and DiBianco lost his grip on the rungs and started to fall.

"*No*, Mr. DiBianco!" Clinton's face went pale.

DiBianco scrambled to grab something; but there was nothing there.

Clinton threw his hands over his head. A split second later, they were falling to the earth.

25

Savanna left at the pre-planned time.

She glared at the bags as she walked by.

Exactly as planned.

She didn't care much for her partner, but had faith that he'd take care of things. He always did.

She glanced at her watch.

Where's the signal?

Pushing a pistol aside in her suit pocket, she found the small device and ran a slender finger along its frame.

All she had to do now, was wait.

26

DiBianco's back hurt. He felt lost, like he'd been sleeping for days. There was a stiffness in his neck and when his eyes opened he realized he had only been out a matter of moments—seconds even.

People were running toward them from Winsland Street, just a block from Paddington Station, there were even a few from South Wharf, a hundred yards away. They must have made quite the spectacle of themselves to cause such a reaction.

If the pain hadn't been so damn real, so horrific, DiBianco may have found comic relief in the lucid vision of himself falling down the side of a building with his testis flapping in the wind.

He looked at Clinton, who laid motionless to his right. His eyes were open. He held his bag at his chest, which raised and fell with choppy, irregular breaths. He was alive, but wasn't making any announcements to the effect.

"Hey kid, you okay?" DiBianco propped himself up on his badly bruised tush. Sitting upright, he looked into Clinton's eyes. "Anyone home?"

Clinton smirked. "Good thing we weren't any higher."

"Can you get up?"

He nodded.

"We're about to have company." DiBianco pointed at the people flocking around them. Yet, DiBianco knew they were the least of their concerns. The dark-faced man in the window would be after them at any moment.

"Come on kid," DiBianco said, raising perhaps a bit to

quickly. Immense pain exploded in his head. A sudden, unbearable migraine—one that could devour every migraine he had ever had. Something spoke, spitting words within his mind.

The Eye. It watches you. Go!

His knees buckled. He barely caught himself on a lamppost before falling to the ground.

"Are you okay?"

DiBianco was silent, holding the post.

"Mr. DiBianco?"

"We've gotta get our asses out of here."

"Yeah," Clinton snickered, staring at the scant hospital gown, "especially yours."

27

Savanna's hands trembled. Her eyes focused on the bags.

The sudden power and fury of the voice screaming—*Don't push the button!*—in her headset startled her; she didn't realize she had pushed the button until she saw DiBianco spring out from a thick of bushes to the left of the hospital's entrance, sprinting like a chetah toward the bags.

It worked.

"Oh shit, it worked!"

DiBianco was barefoot, a hospital gown barely covering his privates.

A lanky young man, dressed in tight jeans and a white polo shirt—a small black bag dangling from his shoulder—struggled to keep up.

Savanna gazed from afar with shocking displeasure.

28

"Mike!" Clinton was out of breath, struggling to keep up with DiBianco's sudden, almost unimaginable energy.

DiBianco didn't say a word. He just kept running; running toward two large black bags.

"Mr. DiBianco, *please!*"

"Call me Mike ... damn you!"

Clinton slammed into DiBianco as he stopped, grabbed the bags, and took off again toward South Wharf Road.

"Mike!" Clinton's eyes rolled in his head. Sucking in a series of deep breaths, he launched himself toward DiBianco. "What the hell's going on? Where are you going?"

DiBianco ran toward Paddington Station like a marathon runner with the finish line in his sights; the black bags hanging firmly at his sides.

"Mike. Hold on. Please!" They weren't going to get far with DiBianco's privates dangling about.

Clinton had a solution. It wasn't great, but it was something. He unzipped his laptop bag, pulled out a thin piece of purple cloth and waved it in the air. *"Mike!"* All he had to do now was get him to stop long enough to put it on.

29

The London Eye. Sitting on the bank of, and towering nearly 450 feet over, the River Thames—its 2,100 tons of steel cables and tubing resembling a gigantic white bicycle tire; and its 32 bus-sized clear egg-shaped capsules giving 800 awestruck visitors the view of a lifetime with each 30 minute revolution—it's quite simply the largest Ferris Wheel in the world.

At the base of London's hottest new landmark the LEO (London Eye Oppressions) Crew, along with members of the Royal Guard, worked to clear the monstrous wheel and secure the area for the evening's media event.

It was a monumental task, preparing an event of this nature. Security would be at it heaviest since 9-11, but fears still brewed. Tony Blair; Prime Minister to be, Brown; even President Bush, were scheduled to appear. It was a fantastic PR stunt. One that easily could turn tragic. Security would have their hands full for sure.

The Eye was just one of many structures being secured. Even in the dark, a sniper could easily fire a shot from the giant wheel, marring Big Ben's face forever. Blair would be speaking at the base of the 150 year old clock tower, certainly within the sights of a master sniper.

The last capsule was emptied.

The Royal Guards—in their bright red and white coats, black slacks, and puffy black hats—were escorting a few remaining visitors off the massive concrete platform, when several black Caddies sped up to the curb, their tires locking with a chirping squeal.

A dozen agents from the US Embassy stormed the London Eye. A tall dark man—fully done up in a black pleated suit, perfectly knotted silk blue tie, dark shades, and tightly cropped hair—approached the giant wheel.

"Take the night off gentlemen."

The head Guard stood straight up, facing the agent, his back stiff, his face ridged. He was a true Royal Guard. "We have orders, Sir."

"You have new orders, captain," the agent said flashing a government citation.

The Royal Guards were baffled but did what they were told. The Embassy *had* jurisdiction too. Sure, England's Prime Minister was England's responsibility, but Bush was theirs.

After several minutes of somewhat confusing, almost confrontational, discussion with London's Royal Guard, the Eye was finally secured.

30

"Did he take them?" The voice crackled in the headset.

"Yes," Savanna said.

"This is *not* good!"

"Who was chasing him?"

There was a long numbing silence. "A serious problem," the voice finally said.

"Oh God," she cried. There was no room for yet another mistake. Fuller would order her banished for sure this time. "What should we do?"

"Kill him."

"Michael?"

" No ... The kid."

"Oh." Her voice was both shaky and relieved.

31

"Mike." Clinton was out of breath; he could barely speak. He prayed he would stop, or at least slow. His knees were giving out, and he fought the constant urge to collapse. It was not like him to be so exhausted, but DiBianco was unnaturally fast.

Paddington Station, with its arched façade, stood tall and largely out of place against the architecture of its neighbors.

The station was crowded, like it typically was. Not just another stop for The Tube, Paddington Station was also a connector for the National Rail System.

Clinton could feel eyes pierce them as they approached the gates.

Without warning, DiBianco stopped and released his grip on the bags, letting them hit the ground with a thud.

Clinton plopped his hands on his knees, trying to catch his breath. In the infancy of his prime and being a competitive swimmer, Clinton was in superb shape; but something about the events of the day, made his head spin.

They stood in front of a crowded concession stand, adjacent a public restroom, a few yards from the gates. The smell of hotdogs and onion rings pushed the looming stench of train grease and sweat from the air.

"Let me see that," DiBianco said, pointing at the purple cloth wedged between Clinton's right hand and knee.

Clinton smiled and tossed him the Speedo.

32

"Where the hell are they?" Savanna stretched her neck, trying to see over the hundreds of travelers cramming their way into the station.

"He must have pushed his way through," the middle eastern voice cracked through her headset.

"Why aren't you here?" she said.

"This is your task, Savanna. You need to prove yourself to

Fuller."

You're such an ass, she thought. "Haven't I proven myself enough, for Christ's sake?"

"*That* is why Fuller is testing you."

"Excuse me?"

"We do *nothing* for Christ's sake."

"It's a damn metaphor." She paused. "Goddamn it!"

"Calm down. Once you take care of *this* I'm sure your standings with Fuller will grow."

Savanna said nothing.

"But if you don't... Fear not. Banishment only hurts a second."

The line went numb with silence.

Savanna's face hardened.

Gripping the pistol she had stashed in her suit coat, she scoped the area with determination.

They must be inside already, she thought, approaching the gate; she inserted her card into the scanner and thought, *he must have rushed his way through. Christ! He could be boarding The Tube to Waterloo by now!*

The gate opened.

Savanna ran into the whirlwind that was Paddington Station.

33

"How do I look?" DiBianco said, standing inside the stall, the door in his hand, held wide open.

Clinton laughed. He couldn't help it. He tried to refrain, tried to see the serious side, but the Speedo had never looked so small—so ridiculously purple—on him. *Or had it?* he thought. *God I hope not!*

"It look's fantastic," he said, a chuckle still tickling his voice.

DiBianco slammed the door. The flimsy stall dividers shook, appearing for a second like they'd fall, fortunately, they did not.

"Just put the gown back on. over it" Clinton couldn't have been more serious. "At least you're covered." He paused. "Hey, what's in those bags?"

DiBianco was silent.

"Maybe there's something to wear."

The door opened, slamming against the wall.

DiBianco was naked.

Hairy son-of-a-bitch, Clinton thought.

He ran from the stall and grabbed one of the bags from the floor. Setting it on the vanity, he slid the long zipper and peered inside.

Clinton was excited. "What's in it?"

"Nothing." DiBianco closed the bag and threw it to the floor, then grabbed the other. Polished aluminum glared in the fluorescent light. "My laptop!" He pulled it out and opened it. The screen sprung to life. "That's odd. It's been over a week. It should be dead."

"Clothes, Mr. DiBianco?"

"Mike!" DiBianco dug deeper and pulled out a suit. Black slacks, socks, coat, white shirt, silk maroon tie, and a pair of shiny black shoes.

"Sweet." Clinton was relieved and impressed.

34

DiBianco left the men's room with a confidence he hadn't had since before he had been approached by Agent Camillin; before he had heard about the disappearance of the Newton Papers.

He didn't know what the road ahead had in store, but he

now knew he was on the right path. Nothing was getting between him and the answers he needed. Savanna's life depended on it. His life depended on it.

"*That's* what I'm talking about." Clinton was awestruck. "Now there's the man on the back of all those books lining my shelves."

DiBianco gazed at Clinton through dark shades, a wide grin invaded his face. "Let's go."

"You see, that's where I'm lost," Clinton said, slinging his laptop bag over his shoulder. "Where exactly *are* we going?"

"Waterloo Station." His voice was confident. "The Eye awaits."

"Are you bloody high?"

DiBianco—sharp, very *Blues Brothers,* large black bag in hand—took off toward the gates.

Clinton grabbed the other bag and caught up. "There's people after you; they probably want you dead; and you're going to The Eye? ... Did I miss something?"

DiBianco looked for the shortest line. They were all long. Picking one, he settled in and rested the bag in front of him.

"Mike?"

"I don't know!" he finally said, his confidence diminishing. "I just know I'm supposed to go there."

"I don't understand."

"Don't sweat it kid," DiBianco said. "Who the hell are you anyway?"

Clinton was speechless.

"You saved me from the *evil nurses* and that stubby English doctor," he said with a chuckle, "but, now it's like you're stalking me."

Clinton's face went white with shock.

"What brought you to Saint Mary's in the first place?"

"I-I over heard, th-the—"

"Spit it out, kid."

"Why are you such an asshole all of a sudden? Reading all your books, I thought... I mean, I thought... I understood you." Clinton dropped the bag and stormed off.

"Hey!" DiBianco shouted, knowing he had made a grave mistake.

But Clinton kept walking.

"Kid!" DiBianco grabbed both bags and ran after him. He didn't understand why he was acting the way he was. It was like something suddenly took over his mind. "I'm sorry."

But it didn't matter, Clinton wasn't stopping.

"I don't even know your name?"

"Peter," he said, not even slowing his step.

"Peter, please." DiBianco followed behind him. "I'm sorry. This has been a pretty screwed up week. I really need your help solving this puzzle."

Clinton stopped. "What's going on?"

"I don't know..."

"And what's in those bags?"

"I—"

"Why the hell did you take them?"

"I—"

"They belong to them—"

"I don't know!" he snapped, questioning everything that entered his mind. "You know," he started, "perhaps it's time we took a look."

35

Camillin landed at Heathrow Airport at 8:57 in the morning. Sleep had not come easy on the flight. It never did. He tried, but struggled to squeeze in a few hours. It would have to do. He had to find DiBianco. There was no time to waste.

Grabbing his rolling luggage from the belt, Camillin made strides for the pickup curb. He hoped his ride would already be waiting. Eleven hours was long enough doing nothing. He did not intend to wait a second longer.

Amidst the slew of white shuttles and taxis was a shiny black Caddy, its windows where dark, like the government issued SUVs back home.

The passenger-side window slid down.

"Agent Camillin?" The Driver said.

Camillin nodded.

"Please. Get in, Sir."

Camillin tossed his luggage in the back and jumped into the passenger's seat, keeping his laptop bag on his lap.

"Have you eaten?" The driver said, holding up a bag of cheesy nacho chips.

"No thanks. Just get me to headquarters."

"Yes, Sir," he said, shoving another fistful in his mouth, crumbs littering his lap. The driver romped on the gas sending the Caddy rocketing into stiff morning traffic.

Camillin grabbed tightly to what his ex-wife used to call the *Oh Shit Handle*—it was the only thing from *that* nightmare he retained—and prayed there was still time.

36

"We need a private place," DiBianco said, looking in a full circle where they stood, outside Paddington Station. He didn't want to wander aimlessly, but he didn't want to spend another minute in that restroom either. "Do you know this area?"

"Paddington? Not really—"

"London."

"Of course!" Clinton said with a chuckle.

"Take me somewhere private."

"I know exactly the place. Follow me!" Clinton took off

towards the station again.

At the gate, Clinton slid his card.

"Go ahead. I'll follow."

He slid his card again.

Clinton took the lead and they entered the heart of Paddington Station.

Trains lined every track.

The smell of hotdogs was gone, replaced by the stench of grease, body odor, and stale cigarette smoke.

The noise was maddening. With its massive arched roof— like the hull of a ship, turned on its mast—the space echoed like an empty cavern.

He followed Clinton toward the opposite end of the station.

"Ease up, Peter."

Clinton slowed, but not much. "We've gotta take the Circle Line to Victoria Station."

"What's at Victoria Station?"

"My apartment."

It was perfect and he knew it. Yet still, something felt wrong. No one would ever suspect to find him hiding at some kid's apartment, but he couldn't shake that feeling of dread.

"Come on!" Clinton sped up. "The train's leaving."

DiBianco hurried, keeping up easily.

"There," Clinton said, pointing at a long white train, a thick blue stripe ran along the bottom, just beneath a set of red doors, which were opened wide.

"Mind the gap!" Clinton shouted.

"What?"

"Mind the gap, between the walkway and the train. It's a terrible way to end the day, but it certainly *will* end it."

37

Shoving the last bit of hotdog into her mouth, Savanna spotted two men dashing toward the Circle Line train. It shouldn't have grabbed her like it did—people run through the station all the time—but they were carrying black bags.

Then it hit her.

It's them!

She swallowed the hotdog in one gulp and took off like a track star to the sound of gunfire.

The men gained on the train quickly. It was preparing to leave.

She ran toward the door closest the front of the train. She couldn't allow herself to be noticed.

The men leapt into the rear door. She heard the hydraulics release. The doors were closing. Her heart raced. Her breathing, so heavy her throat hurt. She could feel her thighs burning.

Just a few feet more.

The doors began to close. *NO!*

People jumped out of her way.

She threw her hands out and slammed into the train's inner wall. The stress was far too much. She didn't want to do what she knew she had to.

She fell to the floor and burst into tears.

38

The steps leading down to Clinton's apartment were flooded with sweltering sunlight. The heavy, sticky stench hovering in the space was putrid. It reminded DiBianco of festering meat.

Sweat poured from DiBianco's forehead. He struggled to breathe. He grew faint. Something about the space haunted him. Shivers swept his spine. He was cold.

"Where's your mother?"

"She's fine, dad. Come on, you've gotta help."

Michael fought to free his father from the snowy grave, but all his father seemed to care about was his wife. "Where's your mother?" he'd ask, over and over. Michael didn't want to lose his father like he knew he had his mother, so his response was simple, "She's fine. Help me, please. You've gotta help me dig."

...and dig they did.

Finally, two hours after finding his father, Michael pulled him out of the crusty crater, and burst into tears. "She's dead. I'm so sorry!"

His father laid quietly for a long time. Tears welled in his shaky eyes. Michael could plainly see that his mind had drifted to another place. He prayed he'd come back.

Forcing himself to sit, his father burst into sobs; he took his son into his arms and, though suffering from many obvious injuries, rose to his feet and walked his son down the mountainside. That was the last memory he would have of his living father. Exposure took him only moments later...

Then it was dark—pitch black. A desk, rich lacquered wood, upon it rested a small black box, a stack of wrinkled papers; the scant light in the room came from a tiny amber flame, a candle perhaps—no, a lamp, oil. Then the box disappeared; the stack of papers rained down from the ceiling; a strange burning on his cheek; next to the flame, now appearing to be dying out, it's light fading quickly. There was a shimmering metal object, impossible to make out—

"It's 2:00," Clinton said, snapping DiBianco from his vision.

Clinton was certain. He pointed at the steps as he walked toward the door, the black duffle bag still in his hand. Wrought iron bars covered the windows flanking the door—one was broken.

He was pointing at the shadow. It hovered over the bottom step. There was a number drawn in red paint; a big red *2*. Two steps higher was a *3*, two higher, a *4*, and so on.

"Someone actually took the time to do this?"

"Pretty cool, hay?"

"And what's wrong with a watch?"

"They turn my skin green."

"You did this?" DiBianco shook his head.

Clinton shrugged. "I was bored."

"I guess so." DiBianco paused. "Get one with a leather strap."

"Too sweaty."

"Did you mark the sidewalks too? How about your living room? Lines running down the wall?"

"I have a clock, wise-ass."

Clinton reached in through the broken window and unlocked the door.

"You *do* live here ... right?"

"There's a key stuck in the lock. Everyone has to reach around."

DiBianco rubbed the tip of his nose and shook his head. *How can anyone live this way?*

Following Clinton through a long hallway, the stench of cat litter and trash assaulted his senses. There was a copy of *The Newton Theories*—one of his largest books—among a pile of crap strewn about in the depths of the hall. That's where DiBianco noticed the door. It was a dilapidated door held closed with a 2x4 nailed at each end. He didn't know then, but it would soon be their salvation.

Several feet before *that* door was the door to Clinton's apartment. Clinton stopped and fumbled something shiny in his hands.

"Ah, a key," DiBianco said with a chuckle.

Clinton said nothing. He inserted the key and turned. It took effort. The bolt slid open with a clang. Clinton shouldered the door open and stepped aside. "Welcome to my pad."

39

Savanna watched the bag-toting men cross Wilton Road and descend into the basement of a rundown apartment complex.

When the men disappeared, she crossed the road, listened carefully for the sound of a door closing, and made her way down.

She had no idea how big of an impact her next move would have on the lives of billions of people.

40

DiBianco couldn't believe his eyes. Besides a slew of papers—some printed, some written—and pictures cluttering the wall at the far end of the spacious room next to a small desk bearing a computer, it was clean and inviting. A small, yet attractive sofa; a quaint oak table for two; and a fancy kitchenette, with everything a single guy should ever need, even a dishwasher. An essence of berries kissed the air.

Clinton slammed the door behind him.

"Sorry," he said. "It sticks."

"I'm impressed."

"Thank you."

"I mean it. You have a great place."

"Enough flattery. Let's see what's in the bags."

DiBianco dropped the bag on the sofa and walked towards the collage of papers on the wall. "What's this?"

"My work."

"Work?"

"It's kinda hard to explain."

"Peter. I know you're a fan of my work..."

Clinton nodded, smiling.

"A person's work speaks clearly about their life. I'd love to learn about yours."

"It's complicated."

DiBianco scanned the countless polaroids and printouts of satanic symbols, crime scenes, murder victims, serial killers; and articles, newspaper clippings, and notes galore.

It's quite a shock seeing this stuff on anyone's wall, much less a young man whose apartment DiBianco was now standing in. He suddenly wasn't sure he wanted to know.

"Why don't you begin with how you found me?" A sudden knot of fear stuck in DiBianco's throat. "What brought you to Saint Mary's?"

"As you can see, I have an attraction to the occult, and the macabre—but it's not the type of attraction I'd call bad, or dangerous."

"How so? This stuff looks pretty dangerous to me."

"I work to expose this stuff. I don't live it—"

"Could have fooled me."

"Mike, hear me out." He was defensive, but confident. "I solve mysteries—shed light on the evil that lurks out there. I'm not one of them."

"I see." DiBianco felt a little better. "You're kinda like a ... like a—"

"—A private investigator?"

"Yeah."

"Only I work for myself ... Oh, and God."

DiBianco walked toward the bag on the sofa and unzipped it. "Let's have a look, shall we."

"You wanted to know how I found you." Clinton reminded, following DiBianco to the sofa, trying to glance inside the bag. "I seem to have this problem, at least that's what I've been told. I can't let mysteries go unsolved. I become trapped by them. It's a minor problem that sometimes gets me into trouble. This time, it led me to you."

DiBianco pulled out his laptop, the purple Speedo and the dreaded hospital gown and tossed them on the sofa.

"That's right," DiBianco said. "You overheard a strange couple whispering in a restroom..."

"Yeah."

"What the hell did they say that so compelled you to drop everything and follow them?"

"I don't know, exactly, something about the tone of it all, I guess. A secret. They were planning something, something mysterious, dark. It was really..."

DiBianco pulled a brand new copy of *God Science* out of the bag; when he did a manilla folder fell to his feet. Something handwritten on the cover.

"What's this?"

Descendants of Lucifer.

41

"I've heard of them," Clinton said.

DiBianco opened the folder. It was empty.

"Why is this in here?"

"How would I know?" Clinton said. "And why should you care? It's not like it's your bag ... right?"

"I'm afraid so."

"I don't understand."

"I'm not sure how it got here, but this is my bag. These are my things."

DiBianco pulled out more books, all of them his own, and sprawled them over the sofa.

"Is that *God Science?*" Clinton said, excitedly. "I've only heard of it. Can't find it anywhere."

That explains the slump in book sales.

"Can I—"

DiBianco handed him the book. "Keep it."

Clinton beamed like a child in a candy store.

"Tell me about this sacred brotherhood."

"They believe they are the literal descendants of Lucifer." Clinton ran up to his collage wall, ripped off a computer printout, and handed it to DiBianco. He was growing fast with excitement. "I uncovered a lot on these guys a few months ago when I ran into some punks claiming to be members. They had been causing trouble around here."

"Were they?" DiBianco said. "Descendants of Lucifer?"

"Kinda."

"What do you mean ... kinda?"

"Their parents are."

DiBianco chuckled. "See, that goes to show how deranged these guys are. If they're *literal descendants* like they claim, then so are their children."

"Not necessarily. But that's not what's important." Clinton's voice grew even more excited now. "The Brotherhood have been around for centuries. This is the biggest mystery I've ever seen."

DiBianco gazed at Clinton with intrigue. Something about this sacred brotherhood was suddenly stirring up butterflies in the pit of his stomach and he needed to know why. "Tell me everything."

"Just read," he said pointing at the printout.

There wasn't much. Just a short blurb. Yet what DiBianco saw took his breath away.

"I thought you might like that—"

DiBianco's throat started to swell. He suddenly couldn't breathe.

"Are you okay?" Clinton reached around and patted him on the back.

"Where did you find this?" DiBianco said.

"On the internet."

"Bring me to the website ... now!"

"I can't."

"Why not?"

"It's not there."

"What?"

"That's the problem with tracking these people. They're always on the move. Their domains are here today, gone tomorrow ... always top secret. I found this little gem completely by accident; the site was gone less than an hour later."

"Is there anyway to prove this?"

"Not likely."

"We need to find these guys, and fast."

"I'm not sure we do. These guys are seriously screwed up; they're like an anti-Christian terrorist organization. They fear nothing and kill anything that gets in there way."

"There's a reason why this folder is in my bag; and if this printout is true ... billions of lives are at stake ... including ours. I see no other choice."

42

Savanna crept down the sweltering brick staircase, her fingers firmly pinching her nose. It was the worst smell she had ever experienced. Sweat dripped from her forehead. She grew dizzy from holding her breath.

She knew what she had to do, but couldn't believe she was going through with it. She had never killed anyone before. She knew now, she was in way to deep. All choice had been stripped away. She worked for Fuller now, and Fuller worked for ... well, he called It, Lucifer in the Flesh. The Antichrist. To Savanna, It had no name, only Master.

Halfway down, her ears were accosted by voices. They came from within the building. Male voices, coming from just beyond the door at the bottom of the stairs.

Without a thought and with extreme vigor, Savanna turned and retreated up the stairs. She stumbled. The heal of one of her stilettos broke. Her right ankle twisted and popped. She fell. Her head struck the battered brink and concrete. A snap shuttered in her ears. There was a sharp pain. Then blackness.

43

"Oh my God!" The shrill voice was a man's, though it sounded to DiBianco like it could have been a woman's. It came from the hall just outside Clinton's door.

"Is she dead?" Another feminine voice shouted.

Clinton rushed to the door and yanked it open. It took great effort, but he was used to it.

"Is everything all right, Frank," Clinton said, recognizing his neighbor. "What's going on?"

"Oh, Peter." His voice was flamboyant, his hands flailed through the air. "I swear, I didn't see anything."

DiBianco gazed at Clinton from the sofa. "What's the hell's happening out there?"

Clinton shot back a look of uncertainty.

DiBianco's curiosity took over and he barreled his way through the door. Clinton stepped aside.

DiBianco made the short trek through the hall in three hasty steps. DiBianco's eyes squinted in the concentrated sunlight of the sweltering staircase. His nostrils were invaded by that gut wrenching stench again, only this time there was a bitter ripeness to it. He recognized the stench.

Blood.

"I swear I didn't see anything," Frank cried.

"She was just there," another man cried.

DiBianco was uncomfortable around this couple.

Frank and the other man—DiBianco assumed his boyfriend, dressed in tight black shorts and a pink halter top, his hair beach blond, bright pink lips and eyeshadow sealing the deal—stepped onto the sidewalk and gazed down at them.

But it was what he saw next that sent him to his knees.

"Savanna?"

44

Her head was bleeding. Sprawled out like a rag doll on the crumbling brick inside the sweltering pit, the scorching sun bleaching all color from her face thin, Savanna looked dead.

"Clinton!" DiBianco's voice was tearful, but strong. "Give me a hand. *Hurry!*"

Clinton propped his door open with an old book from the hallway and ran to help.

Careful not to do further harm to her already frail body, they carried her into the apartment.

At the center of the room, Clinton laid her feet on the floor, cleared away the bag and books from the sofa, and lifted her legs onto the plush oversized cushions.

Placing a pillow under her head, a small silver earpiece fell into DiBianco's hand. It was in several pieces. A three-inch wire with a tiny microphone at the end was snarled in her hair. He carefully removed it and tossed it aside.

Clinton ran to the kitchenette and filled a pan with cool water and grabbed a dish towel from the handle on the fridge.

"Here," he said.

DiBianco took the wet rag and cleared the blood from her face.

"That's her. The woman I heard in the restroom. The one I followed to the hospital."

DiBianco was shocked to she her. Why was she here? Why was she in London? How did she find him?

"She's lucky," Clinton said with confidence.

"What do you mean?"

"Looks like a superficial wound," he said pointing at the

cut in her forehead. "It could have been much worse."

"How pray-tell, would you know that?"

"I've seen my share of diving injuries; that and I'm an avid fan of the Discovery Channel. *Go Doctor G!*"

"She's not waking up. Any ideas, *Doctor G?*"

"Check her eyes." Clinton grabbed a flashlight from the counter. "See if her pupils dilate."

DiBianco grabbed the flashlight and shone it in her face. She squirmed and opened her eyes, only to shut then tightly, screaming in pain.

DiBianco dropped the flashlight and tried to calm her. He placed the towel on her forehead.

"Savanna," he said. "It's me. Michael."

"You know her?" Clinton's tone was critical.

She groaned and winced.

Her eyes cinched shut.

"Bu." Her voice was faint.

She quivered. "Bo..."

"What is it?" DiBianco said, anxiety building.

"Aba," she gasped, her voice exerted.

"What's she saying?" DiBianco glanced at Clinton, who stood behind the sofa, gazing in disbelief. "I don't understand."

She moved her legs. DiBianco held them down. She screamed. The pain was agonizing.

"Bomb!" Her eyes shot wide with terror.

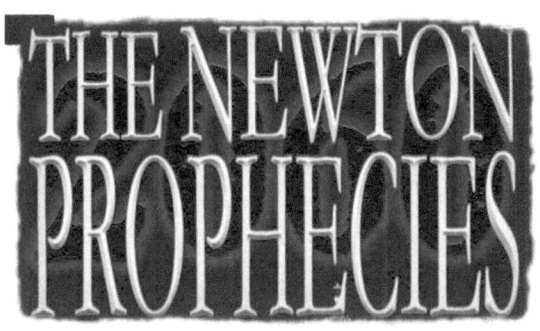

PART THREE

DARK SECRETS REVEALED

45

Pulling into Governor's Square the black Caddy veered off the road, recklessly entering a US Embassy security checkpoint before squealing to a stop.

The driver flashed his badge to security.

"Good morning Agent Packard. Who's your passenger?"

"Agent Camillin. FBI ... Boston Field."

"ID please."

Camillin complied.

"Couldn't have come at a better time, Mr Camillin, the AIC's chopper just landed. He's expecting you."

The tall fence slid open. Men with rifles slung over their shoulders watched them drive through.

Once the gate closed, Agent Packard gunned it, the Caddy squealed around a sharp turn, then sped down a hill into a lower level parking lot.

Camillin felt ill as the car skidded to an abrupt stop in a narrow parking space. Packard's name stared back at him from a white sign over the hood.

Camillin grabbed his bag from the back seat and made strides for the building.

Officers waited outside.

"Good morning."

Camillin nodded.

The officers opened the doors. Camillin's bag dragged behind him while he hustled in.

"Straight ahead, Agent Camillin."

"Thanks," he said under his breath. The large sign on the glass doors made that statement unnecessary.

US Department of Homeland Security.

All he needed now was to find the head of the Bureau—the AIC, or Agent in Charge—and get brought up to speed on the situation.

The moment Camillin entered the double doors, he was approached by a tall brute figure in black slacks, white shirt, and red necktie. He had a gold badge clipped next to his TEXAS belt-buckle and walked like a bull-rider.

"Good morning," the man said with an outreached hand. His voice was deep. Abrasive. Full of fire.

Camillin took his hand. "I'm looking for Agent Fuller."

"I believe you found him." Fuller grinned, his teeth like pearls.

46

Earlier that morning, in the confines of a dark meeting space, hundreds of miles away, two cloaked men spoke in the flickering amber light of a lone flame—its warmth absorbed by the blackness of the room surrounding them. It forged shimmering halos in their dark oil-slicked eyes.

"You are aware that things have changed?" the man behind the desk said, pulling a piece of paper off a large stack, and passing it to the other, taller man.

"Yes, My Lord," the servant said.

Their voices were faint, nearly a whisper.

The paper was old, yellow, the handwriting like nothing the taller man had ever seen; there was another paper, this one white, a clean computer printout, on it ... a list.

"Take these to your men."

The man was obviously growing senile, there was no way it could be done on such short notice; but he was the Master; no one, second guessed Master and expected to live to complain about it.

"Yes, My Lord."

"Due to a formidable change in prophecy, I fear war is imminent. We must be prepared."

"Yes, My Lord."

"Do not fail me."

"What about the missing bags?"

"I trust you'll take care of that?"

"Yes, My Lord."

"And the others?"

"Ready for deployment, My Lord."

"It's a shame it has come to this."

The servant nodded.

"Be cautious."

"Yes, My Lord."

"This will not be an easy task."

"Understood, My Lord."

"Many will be lost."

"Yes, My Lord."

47

The mood in Clinton's basement apartment was solemn.

Savanna sat on the sofa, her feet on one of the chairs from the dining table. Her right ankle was wrapped tightly in an Ace bandage from the first-aid kit given to Clinton when he left home the year before.

DiBianco's fingers grew numb holding an ice-packed towel to Savanna's head. He wiped her tear sodden cheeks. "Where's the bomb?" he said.

"They're going to kill me."

"Who's going to kill you?" DiBianco said.

"I can't..."

"Savanna. You've gotta tell me."

"You don't understand."

"Where's the bomb?" Clinton's voice was exasperated.

"You can't..."

"Can't what?" DiBianco said.

"There's no way to stop it."

"Where's the bomb?" Clinton's voice was stronger now.

"If I tell you, you'll try to find it—try to disarm it."

"Yeah." Clinton sounded sarcastic. "And you'd have objection to that?

"Savanna, please." DiBianco's eyes were calm. "You have to help me understand. You must believe me. We can help—"

"You can't. And why would you?" She started to cry.

"Where's the freakin' bomb?" Clinton shouted.

"They're everywhere," she cried, "even here!"

Clinton paced the apartment, looking for anything that could be a bomb.

"It can't be disarmed," she cried.

DiBianco looked perplexed. "Of course it can."

"Not these." Her voice was stern.

"These?" Clinton said. "How many are there?"

Savanna looked like a suspect who had realized she had said too much. She grew silent. Yet her eyes continued to speak to DiBianco.

Clinton slammed the cabinet doors over his sink. "Damn it! Why won't you just tell us where they are?"

"Savanna," DiBianco said. "What's wrong?"

"I need you to know, I love you."

"You need to help us," DiBianco said firmly.

"It's new technology. The bombs are designed to do one thing and one thing only. Detonate. If you screw with them, they detonate sooner."

"Jesus." The hairs on DiBianco's arms sprung to life and his heart throbbed as harsh reality took root. "What's going on?" DiBianco gaped at Savanna, who gazed back with loving discernment. "What have you done?"

48

DiBianco picked up a duffle bag and dumped it out on the floor, inches from Savanna's feet. There were clothes, towels, books, paper, pictures; loads of crap. No bomb.

He grabbed the other bag and did the same. Pairs of shoes, magazines, toilet paper, more books; a worthless assortment of business luggage now lay scattered on Clinton's floor.

"What's going on here?" Had she been mistaken? Did she hit her head too hard?

"Where's the bomb, Savanna?" Clinton said.

Savanna looked at the pile of junk and lifted a finger. "There." She was pointing at DiBianco.

"Me?"

"No!" she snapped, "The freakin' bag!"

DiBianco was confused. It was just a typical duffle bag. Nothing fancy. Wal-Mart grade. $14.99. 2 for $20 in the springtime. DiBianco glanced at the bag in his hand, then at the other one lying on the floor by the table.

"Yes," she said. "That one too."

"Holy shit!" Clinton said, jumping away from the table like a snake had just made for his foot.

"Don't worry. They won't go off." She paused. "Not yet anyway... Just don't get any crazy ideas and we'll be just fine."

DiBianco laid the bag on the floor and stepped away, then sat on the sofa next to Savanna.

"What's going on? Please, you have to explain this to me." DiBianco laid his hand on her forehead to see if the swelling had gone down. It had. "I couldn't possibly be more confused."

"I know," she said.

"Tell me, and please be honest." His throat choked at the thought of why someone would want her dead. He didn't want to say anything foolish, but he needed to know. "Have you done anything wrong? Have you ... killed someone?"

"Of course not." She laughed. "I'd never—"

"Then what the hell's going on?" He stood from the sofa.

"If you had even the slightest clue..." she started, then paused. "You're not ready."

"What?"

"You'd run away."

"I've never seen you like this, Savanna. You've always been so ... alive ... peppy. You have to believe me. We can help. Whatever it is, we can fix it. We can make it right."

Savanna gazed at DiBianco, glancing at Clinton for a moment, then returning to DiBianco. Then she looked down, clasping her hands together, obviously trying to stop herself from shaking, failing miserably at the task.

"I don't need help."

DiBianco could feel his patience fading.

"I've been hiding this secret for so long." The moment the words began to flow, so followed the tears. "You don't know me; you haven't a clue."

DiBianco was shocked, but eager to know more.

"I love you, Michael, I truly do." Her tears seemed uncontrollable now.

"It's okay. Once we know what's going on, we'll be able to fix it—make it right."

"No. You're wrong." Her eyes sunk into deep despair. "Once you know, it'll all be over."

49

2:30 PM. US Embassy, London.

The phone on Fuller's hip vibrated, sending chills up his spine for the third time in less than five minutes. He had been trying to build Camillin's confidence, determined to get him to return to Boston, convince him things were under control. But he could no longer ignore the call.

"Hold that thought." Fuller stood from his desk, sneered, then grabbed the cellphone. "I must take this. Excuse me." He left his office, closing Camillin inside.

† † †

"What is it?" He said, very hushed. "You know not to call me in my office."

I lost her, Sir. The voice on the phone was distraught.

"What do you mean ... lost her?"

She followed them back to the kid's house. Everything was perfect. Then the signal died. Haven't been able to reach her since.

"That's impossible. The signal can't die. Something's up. Find her, immediately."

Yes, Sir.

"And Afridi ... Treat her with the same respect you're to give DiBianco ... do you hear me?"

Yes, Sir.

"Nothing can interfere—and I *do* mean nothing!"
Understood, Sir.
"You're a good man, Uluba."
Thank you, Sir.

50

"Anything I tell you now, will only be in vain. All this," Savanna said, pointing around at Clinton's apartment, "and everything out there," she pointed out the window at the barren sidewalk, "goes bye-bye at midnight."

Clinton grabbed the last chair from the table and sat, legs spread, backwards, resting his arms on the back of the chair in front of the sofa. " I guess you better start talking," he said.

She was no longer crying. Her face looked battered, sodden with tears and runny makeup. DiBianco thought she had run dry, nothing left. Part of him wanted to feel bad for her, but he was struggling to feel anything more than shock and horror at the moment.

"Please," DiBianco started. "Explain the bombs. Why can't they be disarmed? And how many off these damn things are there?"

Savanna pulled her feet off the chair and hobbled toward one of the duffle bags. "Do you have a pair of scissors?"

"Absolutely!" Clinton jumped from the chair and strode to the drawer, by the sink. There was a large pair, the type designed for multiple use: cutting clothe, paper, cardboard, rope, chicken, etcetera. "Will these do?"

Savanna waved him over. "That's perfect."

Clinton handed her the scissors and retuned to the chair, this time sitting normally, facing the center of the room.

Savanna slowly cut along the bottom of the duffle bag and

then up and around each end. When she finally pulled the bag apart, exposing what hid inside, DiBianco knew what it was they were dealing with, and it wasn't pretty; but it also wasn't the half of it.

"Plastic Explosives," Clinton said.

"Worse," DiBianco said. "Sheet Explosives."

Clinton looked confused.

"This stuff is brutal," DiBianco explained. "The military uses it to destroy tanks. Terrorists have used it to blow up ships, like The USS Cole. Demolition crews use it to take out some of the largest structures ever built; total annihilation, in seconds.

"There's got to be 30 sheets in here. Just one is more than enough to blow a hole the size of a Hummer in the side of a building, perhaps even take that building down, if placed just right." DiBianco began to hyperventilate. Sweat formed on his brow. He was fighting another panic attack. The room began to shrink. He closed his eyes.

"What's it wrapped in?" Clinton said.

In the blackness of DiBianco's mind, there was an explosion; a domed structure, it appeared to be a state house, perhaps the DiBianco House, erupted into a blinding fiery ball of light, then a massive cloud filled the night sky.

"That's what makes it so devastating." Savanna looked hopeless. Her face was sure there was nothing they could do.

DiBianco's eyes bolted open with terror. Why was he having these visions? What did it mean?

"How so," Clinton replied.

"The entire bomb: the plastique, the wires, the timer, the circuitry, memory chips, even the secret ingredient, are all vacuum sealed in this bag."

"Secret ingredient?" Clinton said snidely. "What the hell is this, Martha Stewart?"

DiBianco tried to pay attention but couldn't get the image of the exploding dome out of his head. He was desperate for answers, but instead was flooded with even more questions.

"It's a hypersensitive O2 sensor—"

"Holy shit," Clinton cried. "There's no way!"

"That's what I've been trying to tell you."

"I'm sorry," DiBianco said. "I'm not following."

Clinton gazed at DiBianco with deadly seriousness. His breathing was shaky, and for the first time since meeting the kid, DiBianco sensed fear—real honest fear—in his eyes.

"If that plastic gets so much as a pinhole in it—" Clinton motioned his hands into a monstrous mushroom-cloud, expelling a rumbling, popping wind sound from his mouth.

DiBianco gazed at Savanna. She had cut the bottom of that duffle bag open with a pair of kitchen shears. Either she was crazy, suicidal, or knew a whole lot more than she was letting them know—information they needed if they were going to solve this mystery.

"What time is it?" DiBianco said.

Clinton pointed to a clock on the wall above the table. "Told you," he said, smugly. "No lines."

It was 3:05 PM.

DiBianco was pumped. "How many are there?" It was like a mighty wind swept his soul, clearing his mind, revitalizing his spirit, inspiring him to fight. He didn't understand why, but he suddenly knew the world was depending on him—Christianity was depending on him. "And where are they?"

51

"We have to locate the Holy Land before it's too late," Savanna said.

"Excuse me?" DiBianco contorted his face into a half snicker, half snarl. *What the hell is she talking about now?*

"The plan isn't to destroy the world," she said. "That's the stuff of B-movies and horror novels. We're gathering into the Holy Land and bringing with us those we think are willing to heed his words and fight against theocracy and human suppression."

DiBianco looked on with astonishment.

"But nothing comes easy," she continued. "We're tested. No one knows where the Holy Land is. We must find it on our own."

"Wait," DiBianco said. "I'm lost."

"Could this have anything to do with the folder we found?" Clinton said, his face bursting with a strange combination of excitement, intrigue, and terror. "The Descendants of Lucifer?"

"You're kidding?" DiBianco said.

"Yes," she interrupted.

"My God," Clinton said, "you're one of them?"

She nodded.

"But..." DiBianco's eyes were struck with astonishment. "You believe in God?" he cried. "We..." He was visibly upset. "The books ... We worked so closely on those. What about—"

"I do believe, just not the same way you do."

DiBianco raised his hands to his brow and pinched his temples between his thumbs.

"Why would anyone follow a God as selfish as the one you believe in? The one *you* worship."

DiBianco's blood began to boil. He didn't want to explode, but he could feel it coming.

"A God whose goal is to make every human, like him. One who expects every person to give all they have to him. Who in their right mind would live in a world where everyone is the same, mindless ants fighting for one cause, one purpose, each given only enough to survive and no more, no matter how hard they work, no matter how much they deserve better. Who would live in such a place, where there's one supreme being, and every living thing around that supreme being, works only to increase the power, stature, and supremacy of that one supreme being."

"Enough!" DiBianco's heart was bursting with rage. He could hear no more of it. It was hard enough to listen without knowing where it was coming from. DiBianco paced the room, which started to shrink smaller and smaller until he felt the paint blister off onto his clammy skin.

"I knew you weren't ready."

He had to leave. He had to get away. Away from her. He didn't want to hear another word of it, or believe, even for one-second that those words could be coming from Savanna Campbell, the only woman he had ever been close to, the woman he dreamt he'd marry, and had seen that day rapidly approaching, only to hit this impenetrable wall.

"Michael," she snapped. "Sit down!" Her sudden tone grappled his throat and yanked him toward the sofa. He sat, his knees bouncing in rhythm with his racing heart, the heals of his shoes tapped against the hardwood floor.

"Just because I disagree, doesn't make me a bad person, Michael..."

He wanted to shout; rip her a new place to sit; let her know how off beat she was; but she wouldn't stop long enough for him to get his bearings in a row. He was loosing his mind.

"...I'm a peaceful, loving woman who believes in freedom, self awareness, natural harmony, family, love, peace, all the things you believe in, or at least aught to.

"You're following a false God," she said. "You don't even know it. You don't have a clue. Your Church is nothing but a fake. It's doctrine designed by men to brainwash people into believing that *God the Father* and his son *Jesus* are whom we aught to follow. They brainwash people into believing that

God is wonderful, Heaven is glorious, that righteousness is the path to eternal life and unyielding happiness. Sounds wonderful, until you understand the harsh reality of it.

"It's not a path to eternal happiness. It's a path to an eternity of kissing Jesus's ass and administering to only him, keeping him eternally powerful—the great Almighty God.

"The Church has done an amazing job of brainwashing the world into believing that Lucifer is a demon, some sort of devil, a wicked spirit whose only purpose is to corrupt and pollute the inhabitants of earth.

"*I* know different. *I've* heard the truth. And it is *amazing*... It's wonderful... It's *real*."

Clinton sat, mesmerized by her voice.

DiBianco rose, he needed to speak—

"Sit down!" she snapped.

DiBianco unwittingly complied, his hands shaking even more.

"Lucifer *is* God..."

DiBianco rolled his eyes and gritted his teach, then bolted to his feet. "That's it. I can't listen any more." Without another thought he stormed toward the door.

"Mike," Clinton shouted. "Whether you like it or not, we have to know. We must figure out how to stop it!"

Savanna laughed. "That's why he's here, Michael." She hobbled toward the door, her hands traveling the wall, keeping pressure off her ankle. "He's come. He has told us the truth." She paused. "Your God can't save you. Why is that?"

DiBianco left the apartment and sprinted up the staircase, taking the steps three at a time, finally spilling onto the sidewalk, back into the real world, grim as that now appeared.

Savanna's voice carried through the hallway, out the door, and into the muggy air.

"He's only in your mind, Michael. He's not real!"

52

Standing on the barren sidewalk of Wilton Road, two thoughts raced through DiBianco's mind.

One, why does the world look so different? Victoria Station was empty. Not a soul walked the streets. Not a car passed by. He was alone.

And two, the only way he was going to find out what was happening, and devise a plan to stop it, was to join her at her game. He'd have to become a follower of the Descendants of Lucifer.

DiBianco gazed down the stairs, into the doorway where Savanna stood, gazing back at him.

He smiled. "I love you." His words brought a warm smile to Savanna's lips. "I'm sorry," he said. "I want to hear."

53

Savanna's face was rich with enthusiasm. She acted like she bought his sentiment entirely, though DiBianco struggled to believe that she had. She wasn't that naive, but then again, he didn't know her anymore. He was playing the game. He was listening now.

"How do we find the Holy Land?" DiBianco said, pulling a chair up to the sofa and sitting with Clinton in front of Savanna, who was comfortably perched on the sofa. "Isn't Jerusalem the Holy Land? I've been there once."

"Where's that folder?" she said, seeming to ignore his comment.

"The Descendant's of Lucifer?" Clinton said.

"Yes, where is it?"

"It's empty," DiBianco explained.

"That can't be," she cried, "the pages..."

"What?"

"Son-of-a-bitch ... he took them."

"Who? ... What?"

"Damn him!"

"Who?" DiBianco said again.

"Afridi..."

Afridi? he thought. *Why is that name familiar?*

"He's my partner," she started, then stopped. "was, my partner. We were supposed to find the Holy Land together."

"What do you mean, find the Holy Land?" DiBianco questioned. "Isn't it Jerusalem?"

"No," she said reaching for her headset. "That's what the Church would have you believe. But I assure you ... they're very wrong."

"It's broken," DiBianco said, picking up the pieces of her headset from the floor and handing them to her. "I plucked it from your hair when you were unconscious."

She grabbed them, frowned, and tossed them into the pile.

"We're not only to gather into the Holy Land, but bring truth to as many people as possible before the end of days." Savanna gazed into space, lost in thought. "We have waited for this day for nearly fifty years; it is a day of rebirth; a day of reckoning; yet so many are not ready to hear," she said, locking her gaze upon DiBianco's. "Not even the chosen among us."

DiBianco got a sudden chill down his spine; it was crazy; but something about what she was saying rung true. There was something hidden in the message, something he suspected, even she had no clue about. Something much larger.

"When the clock strikes midnight tonight, only those who have found the way to the Holy Land will stand to inherit the earth.

Oh my God, she's out of her mind, DiBianco thought. *How can I possibly go along with this?* Struggling with his emotions, he pondered and prayed. His mind connected with his heart and for the first time in his life he prayed with pure loving desire. It was a prayer like none he had ever made before. A prayer he hoped would find God, and fast.

Our God, who art in heaven, hollowed be thy name. Our kingdom come, thy work be done, on earth as it is in heaven.

Lord, give me strength. I love thee, of this I am certain ye know. All I am about to do on this day, I do in thy name. I do it to save thy world ... thy people. Please, make me strong. Let thy spirit guide me. Keep the spirit of darkness from me.

Oh Lord. Help us, thy people, in our hour of darkness. I will fight to the end for you. I will do whatever it is you ask of me. I will even die.

In Jesus' name I pray ... Amen.

"...the Newton Papers hold the key," she said.

DiBianco couldn't believe his ears. Had she said what he thought she said? In a heart beat, things were coming together. The blurb Clinton pulled from his wall. It stated that the sacred brotherhood was preparing for war, a war against Christianity—a war against Christ himself, and every soul daring to stand in his name. DiBianco's initial theories had been wrong, dead wrong, this was worse than anything he had ever thought possible.

"Your people stole them?" He realized he had said your people long after the words left his lips, and expected a harsh response. It didn't come. She didn't seem to notice.

"We have the papers," she said, "but we didn't steal

them ... you did."

DiBianco fell ill; a cold sweat chilled his body. He hadn't stolen anything, he knew that with all his soul, he never would have... "Afridi," he said, his eyes lighting ablaze. "I know that name."

Savanna smirked.

"FBI," he said. "He's an Agent!"

"He's one of us." She sounded proud. "So are many others; the world's most important people," she explained. "Like your prized President—"

"Bush?" Clinton interrupted. "Are you out of your mind?"

Was that even up for debate? DiBianco thought.

"...and the Prime Minister," she continued.

DiBianco tried to make sense out of the millions of thoughts racing through his mind. There was no way he had stolen those papers. And President Bush? Blair? It was obvious that Savanna was the poor soul who had been under the influence of some serious brainwashing.

"How about the bombs at Divinity?" she said.

My God, DiBianco thought. "But you were there!"

"I also knew it was coming. We left before—"

"We?"

"Crystal," she said, "oh, didn't you know? ... She's one of us too."

DiBianco didn't know what was right, wrong, left, right, up, down, good, or bad. His brain hurt. He wanted to close his eyes. Wish himself away. Anywhere but there.

"In fact," Savanna continued, "she should be planting her page on a loved politician right now."

"What?" DiBianco's tone was flabbergast.

"It's quite simple. It's one of the ways we communicate our message. After each cryptic key is deciphered, we leave it behind for others to find. It's our way of spreading the word."

"Why are these people being assassinated," DiBianco questioned, "and why leave the keys on their bodies?"

"They, sadly, are those who have chosen to turn their

backs on the covenants they made. They folded in the face of struggle, and threatened to expose the DoL's plans. Through those who have passed on, we expose the truth. Those pages hold the key to finding the Holy Land. The key to salvation."

"Why would the Newton Papers hold any such key?" DiBianco said, still unable to piece together this fast growing puzzle.

"Who do you think founded the DoL?"

54

Outside, dark figures lurked in the alleyways surrounding Clinton's apartment. They had been given strict orders and intended to fulfill them; that was, after all, their only duty in life.

The area surrounding the apartment complex was abandoned. An evacuation order had been given by the head of Homeland Security. Evacuation drills where not unheard of, but this was no drill, and the threat was very real.

Task force vehicles blocked every street, alleyway, and pathway within a quarter mile of Victoria Station. Even the trains in and out of Victoria were halted. Not a single police officer could be seen. This was solely the Embassy's mission.

55

DiBianco sifted through the pile of junk sprawled over Clinton's floor for the folder he had found earlier. The one marked *Descendants of Lucifer*.

Isaac Newton, he thought. *The founder of the Descendants of Lucifer?* The implications were astronomical. Newton despised The Church. He had no doubt. And had written many thousands of papers on how he knew that The Roman Catholic Church had fallen into utter apostasy—a falling away from the truth—after the crowning of Emperor Charlemagne in the year 800.

Many scholars, historians, and yes, conspirators believe Newton had been a Grand Master for the Priory of Sion for decades until his death—a secret brotherhood devoted to keeping the Holy Grail hidden away from those who might wish to destroy it, mainly The Church. But Newton, founder of a satanic brotherhood? *Never.* DiBianco couldn't fathom the thought. Newton was a staunch believer in God, Christ even, though his beliefs differed from that of mainstream Christianity.

DiBianco found the DoL folder, but not a single Newton Paper. He fell to his knees.

Savanna was upset, but held strong to her goal. "We must locate Afridi," she said. "He has the pages. I know it."

"Why is he not with you?" The moment the question left DiBianco's lips, an even more baring question occurred to him. "Why did you come here?"

The sound of tiny plastic keys slapping against the backboard of Clinton's computer keyboard intruded upon the sudden library-like atmosphere of the small space. He was searching the internet for information about the DoL and their possible connection with the stolen Newton papers.

Savanna's face went cold. It was obvious she didn't want to answer the question.

"Hey," Clinton said, excitement filling his eager tone. "I think I found something."

Savanna gazed into space. For a moment she looked lost.

"What is it?" DiBianco said, jumping from his chair, making strides toward the computer station.

"Hold on," Clinton said, grabbing a piece of paper from the drawer beside the printer. "I've gotta print this sucker before I lose the page."

"Good thinking."

Clinton hit a key on the keyboard and instantly the printer screamed to life. DiBianco grabbed the printout and began to read while Clinton read aloud from the screen. "The Descendants have a global network of privately owned satellites—"

"It's how we communicate," Savanna interrupted. "It's what controls the infrastructure of our government. It's what will send The Pulse—"

Just then a crash rattled DiBianco's eardrums and before his mind registered what was happening, the room filled with a choking fog that made his eyes and throat burn.

PART FOUR

THE OLD UNDERGROUND

56

"Tear gas," Clinton shouted. Thinking fast, he ran for the sink. "Quick, cover your faces." He threw DiBianco and Savanna a wet towel and covered his own face, wrapping the towel tightly around his head; then he grabbed a hammer from the side of the stove and sprinted for the door.

"No!" DiBianco said. "That's exactly what they want us to do"

"Don't worry."

"What about Savanna?"

"She's one of them... *Leave her!*"

"I can't!"

"You have to!"

"No!" DiBianco ran to Savanna, who laid unconscious on the sofa. Covering her face with a towel, he hoisted her over his shoulder.

Clinton yanked the door. It swung hard, slamming into the wall. The hall was filled with fog. Whoever gassed the apartment, must have gassed the hallway too.

Clinton disappeared into the billowing cloud of poison. A few seconds later the sound of spikes prying free of their wooden graves pierced DiBianco's ears. He immediately knew the sound. It was a wonderful sound. It was the sound of hope.

Clinton's face peered through the fog as he grabbed Savanna's legs. DiBianco was getting dizzy and his throat hurt. Breathing was difficult. He wasn't sure how much longer he could last. Clinton and DiBianco carried Savanna through the hall, past the splintered doorway, into a dank room; no windows, no light, and thankfully nearly no fog.

Dropping Savanna's legs, Clinton slammed the door and shoved a cinderblock up against it. "It's been years since anyone's been in here," Clinton said, as a beam of light suddenly filled the room.

57

DiBianco hadn't noticed that Clinton grabbed the flashlight, but was glad he did. DiBianco laid Savanna's head softly on the dirt and wiped her face with the towel, then placed it over her nose and mouth.

Keeping the moist towel over his own face, Clinton circled the grave-like room with the light.

"Great plan," DiBianco said, his voice not poised.

"This building was originally a rooming house for workers while constructing the London Underground, nearly a hundred years ago. This was one of many entrances to the tunnels they would use to get to and from work."

"This leads to the subways?"

"Once upon a time."

"How do you know they still exist? Something like that would have been destroyed years ago."

"Not so. It would have been way too expensive to remove. They likely sealed the ends and called it a day."

"I hate to bust your chops, Peter; but if it's sealed, how are we supposed to get in ... or out for that matter?"

"Getting in is not the problem. I've seen the door."

"Where?"

"The owner of the building closed it off. A gang of teens used to break in and hang out. One was bit by something; he was raced to Saint Mary's and died later that night."

"That's reassuring."

"Would you rather use the front door?"

The hallway filled with the sound of running, doors slamming, glass breaking.

"We've gotta move," DiBianco said. The room was littered with wood, cinderblocks, roofing materials, abandoned tools, and workbenches. "There," he said. "Put your light back on that mattress... There. I see something."

There was a breeze. The thin wisps of fog and dust in the room was being sucked out through a hole somewhere behind the mattress.

Clinton charged at the moth-eaten pad and threw it aside, dodging a plethora of dirt, dust, and rodent feces. "There it is!"

DiBianco hoisted Savanna over his shoulder and waited for the door to open, but it didn't.

"What's wrong?"

"It's been nailed shut."

"Where's the hammer?"

"I left it in the hallway."

"Son-of-a-bitch!"

"There's got to be something I can use in here. It's a workshop for crying-out-loud." Clinton scanned the room. He needed a hammer, a crowbar, anything that could pry the door open.

Time was running out. Any second a wave of terror would rush through the door, taking them for a ride. That short, final ride that led to the end of the road.

58

"How about this?" DiBianco held a fence-post.

"Let me see." Clinton took the post. It was badly bent. He recalled the accident that caused the damage. It happened eight months before, but to Clinton, it could have happened just yesterday.

A car veered out of control one rainy night taking out five sections of chain-link fencing that once separated Clinton's apartment complex from a neighboring alleyway. To no surprise it was found that the driver was intoxicated. He nearly killed himself that night—damn lucky no one else was in the car, or the alleyway. The driver's left arm was torn off by the chain-links, he nearly bled to death before paramedics arrived.

Blood stained the fence post; a harsh reminder of the damage stupidity can cause. Ironically, that stupid act, made by a single drunk idiot, Clinton now felt was going to save their lives.

Fate?

Clinton grinned. The pole was cut at the base, there wasn't that massive ball of concrete at the end that you'd expect, and it was bent like a crowbar. "This'll work great," he said. "Come on, hurry!"

The hall was quiet, but DiBianco knew that could change in a flash. Soon who ever was after them would realize the apartment was empty, and would check the only place left. They were trapped. A frail door and cinder block were all that separated them from unimaginable dangers.

Clinton searched the door for a place to wedge the post into. "Right there!" he said, pointing at the lower right corner. A piece had broken away. It was rotten.

Clinton shoved the post inside, the wood fell apart with ease. He felt around, trying to find strong enough wood to carry the weight of the door, but it all just fell apart.

Without a thought DiBianco grabbed the slats and yanked. Chucks of wood fell free in his hands. Clinton dropped the post and followed suit, quickly removing enough to crawl through.

"What about Savanna?"

"Grab her; bring her here." Clinton crawled into the dark frosty void. "I'll pull her through."

† † †

Inside, Clinton felt an icy chill brush his back. There was an odor that didn't sink in at first, but soon would. A sound from behind made his eyes twitch. He didn't want to turn; didn't want to think about what it could be.

59

Commotion flooded the hallway.

"They're coming," DiBianco said, gazing at Clinton through the ragged hole. Clinton was frozen with fear. Without a thought DiBianco shoved Savanna into the hole and Clinton swiftly pulled her through. Clinton was shivering, so was Savanna.

DiBianco climbed through on his hands and knees, feet first, pulling blocks, tools, boxes, whatever he could, toward the door, in an attempt to camouflage their escape route.

Clinton shone the light into the depths of the tunnel. His teeth chattered. His breathing heavy, streams of fog jetting from his nostrils.

As DiBianco heaved the last cinderblock over the opening, the sound of wood splintering, heavy boots, and yelling filled the small space.

"Run!" DiBianco said. "They're coming!"

DiBianco threw Savanna over his shoulder and ran, following the spot of light bouncing in the bitter blackness that seemed to devour everything around them.

The tunnel was more like an abandoned coal mine. Beams were scattered everywhere; over head, leaning against walls, many busted up or rotten. The smell in the air was that of death: decaying wood, dirt, and flesh. There had to be countless animals sleeping an endless sleep in there, somehow making it in, but never finding a way out.

The tunnel seemed endless. A vast winding tube to the end of the earth. Clinton's foot snagged on something and he went down. DiBianco slammed into him, tripping, falling on his back. Savanna flew from his shoulder, hitting the ground with a thud. DiBianco prayed she wasn't hurt.

Clinton moaned.

DiBianco grabbed the flashlight from between his legs and aimed it toward Savanna and froze...

It's teeth were big and sharp, it reminded DiBianco of a wolf. It snarled. It's eyes blank, white, no pupils. It didn't blink, didn't squint, didn't budge. It's large wolf-like body was pale, like a ghost, unlike it's teeth, which were stained in blood.

The beast hissed, then grew silent; listening, waiting. It was blind, DiBianco could tell. It was waiting for someone to make a sound, any sound at all, so it could latch onto its newly found feast.

DiBianco didn't move. His life was dangling in front of the beast like a stake on a stick. It would have to wonder off eventually ... he hoped. But it wouldn't. No, it could smell a meal and wasn't leaving without it.

DiBianco couldn't stand looking at the beast's blank, twitching eyes; he wanted to click off the light ... pray for it to leave, but that would surely be suicide. Any move at all would have the beast lunging, frenzying on his blood engorged flesh.

There was a click—it was the clanging sound of metal on metal. The beast snapped its head backwards, toward the sound.

There was a flash of light. A deafening roar that seemed to ricochet off the cave-like walls like cannon-fire. The stench of sulfur quickly penetrated and hung uncomfortably in the thin air.

The beast fell, blood gushing from its head.

The flashlight swiftly found Savanna, laying on the ground behind the beast, shaking, a small pistol gripped in her white knuckled hands.

Clinton jumped to the sound of gunfire. The beast lay sprawled out across his legs.

Savanna went pale and collapsed, the pistol slipped from her fingers, striking the ground inches from her head.

60

Afridi stood inside the large slatted door, which agents had pulled clear off its hinges, and gazed into the dark shaft that seemed to lead into nowhere.

He had no doubt they had gone in and was certain they would never make it out, but Fuller would never accept anything less than a guarantee.

"You," Afridi shouted, pointing at a couple grunts from the bureau. "After them!"

"Yes, Sir," they said in unison.

61

Whoever was after them would certainly still be on their trail. And DiBianco knew, where there was life, there had to be fresh air, and where there was fresh air, there had to be a way out.

"There's no way that thing got in here the way we did," Clinton said, shoving the heavy carcass off his lap.

"My thoughts exactly," DiBianco said. "There has to be a

way out!"

"Not necessarily." Savanna's voice was faint. "That thing hasn't spent a day outside in its life. I've never seen anything like it. It's like it has adapted to the darkness. Did you see its eyes? Who knows how many of those things are roaming scavenging for food down here."

DiBianco's face sunk with horror.

"We must be still," Clinton whispered.

"We can't stay here." Whoever was after them, would not give up, DiBianco knew that. They were still after them, and would likely gain fast. "We must be quiet, but we must move."

Savanna propped herself on her knees and tried to stand, wincing as her foot touched the ground. "Keep your eyes and ears peeled." She stood, her right knee bent, hands grabbing a beam over head. *I can make it,* she thought. The pain was incredible. She started to walk. "You guys coming? You know, some light would be nice."

62

DiBianco rose to his knees, slipped the pistol into his pocket and stood, shining the flashlight into the vast darkness.

He could not keep his teeth from chattering. The blackness sucked the life out of the light. Its beam was growing weaker by the second.

"Oh no," Savanna cried.

"I suppose I should take the lead."

Clinton nodded, unwilling to offer a rebuttal.

DiBianco approached Savanna who had taken only a few steps and put her arm around his neck.

"Allow me."

She didn't argue.

DiBianco slapped the light against his leg. Its brightness returned, but only for a moment.

"We have to find a way out," DiBianco said. "and fast." He tapped the light again. Again it spurted brightness. Again that brightness faded.

"What are we gonna do?" Clinton said.

The answer wasn't pleasant, but it was obvious.

"I guess we have to—"

Ahhhhhhhhh!

The scream seemed to bleed out of DiBianco's ears like a screeching bullhorn; it was Savanna. Something had jetted across the floor.

"What was that?" he said.

Clinton froze.

"It was another one of those things," Clinton said through his teeth.

Anticipating an attack, DiBianco put his hand in his pocket and clutched the pistol. Sweat pored off his forehead, an icy sweat that felt like needles pricking his skin. His heart raced.

Not now. Christ, please. Not now!

"There!" Clinton shouted.

"For Christ's sake, stop shouting," DiBianco said, nearly shouting himself.

Something lurched from a shadow—

DiBianco's vision was blinded by a sudden flash of white light. The spade shovel cut through the surface. A streak of blood in the snow. A severed head. His mother gazed back up at him—

"*GET IT OFF ME!*" Savanna screamed.

63

"It's just a rat!" Clinton shouted.

"It bit me." Savanna's voice was shaken. "The son-of-a-bitch bit me!"

"Calm down," DiBianco said, trying to put the haunting memory of his mother out of his head. "We have to calm down. There's more of those *things* down here."

"I don't know *what* the hell's down here," Savanna cried, knocking DiBianco's hand away. "But I know we've got to get the hell out of here!"

"Uh, guys," Clinton said. "We have company."

DiBianco spun the flashlight toward Clinton and saw two lights in the distance. Suddenly, they began to bounce and sway erratically.

"It's them," DiBianco said. *"RUN!"*

Clinton snatched the flashlight and took off.

DiBianco scooped Savanna in his arms and followed close behind. The light was nearly dead now. Glancing over his shoulder, he saw the bouncing lights gaining. They couldn't have been more than twenty yards away.

Clinton was pulling away fast.

DiBianco's stamina was draining. His feet tripping on every stone and stick in his way. He had to stop, he was going to fall, hurting himself and Savanna. But stopping would only assure capture, and likely death at the hands of whoever was chasing them. He had to run. *Run, damn you! Run!*

Clinton's light suddenly vanished.

A split second later the ground fell out from under DiBianco's feet and they fell.

64

Time stopped, and for a moment he lost Savanna. He was alone. His heart in his throat. Falling. There was a flash of light beneath him. A splash. The pressure smacked his head like a sledgehammer. He held his breath. Something grabbed his legs. It didn't let go.

Which way's up?

His lungs pleaded for air. His arms and legs cramped, threatening to shut down all together. He had to keep swimming. Keep climbing. But something had his legs and wasn't letting go.

Finally, his head broke the surface of the water and his lungs filled with a painful blend of icy mist and brisk air. It hurt, but his body craved it. It was a good pain. It meant he was still alive.

The grip on his legs released. A moment later something grabbed his head, pulling him under. Under the water he heard something like gunfire. Bullets sprayed the surface around him. His head bobbed in and out of the water. A voice was screaming. *Help!*

Gunfire encircled him. He couldn't believe he hadn't been hit, perhaps he had. His body was so cold, he likely wouldn't feel it if he had been shot.

Help! The voice screamed again. It was Savanna.

DiBianco fought to lift her head out of the water while keeping himself from sinking. But it wasn't working. Every time he'd lift, she pushed him under. His strength was nearly gone. His stamina spent, the freezing water made his muscles seize. He feared for Savanna. Any second, they'd both drown ... or get shot.

Something grabbed DiBianco's arm and yanked him onto a ledge. His back cramped. The pain was agonizing. His spine seized, spasms ricocheting throughout his body. "Savanna!" he cried.

Clinton looked at him with saddened eyes.

She was gone.

65

"She can't be gone."

Fear and anxiety took over, but not like it had so many times in the past. This was different. Adrenaline rammed itself into DiBianco's body. He felt bigger, stronger, invincible. It was a high he had never felt before.

All pain disappeared. He stood and peered over the water. "There's light in here," he said, looking down stream, hoping to see Savanna, bobbing around like a buoy in a choppy sea.

There was no sign of her.

A bright light beamed in from what looked like the end of the tunnel, but they could no longer be in the tunnel. This was a massive chasm, carved into the earth by tons of raging water. "Where the hell are we?"

"It's part of the Old Underground," Clinton said.

"What?" DiBianco's eyes struggled to see how it could be. "This is massive. I've never seen a tunnel so wide."

"In the early 1900s, an entire length of Tube was flooded by the River Thames. It was an unbelievable disaster. The water was so fast, so strong, so sweeping, that it couldn't be stopped. Hundreds died. Most were found days, even weeks later floating in the river, out past Heathrow."

DiBianco was shocked. He'd never heard the tragic story.

"What makes you think *this* is that Tube?"

Clinton pointed up into a dark area behind them.

DiBianco stared a moment. At first there was nothing. Then a hint of red appeared. Then words.

His eyes grew wide.

"Good God..." DiBianco's breath was lost.

He turned his gaze to Clinton, who stared back with a raised brow, smiling.

The words were faded, but still—after nearly a hundred years of desolation, hovering high above the raging waters of the River Thames—it was clear enough to make out.

Newton Station

66

"It's fate I tell you..." A wide grin plastered over Clinton's face. They were sitting on a ledge, their shoes skimming the water's black surface.

DiBianco gazed into the light in the distance. His suit dripping wet, clinging to his skin, making life miserable. "It's so far away," he said.

Clinton didn't seem to hear; he kept talking. "...first I just *happen* to overhear a couple whispering in a dark restroom; then they led me to the greatest author to ever live, only to discover what I'm really finding are the answers to a riddle I bumped into months ago and had been loosing sleep over, and now ... Newton Station."

Clinton's words echoed off the concrete, stone, and rock of an eroded tunnel of the Old London Underground, but DiBianco didn't hear a word of it. His mind was drifting toward the light. How would he reach it? How would he find Savanna and get the hell out of that dreadful darkness? "Do you think we could swim out?"

"Are you out of your mind?"

"We can't stay here."

"My arms are jello," Clinton said, briskly rubbing them, shivering. "I can barely breath. We'll drown for sure."

"There's gotta be something we can do."

"I've got an idea." Clinton stood and pulled DiBianco's arm.

"You don't have to pull on me. Just say it."

"We can find a way out through the old station?"

DiBianco was surprised he hadn't thought of it. The tunnel was so eroded he hadn't noticed, hadn't put it together—even with the old Newton Station sign. They were siting along the edge of a long past eroded rail system.

DiBianco stood with renewed vigor and glanced around for anything familiar. A staircase. A door. They had to be close. The Station sign was right above their heads for crying-out-loud. Then it hit him—

"The sign."

"Yeah," Clinton said. "What about it?"

"It's really up there. I can see the curve of the Tube just above it. It's gotta be 30 feet up. How tall do you figure these Tubes were a century ago?"

By the expression on Clinton's face, DiBianco knew he understood. The raging waters had eroded over twenty feet of concrete, stone, and earth away from the original tunnel.

If they were to find a way out, they'd have to scale twenty feet of unstable earth and dilapidated concrete to do it, and with arms of jello, DiBianco knew it wasn't going to happen. "I can't—"

A blood curdling squeal fired at them, coming from somewhere toward the bright white light.

It was Savanna. And DiBianco knew it. He dived into the frigid water and swam for dear life toward the haunting sound.

Clinton stood a moment, awestruck, lost in the moment

of lunacy, then dived in after him, his arms, even in their weakened state, still moved with the speed and grace of an Olympian gold medalist.

67

Savanna's cries filled the cavernous space.

The bogging weight of DiBianco's suit made it difficult to swim in any direction other than toward the light. Savanna's voice was coming from outside of the water. Somewhere off to his left.

He turned toward the screams. The current was yanking him farther away. He swam as hard as he could, fighting the current.

"*NO!*" she yelled.

Clinton was well on his way. He'd certainly make it before him. He had not been so far down stream when finally changing direction.

"*PLEASE!*" she cried.

DiBianco swam harder. Faster. So did Clinton.

"*NO! ... STOP! They're everywhere!*"

It was then DiBianco noticed. Savanna was standing on the side of the water, about a foot from the surface, grasping the rock wall surrounding her. There was nowhere to go. The ledge, barely big enough for her to stand.

"*GO AWAY!*" She cried. "*Michael please!*"

The current slowed. DiBianco was entering an inlet, an area away from the current. Ripples filled the water around Savanna's feet. Like rain striking the surface. But of course there was no rain and no more screams of gunfire either. Something was in the water.

"Holy Christ!" Clinton shouted. "Something bit me!"

DiBianco saw the creatures swarm toward him. Now was not the time to panic, but he couldn't control it. He never could. His adrenaline faded and was swiftly overrun with panic and dread. His heart raced and his muscles stiffened.

God help me!

68

"Clinton splashed and kicked and shouted at the creatures. "Try and catch me, you little shits!"

As the creatures closed in on DiBianco, their persona became clear and his panic intensified. They were dark black snakes. *Water Moccasins,* he thought. They were mere inches away. He knew then, he was going to die.

DiBianco felt a thud against his chest. Clinton had brought his hands straight down into the water making a percussive splash. The result violently rattled through the water. The snakes changed direction, shooting off with impeccable speed towards the blast—towards Clinton.

"NO!" DiBianco watched in shock as the snakes shot like rockets toward Clinton, who took off into the currents. A noble gesture, DiBianco thought his last. Clinton was their best shot at tapping into the network.

It can't end here, he thought. *Not like this.*

Clinton swam like a champion, the current pushing him along. DiBianco prayed he could swim fast enough. Perhaps the snakes would get caught in the current and lose him.

DiBianco swam with extreme caution toward Savanna, who stood silently on the ledge, tears streaming her cheeks. His eyes focused on the water around the ledge. No snakes.

"You all right?"

"Yes," she said.

"We can't stay here."

"Yes, I can."

"I am leaving this place, right now. I'm swimming into that current and through that hole. I wish you'd come."

"What if they come back?"

"There's nothing here. We need to go, now!"

"I can't"

"If you stay, you'll—"

"I'll be fine!"

"What happens when you fall asleep?"

Savanna grew silent.

"What happens when you drift off and fall into the river. If the snakes don't get you, you'll drown. Either way, you'll die. This is your only chance."

Savanna said nothing. She gazed like an eagle into the water. Her hands were shaking. She looked cold, but DiBianco knew it was fear.

"Come on." DiBianco waved her in. "If there were any snakes in the water, would I be here?"

She smiled; then jumped in.

They swam into the current and let it sweep them toward the light. They held each-other, legs intertwined, taking turns keeping each-other afloat while they flowed within the ripping currents of the chasm.

"Thank you," she said.

"We're not out yet," he reminded her. "Though I'm glad you're with me."

"I love you," she said, her eyes no longer frightened.

"I know."

Something touched his feet sending panic through him. He pulled away, kneeing Savanna in the behind. Her legs wrapped around his waist.

She winced. "What is it?"

"I don't know," he said. "Something—"

It struck again, this time in the behind.

"OUCH!" Savanna shouted. "Something jabbed me in the ass—felt like a rock!"

She was right. They were dragging along a rocky bed. The water wasn't more than three feet deep yet it was still moving along at quite a clip.

The hole was close now. DiBianco could see details. Trees. Hills. The outside world.

But the current was pulling them away.

DiBianco threw his hands and feet down to stop them. It hurt. He dug in deeper.

Savanna did the same.

Finally they stopped. It was dark again, but DiBianco could see light creeping in from behind.

They stood—the water only at their waist—and forced their way against the current toward the light.

A silhouette of a man stood before them.

"Are you guys all right?"

It was Clinton.

69

"What do you mean, gone?" Afridi's face was rigid with anger—tense with the stress of having to answer to Fuller. The gas had completely dissipated. Afridi and his agents were rummaging through the pile of junk in the center of Clinton's apartment. Afridi had a polished aluminum laptop in his hands. It was open, something flashing on the screen.

The agents who had chased DiBianco through the tunnel were exhausted, out of breath, stench pouring off their bodies like a landfill. "They fell into a freezing subterranean river. There's no way they could've survived."

"Fuller will have your heads for this!"

70

After what felt like hours of treading through freezing, snake-filled waters, the sun felt like heaven on DiBianco's face.

Standing outside the partially fenced-off mouth of an old underground tunnel, DiBianco, Clinton, and Savanna loosened their clothing and attempted to dry off. DiBianco removed his coat, shoes, and socks and let the warm breeze filter through the sodden layers.

He gazed at Clinton, who returned a strange look. "How did you..." DiBianco was happy to see Clinton alive. "Those were Water Moccasins."

"Actually, they were Grass Snakes. Completely harmless. We don't get Moccasins in these parts."

Savanna removed her coat, wrung it out, then draped it over a rock. To DiBianco, she looked lost.

"Are you kidding?" DiBianco said. "Grass Snakes?"

"They spend a great deal of time in the water. It's not common to see them in rivers, but they certainly were Grass Snakes."

"How can you be sure?"

"At least three of the little shits bit me." He unwrapped some cloth from his hand and showed off a nasty bite. It was undeniably a snake bite. Clinton stuck it back in the water, rinsing it clean, then wrapped it in the cloth again.

DiBianco understood. One bite from a Water Moccasin could kill a man. Three was certain death. "I'm happy to see you again, Peter."

"It's good to still be here." He smiled.

71

"Where are we?" DiBianco glanced about the stark landscape. "We're not in Kansas anymore."

"Thank God for small favors," Clinton said. "We are, however, still in London."

"We need to pay Afridi a visit," Savanna said.

"So," Clinton said, "you finally on our side?"

"My faith is stronger than yours will ever be, but there is something very wrong here."

DiBianco took Savanna's trembling hands and lifted her to her feet. Her face was sad, raked with betrayal.

"Why did he take the papers?" she said. "Why wouldn't he want me to find the Holy Land?"

"I don't know," DiBianco said. "But I do know, I wanna help you find the Holy Land."

"I know." She smiled. "Believe me, I know."

PART FIVE

HACKING THE NETWORK

72

The Tube was speedy as ever, but to DiBianco, it was painstakingly slow. Time flew by like a fighter jet on a deadly mission. If they didn't find the answers they were looking for soon, they'd be shit out of luck. It was nearly 6:00 PM. The world was going to end in six hours and there wasn't a damn thing anyone could do about it.

Clinton and Savanna sat in the seventies style seat cushions of the District Train, chatting. DiBianco stood, gripping an overhead bar, his mind racing far faster than the train ever could. He was too tense to sit. The end was coming. The train really had to kick it up a notch.

"I have a friend with a Cessna," Clinton said.

DiBianco struggled to see the point.

"Wherever this Holy Land is, I'm sure it's not going to be anywhere on this island."

DiBianco understood and smiled.

"He's been begging me for years to include him in my work. He won't take no for an answer."

"Sounds like you're gonna make your friend mighty happy," Savanna said.

Clinton nodded, then continued chatting.

DiBianco found it hard to believe that just a few hours ago, he was trying to figure out how he got to London—was he drugged and dumped there? Did something happen to give him amnesia?

In a prior life he was a writer, a teacher, a common man—a mundane soul. Why had his life changed so quickly? Why was he suddenly trying to fill the shoes of some biblical action hero, on a mission to stop the Antichrist from destroying the world? It was all very absurd.

The lights flickered and the train stopped.

The voice on the loudspeakers announced *Saint James Park* as the doors slid open and piles of travelers scurried into a typical busy station in their typical busy way.

But life was far from typical.

In a matter of hours the world would have a new purpose. DiBianco knew that the *End of Days* brought with it change ... change no one on earth could possibly be prepared for.

Savanna and Clinton stormed off the train; DiBianco followed. They needed access to the Descendants' Network. Clinton knew hacking into Afridi's computer was the best shot they had.

Savanna's pace was brisk. Without a word she led them down St Ermin's Hill, then sped left onto Broadway.

The streets were full of pedestrians. The temperature, like hell. The sky was thick with a heavy haze. It was difficult for DiBianco to envision the world, come morning, if they didn't succeed.

They hustled through a busy traffic circle and ran up Tothil Street. The traffic was heavy. Many vehicles honked as they cut across, nearly getting hit by a double-decker bus. Traffic on these streets went in one direction; they seemed to be constantly against the flow.

Clinton effortlessly kept up; those swim-team legs obviously good for more than just swimming.

DiBianco, however... The day—the entire week—had caught up with him, bringing him down. He pushed himself but kept falling farther behind.

For what felt to DiBianco like an eternity—in bleak reality a mere five minutes—they walked; more like a vibrant dash, in all fairness. DiBianco's feet and ankles pulsed with pain, so did his knees, thighs, and lower back. He was far too old for this Indiana Jones crap.

Except for the newly deposited sweat under his arms and around his collar, DiBianco's suit had all but dried out, but that brought no comfort. He needed a drink, and he needed one soon, and a soft cushy seat while he chugged it back would suffice him well.

He followed Savanna and Clinton the best he could down Dartmouth Street. Now and then Clinton would look back and shout for Savanna to slow down. She never did. After a long exhausting block, they cut over to Old Queen.

Graciously, Savanna stopped and pointed at a gigantic complex of many different styled facades, all seemingly connected like one enormous six-story, block long structure hanging out on the left side of the road. Businesses laced throughout. Vehicles of every type lined the road.

"There," she said. "That's the place."

73

"There's a house in there?" DiBianco said, hunched over, hands on his knees, sucking in breath after breath of sticky air.

"He's in the first unit," Savanna said.

"They look like government buildings."

"You're not far off," Clinton said. "Much of this was government owned. In the last few years they've been sold to private businesses who've been modifying them into period Georgian houses. I've seen the website. They're stunning. Wish I could afford one."

DiBianco wasn't impressed. "How are we going to get in?"

"Follow me," Savanna said.

"Not again," DiBianco cried.

She ran up a grassy embankment to the left of the first building and ducked behind a bush.

Clinton and DiBianco followed.

"This side of the building is his."

"All six stories?" DiBianco said.

"Holy crap," said Clinton. "What does anyone need with that much space?"

The windows on the ground level were covered with iron bars about three inches apart. Only ten feet higher was another set of windows that not only were bar-free, but one was wide open; a white curtain blew in the heavy breeze.

Savanna smiled and grabbed the bars. "I can get myself up there, but I'll need help getting in."

"I can climb like spiderman," Clinton said.

All those trips up the high-dive? DiBianco wondered.

"I used to climb trees when I was a kid. Really tall ones. I once climbed to the top of the tallest Plain Tree in London, you know, the one on Festival Walk..."

DiBianco shook his head. He hadn't a clue what he was talking about, nor did he much care.

"...by the ponds in Carshalton?" he continued. "Anyway, I can climb in there without breaking a sweat. I'll go in and open the front door for—"

"NO!" Savanna said. "I'm certain there's a security system. I'll go. I've been here before. I know my way around. I'll find what we need and let you guys in when I'm sure the coast is clear."

"Fine," Clinton said.

She grabbed the bars and pulled herself up. She climbed fast, getting to the top of the window quickly. Clinton followed, grabbed her foot, and hoisted her a couple feet. She caught the sill and hoisted herself inside.

Clinton leapt to the ground. "Now what?"

"I guess we wait," DiBianco said, "and pray we don't hear sirens anytime soon."

Clinton snickered lightly, then gazed upward.

74

The room was simple. Elegant. Pure white curtains draped the two windows, the one she had just entered and another one about twelve feet to her left. Several black and white prints of London landscapes and royal landmarks, bordered in black, stuck out of the stark whiteness of the walls like modern art in a brightly lit gallery.

Savanna recognized the room. On the far wall, between two oak doors, was a fireplace with shelves full of hard-bound books flanking both sides. Pearl-white vases filled with towering white flowers topped the white marble mantle, along side their neighboring pictures of individuals unknown to her.

At the center of the room was an oblong table, black, like the frames surrounding each print—its high gloss sheen capturing the reflection from the polished aluminum and crystal chandelier that hung over the center of it. Sixteen black high-back chairs with pearl-white upholstery circled the table in reverent homage.

It was the room where she first learned of the sacred brotherhood—the DoL. She doubted they would have brought her in, had it not been for Michael. It was her relationship with him that attracted them to her; but she was so eager to learn about the Descendants. She wanted to hear.

That was sixteen years ago. Not until now had the uncertainty felt so strong. For so long she believed in the DoL's vision. For so long she let them drive her towards their future. It was a future she believed in. A future she felt was not only justified, but forthcoming and right—if not righteous.

But the events of the last few weeks had her deepest fears and questions resurfacing. She found herself questioning everything, and those questions were beginning to shed light on the last sixteen years. She loved Michael—with all her heart she did—but how could she have been so foolish.

She needed to figure it all out; why did Afridi take the papers? Why had they brought Michael here? It was all wrong, and she knew it. The prophecy clearly said he would come of his own free will and stand with them in the last days.

She doubted not only the scornful words of her superiors, but the very core of the DoL creed. How could she have been so wrong? How could she have fallen for such notions of grandeur?

She had written books about God and science with Michael and had studied mounds of evidence from both sides. Deep down she knew that the DoL were fighting a losing battle. The bible had predicted such a battle in the *Book of Revelations*. She recently wrote a book on the subject with the help of Michael.

"HEY!" Clinton's voice carried through the open window, startling Savanna out of her dreamlike state. "What's going on in there?"

Savanna ran to the window and shot Clinton an impatient glare. "Hold yourself, damn it! I'll let you know when you can come in."

Clinton frowned. "What's taking so long?"

She didn't answer.

She also didn't notice any security devices. No motion detectors, no cameras; no sensors of any kind. *That's odd*, she thought. *I could have sworn this place would be loaded with them.*

She walked toward the door directly in front of her—the one to the right of the fireplace. The floor was carpeted in the most plush white carpet she had ever seen. It felt like a cloud. Approaching the door she grabbed the jamb and peeked into the grand hallway.

She glanced around for motion detectors, cameras, anything with flashing lights. Remarkably, there wasn't anything—nothing at all.

Stepping onto the maple, her heals clicked on the floor sending echos throughout the starkly decorated hallway. Tall vaulted ceilings, arched doorways, elegant circling stairways going both up and down. Four huge windows—two to her left and two to her right—lighting the vast space with immense whiteness. It was more like a temple than a home.

Savanna walked toward the staircase leading down to the living quarters. It was where she recalled seeing his office and computer. Her hand traveled along the black handrail, which hosted dozens of white, beautifully spun spindles. Small silver lamps with flame-shaped light-bulbs, spanned the walls throughout the home.

Looking over the banister she again searched for security fixtures and found nothing. She spotted the front door, its arched top, framing a fantastic piece of stained glass, casting an array of prismatic color over the living-room's luxurious furnishings.

She looked for a security pad by the door. There was nothing. It was too good to be true; but there was truly nothing, not even a single blinking light.

Something tingled in her chest—speaking clearly to her, *something is wrong with this*, but she knew they had to hack the network, and to do that she needed to get Clinton into his office.

She made her way back through the temple-like hallway, making strides toward the stark white meeting room, and jetted across the plush carpet toward the open window.

75

Not far away, in a dark and silent room, a tiny red light started to blink. A moment later, a dial-tone filled the small room. A sudden string of digital tones rung out. The cacophony of harsh *shrieks, beeps,* and *scratches* that followed fired like a heat seeking missile across the open phone-line.

76

"What the hell took so long?" DiBianco said.

Clinton hoisted DiBianco through the window, then pulled himself in behind him.

DiBianco's eyes popped with amazement at the impressiveness of the home. It was like nothing he had ever imagined.

"I had to check for security," Savanna said. "Believe it or not, everything looks clear."

"I wouldn't be so sure." DiBianco glanced around the room himself. He knew it couldn't be so easy.

"Where's the computer?" Clinton said. "My mind's achin' for a break-in."

"Come on. I'll show you."

Clinton's face was awestruck. "The pictures on the internet do nothing for this place."

"Just focus on what we're here for."

"Right. The computer."

They started down the large spiral staircase. The steps were wide and many and not a squeak could be heard. It was the most superb construction DiBianco had ever seen. "This place must be worth five-hundred-thousand pounds."

"And that's just the house," Savanna said. "The articles in here top that, I'm sure."

Half way down, DiBianco focused on a huge bronze statue. "Why would a life-size ornament of the head pontiff be in this guy's living room?"

"The same reason Muslim extremists would have a Christian crucifix dangling over their sofa," Clinton explained, "or a Holy Bible propped on their coffee table." Clinton's eyes drifted. "My God," he said, gazing at the arched cathedral ceilings, fine architectural embellishments in the moldings and window treatments.

Not a curtain could be found on a window in this room. The glass seemed to change shades of tint with the coming and going of the sun. The woodwork resembled angels, two on either side of each window, facing each other; their glorious wings draping like feathering white curtains, caressing the panes of glass slightly then curled back into their sides. "This place is amazing."

Savanna took the last few steps and hustled into a small room. Afridi's office. "In here," she said, peeking back into the main living quarters.

Clinton jumped. His hands pulled away from the magnificent statue of the head pontiff.

DiBianco explored the spacious kitchen for a glass. "Go on; do your thing. I'll be there in a second." He paused, opened another cabinet door and frowned. "Better make that two."

77

Afridi's office was an amazing sight to any computer geek. But to Clinton it was like he had died and gone to heaven.

The man had three computers: a PC and two Macs—all the latest models. There were two laser printers; stacks of computer paper; scanners, six of them; and four large flat-panel monitors—Clinton thought, maybe thirty inches each—mounted to the wall, all linked to form one huge monitor.

It was the Mac that was running. A screen-saver depicting the biblical stories of the birth of Christ, the Crucifixion, the Resurrection, and the end of days filled the makeshift monstrosity of a monitor, on the wall just above a massive ebony desk and high-back leather chair.

Clinton sat in the chair and spun to face the computer. It was the most comfortable he had ever sat in. "Now I know where all the money is."

He grabbed the mouse; at once the screen changed. The image on the desktop was the logo of the Department of Justice. A dialog box appeared in the middle of the screen asking for a user name and a password.

"Damn," Clinton said. "This guy doesn't mess around."

78

DiBianco took another gulp of water, nearly emptying the elegant stemware he had discovered, and fell into one of the three plush sofas surrounding the pontiff. His tired body sank nearly a foot into the down pillows and silk cushions. It was a little piece of heaven.

DiBianco gazed at the bronze pontiff and prayed for the man who had done so much good in his fifteen years at the Papal helm. He was home now. *Couldn't have picked a worse time,* he thought. But it made sense that the Antichrist would pick this moment to attack. The Church was always at its weakest during this brief time of transition. DiBianco could have fallen asleep in the plushness of the sofa, and probably would have, if not for the sudden shriek of sirens invading his peace.

DiBianco struggled to get out of the sofa. It was like a starving monster, holding on to its prey. The stemware fell from his hand, shattering on the hardwood floor, water hitting his legs and the base of the pontiff. He finally pulled free and made strides toward the large window.

The street was clear, and it was a damn good thing; DiBianco felt completely exposed in the massive picture window. He might as well have been a mannequin, posing for his capturer. *Here I am. Come get me!*

The sirens were getting closer. He had little doubt where they were going. *Son-of-a-bitch,* he thought. *There is a security system.*

A line of small black cars with single red strobes flashing on each, raced around the corner of Dartmouth and Old Queen—yards from where he stood.

DiBianco dove from the window, his elbow struck the floor, sending shooting pains up his arm and into his chest.

The sound of cars skidding to a stop outside drove him to his feet. With haste he ran for Afridi's office.

79

"Damn it! That's not it either." Clinton was sweating, his hands shaking.

"I thought you were a pro?"

"I can't work with you breathing on me!"

"Fine." She backed away, but only a few feet.

Clinton mumbled through several more ideas, tried a couple, then took a deep breath. "If I try another, and it's wrong, the system will block me out. Any ideas?"

"I don't know. I mean, I think so, but—"

"What is it?"

"Try typing, white."

"This is not the time for playing—"

"Just try it!"

Clinton reluctantly typed in the word, gazed at Savanna with unsure eyes, then hit return.

With a flicker, the screen changed. Instead of the Department of Justice seal, there was a new desktop bearing an image Savanna seemed to recognize immediately.

"It's the crest of the DoL," she said.

It pictured the head of a bull with long curling horns, with a face like a man with a long narrow chin and high cheekbones, the numerals 616 in a bleeding bold-faced font dripping beneath it.

"616?" Clinton said. "That's odd."

DiBianco stormed the office, his right elbow in his left hand. He was out of breath. Sweating bullets. "We've gotta get out of here," he said. "Now!"

80

A string of beeps and dings rang from Afridi's computer. A second later a dialog box appeared at the center of the screen.

DiBianco knew what it was right away. A Mac user himself, he often used the same software to remind him of upcoming events in his crazy life.

"It's an *iCal* alarm," he said. "Open it."

Clinton did.

Gazing at the screen DiBianco's eyes grew large. "That's tonight." Then he looked at the clock in the upper right-hand corner; it flashed 6:38 PM. "My God, that's less than thirty minutes. Print it!"

Two keystrokes was all it took for the laser printer to roar to life.

"What's taking so long?" DiBianco said.

"It needs to warm up."

There was a pounding on the door. A man shouting. DiBianco couldn't tell what was being said, but it didn't matter.

"There's no time," DiBianco said. "Let's go!"

Just then the printer spit out several pages, text and pictures. Much more than shown on the screen. The printer was fast. A dozen pages spit out in seconds. DiBianco grabbed the pages and ran out of the room.

Savanna followed.

The high back chair spun in circles as Clinton lurched from it, racing to catch up. "Wait!"

81

DiBianco ran through a short passageway, passed a large bathroom finally spilling into a strange room; small, covered in cedar boards and shingles, it was more like a shed.

Lining the walls were weapons: riffles, hand guns, rocket launchers, magazines, ammunitions of all sorts, grenades, C-4; everything you'd expect to see at a terrorist training camp, or police headquarters, certainly not someone's house. This guy was fanatical; and DiBianco knew, incredibly dangerous.

"Holy shit," Clinton said, jetting through the door. "When did we arrive in Afghanistan?"

"Come on," Savanna shouted. "There's no time."

A massive crash shook the house. The sound of heavy tromping echoed into the cedar room.

Clinton grabbed a hand gun, some bullets, and a grenade and shoved them into his pockets.

DiBianco pulled the drapes back on a small windows beside a steel door and gazed at the busy street; beyond was a row a trees and an endless open field. It was Saint James Park, one of the only places in London DiBianco was familiar with.

"I don't see anyone," DiBianco said. "We should make a run for the park."

Savanna looked at ends. "Are you sure?"

"Do you have a better idea?"

Shouting filled the house. The scurry of boots was growing closer.

"Don't you find it odd that there's no one out there?"

DiBianco stopped to think. She had a point.

"Through those trees is a police station," she continued. "Shouldn't they be littering this side of the building by now?"

DiBianco knew she was right, even more, he knew what she was thinking. It made sense, but was it worth the risk?

"I know Afridi has nothing to do with the cops. That's why nothing's happening out there."

Without another word DiBianco stormed out the door.

Savanna and Clinton followed.

The door closed itself behind them.

PART SIX

FINDING THE HOLY LAND

82

DiBianco ran into busy traffic without hesitation, cars skidded to a halt, barely missing him as he hustled across, the computer printouts in his tightly cinched right hand flopping in the wind.

DiBianco jetted through the trees and into the wide open fields of Saint James Park. Up ahead was a large pond. To his left was Buckingham Palace, and the House of Parliament and the London Eye were maybe three blocks to the right. Yet it was the police station on Duck Island directly ahead that was locked in his sights.

Over his shoulder he spotted Savanna and Clinton; but no police, no agents, no sacred brotherhood, or whatever the hell was after them.

Taking a long path leading to a small bridge, DiBianco crossed the pond and made way for the entrance. Coming up on the door he slowed his pace, shoved the papers in his waistband and ran his fingers through his crow's nest. The grim reflection in the glass reminded him of his day.

83

The police station was calm, quiet, seemingly deserted, except for a woman wearing a simple white blouse, tight black skirt—cut just above the knees—and a small silver badge clipped at her waist, which DiBianco noticed was so small that he imagined wrapping his hands around her middle, his thumbs resting on her soft hips, his finger tips caressing the small of her back. She was elegantly made and filled the room with the light scent of musk and jasmine.

"Can I help you?" She said, standing from her desk.

A sharp elbow in the side snapped DiBianco from his gaze.

"We need to report an assassination attempt," Savanna announced, smirking at DiBianco, who looked like he was in pain.

"Oh really," the woman said, her voice sinking into a pit of sarcasm. "And who's the victim?"

DiBianco wasn't sure this was the right approach. He gazed at her. *What are you doing?* The thoughts bled from his eyes.

"The Prime Minister," Savanna said.

DiBianco's face dropped. He wasn't the target. She knew that. Perhaps she was raising the stakes so the woman would take her seriously. In any case, it worked.

The woman's face went pale. She glanced at the clock on the wall and hustled toward another desk and grabbed a phone. It shook in her hand as she pressed a series of numbers.

DiBianco looked out a window, towards Afridi's place. The coast was clear, remarkably, but it was a long three blocks to the House of Parliament. DiBianco wasn't sure they could make it. He knew they wouldn't stop until they found him—and quite possibly killed him.

"A-Ag-gent F-Fuller please," she stammered.

DiBianco watched Savanna's eyes go wide with terror. She yanked on his arm, demanding his attention. *"We've gotta get out of here,"* she said under her breath.

"What's wrong—"

"Shhhhh!" She put a finger against his lips. "Fuller's with the Descendants. We must go, Now..."

DiBianco gazed at the woman. She glanced back, then turned away, covering the receiver with her trembling hand.

DiBianco looked at Clinton who obviously heard what Savanna said and was looking for DiBianco to give the word.

DiBianco nodded and the three of them ran toward the door.

"Wait!" the woman shouted. "Come back..." her voice disappeared as the door slammed behind them.

84

They ran through the line of trees, across Horse Guards Road toward the House of Parliament. They had less than fifteen minutes before the assassination took place. They must keep moving. No more pit-stops. Death would be the only thing to stop them.

DiBianco ran down Horse Guard Road—Savanna and Clinton catching up quickly—and shot left down Great George Street, running toward Big Ben, now in his sights. But the final block hit him hard.

Clinton passed him. "You gonna make it?"

DiBianco waved him on, nodding.

The crowd around the House of Parliament, in the area of Big Ben was invasive. Royal Guards and US Special Service secured the area where the Prime Minister was scheduled to speak. President Bush was also planning a few words, so security was enormous.

DiBianco was swallowed by the monstrous crowd. He glanced about, franticly, found Clinton and pulled him close.

"Where's Savanna?"

"I don't know."

"Peter."

"Yes?"

"I'm going to stop this."

"How do you plan to do that?"

DiBianco pulled the papers from his waistband and pointed at the London Eye.

"Oh no," Clinton said. "There's no way you can do that. Besides, it's secure, I doubt you could even get close."

"I have to try."

"No," he declared. "You find Savanna, get that damn paper. I'll stop the assassination."

"Peter!"

"I give my word. I'll stop it."

Clinton's face was stern ... confident. It was *that* look that reminded DiBianco so much of himself; it was also *that* look that had DiBianco worried he'd never see his new friend again.

DiBianco patted Clinton on the back and smiled.

Clinton threw his arms around DiBianco in a monstrous bear hug that took him by surprise, but left him in tears.

"Be safe, my friend."

All Clinton did was point and wink. Point and wink. DiBianco took it as his way of saying, catch you later. He really hoped he'd have the pleasure.

85

The hands on Big Ben's face were readying themselves for that 8:00 hour. The podium was cleared. The British flag stood tall to its left, the American flag to its right. Cameras aimed at the podium from all angles. The press crowded in, while onlookers were forced back behind the lines of personnel drawn by British and US security.

Prime Minister Blair would soon be escorted onto the podium along with Prime Minister elect Brown and President

Bush. The speech was expected to be brief—thirty minutes, at best. DiBianco knew there wasn't much time.

He searched for Savanna. He needed to find her. He had no idea who or what to look for—who would have the Newton Paper? He had hoped Savanna would search, rather than him.

"Savanna," he shouted.

Protesters pushed their way to the security line. They held signs and banners reading, *Blair loves America!* and *BUSH Lover!* DiBianco recalled a day when—*BUSH Lover*—wasn't necessarily a bad term, though he personally never was much of a *BUSH Lover* in that regard; though, he certainly didn't side well with the *BUSH Haters* of today.

As for Blair, DiBianco knew very little about the leader, other than he stood strong with his greatest ally and didn't back down simply because it was unpopular. That took balls and courage, and DiBianco believed it was the right thing to do, so he respected the man, for what he knew of him.

The street and the lawn around the 250 year old clock tower was chockablock. DiBianco had an increasingly difficult time spotting anyone of interest. He scoped the press area, looking for anything suspicious. He knew that anyone able to plant something on this particular victim was going to have to be close—real close.

Even though the intended target wasn't the Prime Minister, it *was* one of his right hand men. Only the press—*or perhaps someone closer,* DiBianco thought—could have a shot at planting the paper. But he saw nothing out of the ordinary. Guards came out of the masonry, Police patrolled the civilian areas, special agents cluttered around the podium. It was difficult to see beyond the wall of black suited men, wearing the typical black shades and earpieces.

The crowd began to stir and the suited men thickened around a small cluster of individuals making their way toward the podium.

DiBianco saw a glint of Blair's face peeking out between

the suits. At his sides were both Brown and Bush. They were walking breast to breast, marching like the commanders they were, at least in DiBianco's opinion.

DiBianco shot a frightened gaze toward the London Eye.

Please God, let your spirit be with him. Give him the strength to stop this evil before it strikes again. And God, please bring him—

"Mr. DiBianco?" The soft female voice was surprised, but pleasant.

DiBianco shook his head and spun at the familiar voice. He couldn't believe his ears, or his eyes.

"Crystal?"

86

Clinton watched from the edge of the River Thames as the black suits guarding the London Eye shifted their places. Two of the men jumped onto the giant wheel and scaled the ladder circling the massive structure, climbing swiftly, one after the other, toward the summit with a deadly mission in their spirits.

Clinton knew what they were up to. It was time to kick into high gear.

The remaining four guards covered the street entry points to the wheel. No one from the street was getting through, no chance in hell. Clinton had no intention of gaining access from the street. He pulled off his shoes and socks and gazed down at the River, nearly twelve feet below.

Clinton swooped silently into the river and swam under the water toward the wharf on the back side of the wheel. The water was freezing, even colder than the subterranean river they had fallen into hours earlier. But he propelled his way with ease and several moments later popped his head up beside the wharf.

He took in a huge breath and scoped the area. There were no guards on the wharf. He saw the four on the street facing the crowds on the east bank of the River, wielding signs of protest, smoking, drinking—and not just *Camels* and *Cokes*. He gazed up and spotted two men climbing, approaching the halfway point quickly.

He had to move.

Clinton carefully pulled himself up onto the wharf and without hesitation ran to the wheel and climbed into the mesh of steel cables and hid out of site for a second. Drying his hands and feet the best he could, rubbing them down and blowing warm breath onto them, he readied himself for the challenge. He knew he could do it.

Piece of cake, he thought.

He grabbed one of the massive steel spokes and scaled it like the London Plain Tree he climbed when he was seventeen. Only the tree was a mere one-hundred feet and had rough edges to grab on to. The Eye was nearly four-hundred-and-fifty feet and had just the slight roughness of braided cable. Still, he knew he could do it—and would, even if it meant death, which he held to that constant prayer, that God would protect him. He had given his word; and Clinton knew, there was nothing more important for a man to follow through with, than his word. Yet he also gave his word that he'd be back, and he had every intention to keep that word over all.

He scaled the cable quickly, his back to the River so the guards on the street couldn't see. He no longer saw the men above, he knew he was safe for the moment. In less time than expected he reached the center spindle. It was massive.

It looked like the spindle of a bicycle tire, only larger, it was the size of a large man. With his arms stretched high above his head, he rested his feet in a grove in the lower ring and grabbed the upper rim with his hands. It was an awkward stance, but a much needed break from the monkey-climb up the spoke.

At the center, two-hundred-and-twenty-five-feet in the air, the wind was violent, and was getting stronger with each step he took. A few of the gusts nearly ripped him from the steel cables.

The sound of metal clanking and men talking grabbed his attention. He tried to listen to what they were saying but they were too faint, and the wind was whistling in his ears.

With his brief rest behind him he started up another spoke, this time, picking one that was slightly angled—somewhere between 10:00 and 11:00—so he could climb faster and without so great of a chance of sliding. His arms and legs were getting tired ...and numb, but he was not going to stop. This was the most important mission he had ever set out to complete.

Reaching the outer rim of the wheel, nearly two-thirds of the way to the top, Clinton hid behind one of the huge glass capsules where riders typically stare out in awe at London, from their safe air-conditioned space, no fear of falling or of anything horrible happening. Clinton wished he was inside, simply enjoying the spectacular view.

The sound of gunfire snapped at his ears and the spray of paint chips and metal shavings blew in his face.

"Shit!" Clinton tucked behind a thick steel cross-member, one of the main supports around the wheel's perimeter, and behind a non-transparent piece of the glass capsule, breathing heavily, waiting for another shot. None came.

He glanced around the beam, toward the suits who were readying themselves at the wheel's summit. There was only one now, he was laying under the pinnacle capsule, wedged between the underside of the capsule and the steel support of the wheel. He had a large rifle, looked more like a rocket launcher, with a large sight. The suit was aiming at the base of

Big Ben, at the podium that would soon support the greatest leaders of the freest lands of earth.

Clinton looked for the other suit.

There was a gunshot. More paint chips and metal sprayed in his face. His ears began to ring. He grabbed the hand grenade out of his pocket, put the pinned trigger in his teeth, and climbed the ladder.

Another shot screamed in his ear, this time he felt a searing heat in his right leg. The suit firing at him was on the other side of the wheel, at around 2:00. Clinton saw him clearly now. He had to move, and fast.

He slipped, hooked his arm around a rung on the ladder, and stole a breath. *Shit.* Swinging behind one of the massive cross-members, he grabbed a quick glance at his throbbing leg. It was bleeding badly. Feeling was slipping away.

He hurried up the ladder, taking a dozen steps and ducking for cover behind another steel cross-member. He peeked around, saw the suit, he was climbing toward the summit—toward the sniper.

Clinton took advantage of the opportunity, knowing the suit was moving, and did the same. He shot up several rungs at a time. His leg was gushing blood now, but it did nothing to stop him. Between 11:00 and 12:00 were four capsules, he passed two of them within minutes.

Clinton felt faint. He was approaching the last capsule, next to the one the sniper was set up under. He had to act fast if he was going to pull it off before falling to his death. He pulled the grenade from his mouth, the pin still dangling in his teeth, and suddenly found himself bombarded by another spray of bullets. He tucked behind the capsule—the glass surrounding it shattered, spraying over him—and repeated that soft prayer.

Please God, don't let me die. But he knew he was going to. At least he wouldn't be dying alone.

87

On the ground, a few feet from DiBianco and Crystal, President Bush had begun commemorating Blair on his achievements over the last decade of service for his country. Under different circumstances, DiBianco would have listened to the talk, he was a fan, even if he screwed up the War.

"...I came with Savanna," Crystal said. "I suppose, by now you must know..." Her amazing blue eyes penetrated DiBianco like shards of blue ice, exploding in his chest, filling him with the vibrant chill of ecstasy. Mesmerizing. Hypnotizing. Dehumanizing. He couldn't pull his gaze away.

"Mr. DiBianco?" She said, snapping him back.

DiBianco shook his head. Exhausted. Lost.

"Sorry," he said. "Have you seen her?"

"Savanna? Sure. She's right—"

An explosion rocked the still purple twilight. Flames and smoke billowed up and away from the London Eye. Shards of glass pierced the sky like Chinese stars, sinking into the earth, crashing into neighboring buildings, breaking windows, plummeting down like razor-sharp chunks of hale on the spectators and protesters below the giant wheel.

Deafening screams overpowered the sound of falling debris. Dozens of black suits lurched in front of the President, sweeping him out of site. Blair and Brown also disappeared, escorted by Royal Guards and their version of the Secret Service, the Secret Intelligence Service, or SIS.

Total pandemonium swept the streets. Police drew nightsticks in an attempt to create order. It only made things worse. Many of the protesters threw themselves into the crowd, and onto the police. It was a violent gesture of their spirited message. This was just the type of terror they accused Blair of bringing home with all his mindless political ass-kissing.

DiBianco took Crystal by the arm. She winced in pain. He didn't loosen. "Where's Savanna?" He shouted, trying to be heard over the mayhem. He glanced at the London Eye, it's summit capsule gone, along with much of the supporting structure around it. The giant wheel swayed in the wind. DiBianco thought it would topple. His heart sank.

Clinton was gone.

"Where is she?" He shouted, tears forming in his eyes.

"Let me go!"

"Son-of-a-bitch!" DiBianco felt his life falling apart. Not only had Clinton sacrificed his life saving some good-for-nothing politician, but they had failed to get the Newton Paper. How would they find the Holy Land and stop the DoL? How could they get to the Holy Land, without Clinton, and his pilot friend?

"We need to go," Crystal said, yanking her arm out of his grip.

"What about Savanna?" DiBianco could only hope she had found the Newton Paper. At least that would keep his spirits alive.

He looked up at Big Ben. It was 8:20. Three and a half hours. *There's no way.*

Crystal grabbed DiBianco's hand and ran through the crowd. He didn't know where she was taking him, but at this point it didn't matter. Anywhere was better than there. Besides he had a feeling, she knew something he didn't.

And she did.

Civilians on the street were being replaced with officers of every type imaginable: police, fire, special agents, royal guards, SIS, you name it; it was a mad house of activity.

She pulled him out of the crowd, up Parliament Street to a slew of taxis lining the side of the road.

DiBianco's eyes lit up. "Savanna?"

"Thought you'd never make it," she said, gazing at Crystal. "Thank you."

Crystal nodded.

Savanna opened the door to one of the taxis and motioned for DiBianco to get in.

He did.

Crystal scooted him over and plopped herself next to him.

Savanna took the front. "Heathrow Airport," she said, with a smile.

Crystal glanced at him; her smile was wide.

DiBianco would come to realize, everything Crystal did, came with a smile. It was one of the reasons he found her so attractive. Another reason—probably most important—was that in many ways she reminded him of his wife, what he imagined she would have been like at nineteen; and what he hoped she would have still been today, if she were there. The sudden loss of a new friend only made the loss of his wife more prominent.

DiBianco looked perplexed. "Where're we going?"

Savanna turned her head, glanced at DiBianco, then at Crystal. Then nodded.

Crystal pulled something out of her pocket.

DiBianco's eyes filled with renewed hope.

"You found it!"

88

The taxi sped north on Parliament Street to King Charles. The road was remarkably clear, but not for long. Soon every street surrounding the incident would be jammed. Thankfully, this taxi driver was having no part of it; and for that, DiBianco was exceedingly grateful.

As the cab fired through The Mall Rotary and headed west on Trafalgar Square (which was also Route A4), DiBianco grabbed the crumpling paper from Crystal's hands and carefully unfurled it.

It was delicate; and like the photocopies he had seen back in Boston, the vast majority of the page was blacked out with a black magic marker. DiBianco gazed at the written text that remained.

"I thought it was supposed to be decoded?"

"It is," Savanna said. "What does it say?"

DiBianco looked at the defaced Newton Paper. What it read, at first, made little sense. He wondered how long the trip to Heathrow would be. He was going to need time.

He'd have plenty. The trip was nearly seventeen miles and under ideal conditions could take upwards of thirty minutes.

His eyes studied the text. In time it would begin to make sense, though what it said, DiBianco found difficult to accept.

And they shall gather into the Holy Land, which is that same Holy Land considered apostate to His Greatness. A land which liveth in the shadow of a great and mighty key; the greatest and mightiest of all Lords. A land which hideth behind a vail of righteousness, though remaineth trapped in utter darkness.

DiBianco gazed at Savanna, who turned slightly in her seat, facing him, her eyes beaming with life.

She knew; she had to.

A few things revealed themselves then. Not only did DiBianco know that Savanna found Crystal in the crowd while they were separated, but she had discovered the paper too; she had studied it. She must have sent Crystal to find him and bring him to the taxi. *But why?* Where did Savanna go before meeting them? What was she up to?

"What does it say?" Savanna's eyes were mockingly curious.

DiBianco gazed at the paper, struggling to accept its message, though in his heart he knew it was the answer they needed; the answer they had been searching for; the answer that would guide them to the Antichrist, and to a way to stop The Pulse.

DiBianco glanced at Crystal—who sat with her legs crossed, smiling—then at Savanna.

"Looks like we're going to Rome."

89

DiBianco gazed through the open window of the cab at Saint James Park. The oldest of the Royal Parks, Saint James was also the most spectacular, at least in DiBianco's opinion. Buckingham Palace crested the horizon like a fortress.

DiBianco squirmed in the cab's leather seat and fished out the computer printouts from his waistband and spread them over his lap. It was the first time he had the opportunity to study them. He had to make sense out of the mass of information he had gathered. It was very confusing; and though pieces were coming together, none of them seemed to fit.

The only thing clear was that the Descendants of Lucifer planned to destroy the world, mainly Christianity, in less than three hours and DiBianco still had little to work with. How was he going to stop it? How were they going to make it to Rome? With just three hours, he saw no way they could find a flight in time.

The printouts were plastered with dates and times. A schedule of the entire month of June. But with June now at an end, very little seemed of any use. There was the timing of the assassination of Lowrance Hateeb, the Parliament Member whose life was just spared at the expense of his new and dear friend. But there was something else. Something

DiBianco hadn't noticed before, something vital.

Included in the printout was an image. A long face, a narrow chin, high cheekbones, long curled horns like a bull. The image had the appearance of blood and smoke. However, it was the numbers plastered along the bottom of the image that grabbed DiBianco's attention.

616

DiBianco gazed up.

Savanna was looking out the passenger window at vast amounts of farmland. It reminded DiBianco of the month he spent canvassing the midwestern states campaigning for Bush senior back in the early nineties. It was then he realized how amazed he was that he could have befriended a Clinton. He wondered if there could possibly be any blood there. *Likely not,* he thought. Though he knew how important bloodlines could be; it was, after all, the basis of his *God Science* theory—the theory, which he suspected had gotten him in this mess to begin with.

They were getting close to Heathrow now.

Crystal glanced at him and smiled. She had been watching the whole time, intrigued by what he was doing, seemingly unaffected by the obvious discernment in his eyes.

"What is this?"

Savanna turned to the sound of his voice, gazing at the image gripped tightly in his hands.

"It's the symbol of our faith," she said.

"What is this number?"

"It symbolizes the coming of Lucifer."

"The number of the Beast? ... Isn't that 666?"

"That is what The Church would have you believe," she said. Something about the use of the term *The Church*, had him glancing at Crystal. *If you truly believe that The Church would kill to keep these findings secret, then please explain, Professor, how could anyone possibly find out?*

DiBianco looked away. His mind racing with indecisive thoughts and theories. He must figure this out. He had to, so many lives depended on it.

Out his window, off in the distance, he saw the airport.

The taxi turned off the highway and sped down the ramp onto Tunnel Road East. The airport was directly in front of them now.

"How are we going to find a flight to Rome at this hour?"

"Don't worry Michael," Savanna said. "There's more I haven't told you ... a lot more."

90

A massive, long sign, perched at the center of a grass covered island at the center of the road, announced their arrival at *London Heathrow Airport.*

At a distance beyond that, after passing beneath an overpass, at the end of the roadway island rested a large jet-plane. It was perched in the grass with a large plaque sunk in the ground in front of it. DiBianco couldn't make out what it read, if anything; though he craned his neck, trying to make out the inscription.

As the roads came back together on the other side of the island, the cab raced through a long amber-lit tunnel. It ran under several thousand feet of runway and terminals.

Out the other-side, the cab shifted into the far right lane and sped up a ramp toward the Heathrow Main Terminal.

"Not here," Savanna said. "South Perimeter, please."

"Where to?" the taxi driver asked.

"I'll point you in the right direction once we get there."

† † †

"I never knew this place existed," the cab driver said.

"And in a few hours, none of that will have changed," Savanna declared.

Even though doubt had struck her; even though she had helped *him* find the Holy Land, perhaps more than he had helped *her*, Savanna was clearly not turning. She was still a believer in the Descendant's and clearly intended to help fulfill their plans.

DiBianco knew he must play along. And though he couldn't bring himself to say that he was willing to let the events follow through, he certainly wasn't about to announce his plans to stop them either. Sadly, however, with Clinton gone, DiBianco knew he was on his own in that department.

"Ten pounds," the driver said.

Crystal pulled twenty out of her pocket, passed the wrinkled bills to the driver, and stepped out of the cab.

DiBianco gathered the printouts and the Newton Paper and shoved them back into his waistband.

Savanna opened the door and reached inside.

He grabbed it.

"Come with me," she said. "There's something I need to show you."

91

Savanna lead DiBianco down a long concrete walkway toward an aluminum vaulted hanger. Several planes were parked outside; single engine Cessnas, mostly.

Entering a small door at the front of the hanger, DiBianco's eyes struggled to adjust to the poor lighting while Savanna approached a gentleman wearing a greasy blue jumpsuit, cracking a black smeared grin.

"Miss Campbell," the man said, wiping his hands in a blue shop rag before reaching to grab her hand.

She didn't take it, she smiled and glanced about. "Where is it?"

"It's been done for some time, Miss Campbell. We tried calling, but had no luck. I was about to ship it back to Athens."

She looked frustrated. "Where is it, Mitch?"

"It's out back," he said, pointing toward a string of large hanger doors. Two of which were open.

DiBianco watched several aircraft, large and small, taxi about the tarmac outside.

Savanna stormed toward the open doors.

"Miss Campbell. You might need these." He threw a large metal ring, with several keys attached.

She caught it without a flinch, then continued out the door and onto the steaming tarmac.

DiBianco followed. She raced toward a small plane. In his hasty strides to keep up, he didn't notice the computer printouts slip from his waist, falling to the tarmac behind him.

"Are you going to tell me what's going on?"

"Relax," she said, approaching the single engine plane.

"We'll never make it to Rome in that thing."

"No, you're right," she said walking past the Cessna. "But we'll surly make it in that."

92

It had to be the largest personal jet DiBianco had ever seen. He had flown on commercial airliners not much larger. It was at least fifty feet long, and stood twenty feet tall. Two massive jet engines were propped in front of the tail; the name CITATION: XLS+, predominantly located in red on the side of each. There were five rows of dark windows, not including the windows surrounding the cockpit.

The design was simple, yet elegant. High-gloss white, with blue and red pinstripes, starting at a point at the tip of the plane's long nose, running the plane's length, before disappearing behind the engine; then shooting out from behind, returning to a point behind the tail-wings.

DiBianco watched an attendant drive a mobile staircase out of the hanger to the side of the jet, climb the dozen or so steps and open the door—the same type you'd find on a commercial airliner.

"Who's going to fly that thing?"

"Why, me, of course," Savanna said with a wide grin.

DiBianco couldn't believe he was about to climb aboard a plane with Savanna Campbell piloting. It both unnerved him and excited him. They would make it to Rome. But would they make it on time?

Savanna and Crystal climbed the dozen steps to the fuselage and disappeared into the dark hull.

"You coming?" Savanna shouted—her face peeking out from the darkness.

DiBianco stood on the tarmac a second longer, shocked, then broke his gaze from the jet's engine and gawked up at Savanna. "Of course."

93

The interior of the CITATION XLS+ was no less impressive than its exterior.

Savanna stood by a well lit—and well stocked—drink bar.

Stemware hung in front of a large lit mirror. The wood encasing the bar was a deep mahogany—a classy wood that matched the other accents throughout the plane's interior.

There were eight extra-large tan leather captain's chairs—the type you'd expect to find in a full-sized luxury van. They made the first-class seats on his last flight to California the year before look like economy-class.

Crystal was seated to his right in the second row facing front. She watched Savanna grab stemware from the overhead rack and start pouring drinks.

"Just Scotch this time," Crystal said.

DiBianco glared at her. She was only nineteen and had no right drinking—at least in *his* mind—and he had no right letting her.

"Have a seat Michael," Savanna said. "There's a lot we need to tell you before we leave."

DiBianco sat in a front seat facing the back of the plane, facing Crystal.

Savanna passed the Scotch to Crystal and rested a tall glass on the tray beside DiBianco. The citrus scent of orange mixed with the slap-in-the-face punch of vodka brought a smile to his tired face.

She remembered.

It had been years since he'd had a drink, and though his mind was screaming *No!* The day; the situation; his mood, demanded he drink it; and he did, in one slug.

Crystal raised the Scotch to her lips and sipped slowly, then returned the sparkling stemware to her mahogany tray.

After slugging his Screwdriver, DiBianco felt odd saying anything about her baby sips of Scotch.

"What do we need to talk about?" DiBianco said, resting the empty stemware on his tray.

"You know nothing about me ... or Crystal." She took the glass from DiBianco's tray and filled it again. "I think you should have another."

He didn't argue. This time he sipped the bittersweet

mixture slowly, and perked his ears for what was to come.

Grabbing her drink from the bar, Savanna sat in the seat beside Crystal and took a sip. DiBianco could tell it was her usual. Diet Coke with a pinch of lime. She never drank—or did she. *Christ,* he thought. *I have no idea anymore.*

Savanna crossed her right leg over her left, her skirt barely covering her knee, and tapped her long red fingernails against the crystal stemware.

The silence in the cabin was too much to bare. He wanted to get to the Holy Land; he had to stop The Pulse; but he was intrigued by Savanna's strangeness. What in the world was she about to say, and was it important enough to justify being late, or perhaps that was the point.

"Michael," Savanna said. "I haven't been honest—"

"Oh, that's an understatement."

"Today, Michael." Her demeanor changed, along with her gaze. A look, so stern, so serious, she almost looked like a different woman.

An odd sense of déjà vu swept DiBianco while she spoke. He felt like he had been on that plane before, though he knew he hadn't, he would have remembered. He'd only been on two flights in his life, that was getting to and from Jerusalem only months before.

He gawked at the plush seats in front of him. Where Savanna sat, he saw himself, naked, Crystal on top of him, riding, crying, shouting—a wild beast feasting on her prey.

"Michael," Savanna shouted, waving her hands, snapping him back to reality.

DiBianco gazed glassy-eyed at Savanna.

What is going on here?

"I thought I lost you for a moment," she said.

DiBianco shook his head, glanced at Crystal, who grinned back, then chugged down the rest of his drink.

"It's true, I'm a member of the Descendants of Lucifer, but I joined sixteen years ago, not because I wanted to, but because I had to."

He didn't care how she joined or what made her, none of that mattered, but he played along, he saw no choice.

"I don't understand?" He said.

"Crystal has been a member going on ten years."

"She joined at nine?" DiBianco was flabbergasted. "How does a child of nine suddenly—"

"Michael," she said. "Crystal is not what you think."

DiBianco gazed at Crystal, who took another sip of Scotch, smiled sweetly, then winked.

DiBianco felt dirty. He knew he never had sex with the young woman. His overactive imagination and deprived sex life had every part in that little joyride. Yet he couldn't brush the feeling—the feeling like he had been on that plane before.

"The only thing she attended Harvard Divinity for, was to learn about you. She was majoring in Michael DiBianco."

"Why would she want to learn about me?" DiBianco knew he was well known around the world for his writing and his belief of God and Science. Outside of that, what else was there to know?

"You're a very special person," Crystal said.

"Like I said." Savanna's eyes were bright. "There's a lot you need to know. The question is ... are you ready?"

94

Hundreds of miles away, Camillin prepared for DiBianco's arrival. Fully accepting the information retained from his source as fact, Camillin made several phone calls and boarded the next flight to Rome. He had no doubt it was true.

His army of nearly one-hundred foreign and domestic agents gathered at a secret meeting place outside *Leonardo da Vinci - Fiumicino*, Rome's largest international airport.

It was all coming together now and Camillin knew without a doubt, DiBianco was the final piece he had been searching for.

He just hoped it wasn't too late.

95

"What we're about to tell you can never leave this plane; do you understand?" Savanna said, leaning closer to DiBianco.

DiBianco nodded.

"Don't even speak of it to me. Am I clear?"

He nodded again.

"Say it!"

"Yes," he said. "Perfectly clear."

"Good." Savanna rose from her seat and topped off her glass, squeezing a lime wedge in to it and dropping in the peal. She gazed at Crystal.

"First," Crystal said. "I'm thirty-three, not nineteen—"

DiBianco's grin exploded on his face. "I—"

"—but I'm happy you thought so."

"She is beautiful," Savanna said, "isn't she."

DiBianco's face went flush. He tried to hide it but couldn't. "Why aren't we leaving?" he said, trying to change the subject. The question was good. They only had a few hours.

"Relax," Savanna said. There's plenty of time.

Sure, he thought. *Plenty of time to reach Rome, and watch the rest of the world get blown to pieces.*

DiBianco's frustration intensified. He needed to stop The Pulse. He wasn't about to sit back and let it happen; he couldn't live the rest of his life with the death of the world on his shoulders like a life-sentence, knowing he could've done something.

"I think it's time we spit it out, don't you," she said, glancing at Crystal.

Crystal nodded.

"Smile," Savanna said. "This is *good* news."

Nothing about this was sounding good at all.

"I suspect the events of this day have brought you a long way from where you were this morning; I don't mean fisically of course; I mean, I bet you were questioning how you got here, weren't you?"

DiBianco nodded. He didn't see the relevance, but he did want to know.

"You came to London on this plane, Michael," Savanna said with a smile. "We brought you here."

"What the hell are you talking about?"

"When you were a boy," Savanna continued, "you were adopted by a priest..."

"Yeah?"

"Do you know why?"

"Because my parents were killed in an avalanche." DiBianco was positive. "I watched it happen. That man was kind enough to take me in."

Savanna fished a small device from her coat and fumbled it in her fingers. "Your parents were told of the prophecy, but wanted no part of it. They refused to obey, Michael."

"What are you talking about?"

Crystal's face was stern. "Your parents were very important—"

"*Very* important," Savanna interrupted. "Yet the moment their power was stripped away, they fell, just like the rest."

DiBianco gazed at the device in Savanna's hands.

"Your parents didn't die in an avalanche, Michael," Crystal said sadly. "They were murdered."

"You're out of your mind!"

"Tell me," Savanna started, "can you recall anything, anything at all from before your parents died on that mountain?"

He racked his brain for the answer. *That's odd*, he thought. He couldn't. He couldn't remember a damn thing from before the accident; the accident that stole his parents away and spawned the beginning of Michael DiBianco, *this* Michael DiBianco, the one who stared inquisitively back at him in the mirror every morning before he'd jump in the shower and start his hectic day.

"Shortly after your parents died," Savanna said, "you were brought somewhere, do you remember where, Michael."

Still he couldn't. Then all at once his past seemed to blur into a blood-red streak. Nothing at all was clear anymore.

"They planted something in your head, Michael. A nanoprocessor. It reprogrammed you—"

"Bullshit," he shouted, "I watched my parents die. I was there!" Tears welled in his eyes. "I dug my father out of that mountainside, just to have him die on me hours later of hypothermia. I watched my mother's head get chiseled out of the ice; the rest of her remains weren't found until the following spring. They were half eaten by wild animals!"

"Those memories were planted," Savanna said. "The nanoprocessor has been slowly preparing you—"

"For what!" he interrupted.

"Your destiny ... your fate. The future, Michael."

DiBianco stormed out of his chair and paced the cabin. "I need to get off this plane ... now!"

"It's true," Savanna said. "I'm not making this up."

"If it is true," he paused, knowing that his next words might get him into even more trouble. "—prove it!"

Savanna took the tiny device in her hands and caressed the red button. "I signaled the nanoprocessor when you were escaping the hospital. Do you remember? There would have been a sharp pain in your temples. Then a message. You heard something ... didn't you? You have to remember."

He did ... clearly, too. The migraine that had hit him back then, returned along with the recollection of it.

The Eye. It watches you. Go!

"Your friend foiled our plans," Savanna said, "but he suffered the ultimate price for his misdeed, didn't he?"

DiBianco's pulse raced, but it wasn't anxiety he was feeling, it was fury. He struggled to refrain from lashing out. "He did nothing to hurt a soul," he cried. "He was doing what he felt was right—what we *both* felt was right."

"Soon you'll understand," Savanna said. "Soon you'll see the truth. You'll see with such clarity and divine force that your clouded beliefs will no longer blind you." Savanna passed the small remote to Crystal. "It is time."

DiBianco gazed at the device with sudden terror. He wanted to lurch toward Crystal and grab it from her hands, but before his mind sent the signal to jump, her finger tapped the red button.

96

Am I dead? Did I pass out?

Darkness fell the moment the button was pressed. But there was no pain. No messages. Just pure and utter darkness.

What's happening? he thought.

"Relax," a deep voice said. "It will come."

When it did, DiBianco knew he had always known. The images flashing through the darkness were new to him, yet he remembered seeing them before; he had known; he had always known.

He tried to close his eyes, will his mind away, but the images remained. Terrifying images. Hundreds of skyscrapers flashed before him. It was like watching a three-dimensional movie, he flew through the air like a hawk. Some buildings he recognized, most he did not; black duffle bags were carried through the front doors. It was like he was watching the world through his mind's eye.

The bags passed into museums, government buildings, security checkpoints. Officers emptied them, inspected them, dogs sniffed them. The bags passed through every gate. Carried by lawyers, doctors, senators, judges, priests, teachers, police, bankers, students ... just plain common-day people.

Nuclear power plants from around the world invaded his dark vision: Seabrook, Opal, Tianwan-1—just a few he recognized. Nuclear warheads—missiles. In a bat of an eye he saw every one of them in every part of the world flash through the darkness, fired on a path to certain destruction. He recognized the Russian landscape; the middle-eastern deserts; the oceans of America. It was all part of the plan. It wasn't just about sheet-explosive-laced duffel bags anymore. The entire planet was wired and ready to blow.

Somehow the Descendants had infiltrated every layer of the world's infrastructure. They were using the world's own arsenals against it. It was then he realized. The Pulse was going to melt power-plants, launch missiles, nukes ... every weapon connected to a computer system was going to be armed and fired by The Pulse.

Then, in the peripheral of his vision was a great and mighty gathering. A land untouched by the devastation. A land with no warheads aimed at it. A land without nuclear reliance. A land that would live to ultimately inherit the earth.

There was a man, whose face was unclear, distorted by unnatural brightness. A man who spoke with a mighty tongue; speaking of a war; a battle to succumb all battles. In his soul, DiBianco knew this war was to be fought against Christ and his concourse of angels in the latter-days.

"That man is no stranger," the voice said, sending a chill through DiBianco's paralyzed body. "Actually, you know him quite well."

A violent shake jolted DiBianco out of his hypnotic state. His eyes blurred, his head spun, then came the throbbing.

Grabbing his head with both hands by the temples, he

grimaced and glanced about the dim cabin.

He was alone.

The plane bucked.

We're airborne!

He glanced out the window. It was dark. With the pulsing strobe of the wing-tip-light came a sudden streak of a dark cloud. Rain channeled sideways across the window.

DiBianco looked at the clock on the wall by the bar and his breath became lodged in his throat.

11:49!

97

DiBianco bolted toward the cockpit. The door was shut, locked. Voices rang from within, too faint to be clear. DiBianco knocked. The door was hollow. He could kick it in, if needed. *So much for security,* he thought.

"Hey!" He knocked again, this time harder. "You realize we have less than ten minutes—"

The door opened. Crystal gazed at him from the brightly lit cockpit. "You're awake!" Her eyes were shockingly blue, her smile pleasantly wide.

Just beyond her, seated in the lone captain's chair—both hands strapped to the controls—was Savanna, "We're nearly home Michael."

Home? he thought. DiBianco's chances were slipping away. *There's no way we'll make it in time.* He forced a smile. "How much longer?"

"We'll arrive just in time," Savanna said.

It was the answer he dreaded, yet expected. He slipped away to the chair he had awakened in.

Crystal followed.

98

Crystal sat across from DiBianco and gazed at the open cockpit; she should have closed it. *I must tell him,* she thought. Shifting focus to DiBianco's shaky gaze she reached in her pocket.

DiBianco's eyes flared with panic as she slipped the device from her coat, her fingers caressing the bright red button.

Crystal retreated her fingers; she didn't intend to press it again. She just needed time to explain. She wanted to tell him. *But Savanna will hear.* Or worse, she'd come out of the cockpit and see. Crystal couldn't risk it, though she also couldn't stand to keep DiBianco in the dark any longer. *Please, God, help me.*

99

DiBianco's pulse raced when Crystal's fingers brushed the button, then retreated abruptly. He didn't notice the sudden look of concern in her eyes; his focus was locked on the device; he knew it would bring more darkness and pain. He did *not* want to experience *that* again.

"Michael." Her voice was soft, a dull whisper, he barely heard it. "Michael," she said again, this time more pronounced.

DiBianco shook his gaze from the detonator and met Crystal's piercing blue eyes. Her concern became clear and stung like a swarm of bees. His pulse raced. His breathing labored. Something was different now that she was alone.

Crystal moved her lips, shaping words without speaking; she mouthed the same phrase over and over. What at first was unclear, struck him with a force so powerful, it stomped out his panic and filled him with an excitement so immense, it nearly made him shout aloud.

I work for the FBI. We're going to stop this.

A noise from the cockpit grabbed his attention.

Crystal's gaze shot up at Savanna, who walked out of the cockpit and poured another Diet Coke.

"I see we're ready for phase two?" she said.

Phase two? DiBianco's mind started to ache.

Crystal glanced at the detonator, then at DiBianco. Another phrase, this time terrifying, crossed her silent lips.

I'm sorry.

100

"What you're saying," Father Fredrick started, surprised to hear from a long missed voice from his past, "it's lunacy!"

"Father, you know me well. Too well. This is no joke!" The voice on the phone was the epitome of seriousness. The Father had never sensed such sternness excrete from his son's soul.

"Of course, my son," Father Fredrick said, his voice solemn, yet uncertain. "I'll have things ready for your arrival." He sighed. "I pray you're wrong about this."

"Me too, Father. Me too."

With a long hesitation, The Vatican Secretary of State dropped the heavy receiver on the phone's base and attempted to stop his hands from shaking.

"What is it, my child?"

The voice brought a sudden chill upon Father Fredrick. He had no idea anyone else was in the room. "I-I'm fine."

"You're shaking. Is everything okay?"

"Yes, Sir." Father Fredrick turned toward the shadowy figure, standing motionless in the corner.

"Come," he said, "there's work to be done."

101

A few moments later, Father Fredrick entered a small study where a dozen cardinals stood silently, reading and praying.

"Gather the College," he announced.

"But it's so late," a cardinal said, moving from the darkness into the scant light from the window.

"We must meet at once."

The man's eyes glassed over with concern as he turned and gazed out the window onto a lamp-lit Saint Peter's Square.

"This is unexpected, should we not wait—"

"Hurry!" He snapped. Father Fredrick didn't want to succumb to the stress, but he had little choice. This was proving to be the most difficult situation he had ever dealt with; certainly the most difficult in the history of The Church.

"We have less than an hour," he declared.

Several cardinals gathered into the light. Father Fredrick could sense the shock in their eyes. The men were strong with spirit; he could feel them demand—if only with that spirit— to know what was going on; but Father Fredrick was not

188 † Keith Katsikas

about to tell them.

"We must gather in the Sistine Chapel," Father Fredrick said. "Please, hurry, my brothers. We haven't much time. Have everyone there before midnight!"

Without hesitation the men scattered.

As the room cleared, Father Fredrick lowered to his knees and closed his eyes.

He was alone, in a room which still encapsulated the uncertainty and panic of a dozen holy men. Their spirits weighed on his thoughts as he bowed his head.

Oh Lord, forgive me for what I am about to do.

102

The squealing of jet tires, combined with the plane's sudden impact with the runway, jolted DiBianco from yet another unwanted vision.

He tried to clear the images from his mind but it was futile. He feared he would suffer flashbacks of these visions, even more often than the memory of the death of his parents, which oddly felt less remarkable now. In fact he welcomed the memory of that day; anything was better than what he had just experienced.

The jet skidded to a stop. He had never been on a small plane before; he had never felt anything stop so abruptly. It was then he realized. *I can't see. Am I awake? Am I blind? What's happening?*

There was a series of clicks, then a sudden chill rushed the cabin. The door was open. A vehicle in the distance grew closer and closer until finally something nudged the plane.

Soft voices grew louder, more pronounced.

"Is he ready?" a man said.

"He is." The voice was Savanna's.

"Good," he replied. "Is he still sedated?"

Sedated? DiBianco thought.

"He should be."

"Why don't you make sure?" The man's voice was stern. "We cannot have him waking up."

A soft voice whispered in his ear. *"Michael."* It was Crystal.

DiBianco still watched as horrific images flashed in the darkness of his mind. He *felt* awake; he could hear, yet; he felt like he was dreaming.

"Don't worry," Crystal whispered, *"everything will be fine."*

But nothing was fine. How could it be? The end had certainly come and gone. He was sure of it. All that remained was the, so called, Holy Land and the Descendants of Lucifer. *Nothing was fine.*

DiBianco felt himself being hoisted; he was quickly enveloped by the frigid cold. The hands grabbing his arms, legs, and middle were strong—large; they had to be men, but who? And did it even matter anymore?

As devilish images flashed through the darkness, DiBianco felt himself float through space. Soon the hands were gone and he felt himself moving in a more familiar, yet nauseating way. He was in a car. And it was driving fast. Very fast.

103

"Michael." The voice was faint. Soft. Female.

Have I been sleeping? he thought.

"Michael," the voice said again, "please, wake up."

He *had* been asleep, but for how long? Were they still on

the plane? Was there time? *Christ, Please! Let there be time!* DiBianco's eyes cracked opened, and when they did it was clear. "It is too late." He didn't intend to speak, but he did.

"What's too late?" Crystal said.

DiBianco turned and faced her; she was seated to his left in the back of a dark stretched limo. Her legs crossed, she was smiling, her left hand dangled lightly over DiBianco's right shoulder. He tried to clear his thoughts. He still felt sedated. All at once, the experience of being lifted out of the plane flooded back. "Where's Savanna?" He said.

"She's no longer with us," Crystal assured him. "I told you ... everything is fine."

DiBianco's confusion peaked. "How can anything be fine?" He said with perhaps an excessively impatient tone. He gazed ahead, trying to make out who the two men in the front seats were. The back of the head of the man sitting in the passengers seat didn't strike him in the least; however, the driver's eyes, gazing back at him through the rearview sent chills down his spine.

"What's going on?" DiBianco panicked.

"I tried to explain earlier but my chances kept getting thwarted. Please understand, I couldn't risk blowing my cover, especially in the air." Crystal paused for a moment, softly brushing DiBianco's shoulder with her fingers. "Smile Mike. It's over."

"How do you mean?"

"We know about the DoL's plot; we're on our way to stop it right now."

A surge of energy flooded DiBianco as her words registered. But then it struck him.

The clock! "But it's too late," he said again.

"How so, Mike?" A familiar voice fired from the front of the limo, yanking DiBianco's attention away from Crystal and her soft hand, now massaging his tired neck.

"According to the DoL Network, and all that Savanna had told me, The Pulse was scheduled to fire at midnight."

"And?" Camillin's voice questioned.

A clock-face entered the entirety of DiBianco's mind. The same clock he saw on the plane moments after awakening from his first vision.

11:49, it displayed. He knew it was too late.

"Midnight had to have passed long ago. It's gotta be ... what, one in the morning ... maybe later? How long have I been out?"

"Michael," Crystal interrupted with a look of despair. She yanked her hand out from behind his neck, focused in on the small silver-faced wristwatch and pressed a tiny button on the side.

DiBianco felt his blood run cold when the face of the watch lit a holographic blue. His eyes focused on the brightly lit numbers and a sudden burst of adrenalin filled his soul.

10:58 PM

"But, the clock on the plane—"

"That?" Camillin said, chuckling slightly. "That jet is one of our latest acquisitions from the embassy in Athens."

DiBianco knew immediately. Greece is an hour ahead of Rome. An invigorating sensation swept DiBianco's body. They had time to stop The Pulse. But how? He never figured out much more than where the Holy Land was. Sure that was helpful, but where the hell is the source of The Pulse?

"How do you plan to stop this thing?" DiBianco asked Camillin.

"We know the hub to the DoL Network is located somewhere within the Vatican. When your friend hacked into the network we also got in and dug around. Much of what we found didn't make a whole lot a sense, but we did find something."

"What?"

"We know that the brotherhood has penetrated the Vatican. We're sure the information pulled from the network points to one man."

"Who?"

"The Pope's closest, most personal assistant."

"The Chamberlain?" DiBianco said. "That's odd. How can you be sure?"

"The DoL Network stored tens of thousands of emails, years of phone conversations between the Chamberlain and DoL members throughout the world. Some of the messages were, well, I'm not sure how to put it. Unbelievable? I have no doubt he's our man."

"How do we get to him?"

"I've made a few calls."

"Who?" DiBianco's head was spinning.

"Let's just say, I have friends in rather high places."

Crystal brushed DiBianco's shoulder with her fingernails and smiled. "The Vatican Secretary of State."

"Oh," DiBianco said with a smirk. "*That* high."

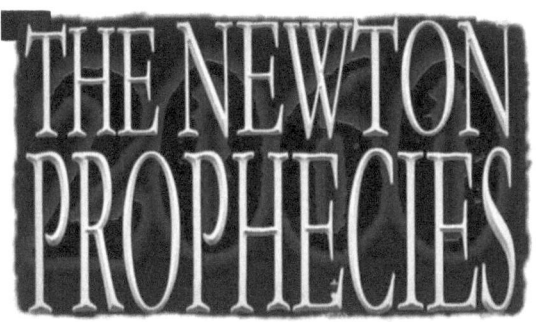

PART SEVEN

TIME'S UP!

104

11:00 PM

By droves, the world's holiest men flocked into Vatican City. By order of Father Fredrick, they gathered in the Sistine Chapel for an unexpected meeting. It was obvious what it was regarding—the Pope *had* just died—however, the timing was odd, to say the least. It Should have waited until morning, like the Chamberlain had scheduled; but the cardinals obeyed; it was not in their blood not to; especially a man like Father Fredrick, he was, after all, the man in charge.

105

11:01 PM

Father Fredrick welcomed himself into the Chamberlain's study and sat in the large leather chair at the front of his desk. He wasn't surprised to see him awake, he had been up most nights since the sudden decline of the Pope's health, and now that he was gone, he knew the Chamberlain still had a hard time sleeping.

He hadn't wanted to confront the young assistant, but knew he would never come if not personally recruited.

"To what do I owe this pleasure, my brother?" the Chamberlain said with an exhausted smile.

"We have a problem."

"What type of problem?"

"We must meet in the Sistine Chapel at once."

"What?" The Chamberlain's voice grew stressed. "I have already arranged for the college to meet at first light."

"I've recruited the college. They're on their way now."

"What is the meaning of this?"

"It's of vital importance that you join us within the hour."

The Chamberlain took in a mighty breath and stood from his chair. Father Fredrick could sense he didn't want to oblige; however, the Secretary of State's power was far greater than the Chamberlain's. He had no choice.

Father Fredrick followed the Chamberlain's gesture and stood. "Thank you," he said. Then swiftly left the thick weight that had fallen over the Chamberlain's office.

106

11:02 PM

Just outside the Vatican, in a dark building somewhere along the outer rim of the city, a phone rang, jolting Afridi from a sound sleep.

He grabbed the sticky receiver with his non-obstructed hand and grunted, "Yeah?"

"You were right," the voice said. "Get here, *quick!*"

"Yes, sir." Afridi slammed the receiver hard and rolled off the bed. He stood quickly, brushing empty food wrappers and crumbs from his clothing, then smashed his cast on the night-stand causing him to reel in pain. "Couldn't have put me in a goddamn hotel?"

107

11:03 PM

Heavy rain now fell over Vatican City. It was a soaking downpour that coated the streets in what looked like sheets of ice. DiBianco could feel the tires hydroplane as the limo sped up *Via della Conciliazione*, spilling into *Piazza Pio XII*, then into *Saint Peter's Square* itself, passing between the towering Vatican obelisk and one of the two tiered fountains—still running, even at this hour, and in this weather, its mushrooming waterfalls lit a pale green by the lights within the base—finally skidding to a stop feet before the Grand Staircase, leading up to Saint Peter's Basilica. A towering statue of Saint Peter gazed down upon them, disgusted with the sudden intrusion—or perhaps pleading, *please hurry!*

Within seconds the doors sprung open and DiBianco was hustled out of the limo, back into the brisk night air; only now rain pelted his face, stinging his flesh, snapping him awake, if only for a moment.

DiBianco hadn't noticed the line of black limos racing behind them on the way to Saint Peter's, but now they were skidding to a halt all around him; they filled the square—dozens of them.

108

11:04 PM

The sight of Saint Peter's Square and the facade of his Holy Basilica, lit at this time of night was stunning—the square's two fountains and towering obelisk; the basilica's roman columns, intricate carvings and decorative windows, Michelangelo's dome—which reminded DiBianco of the dome perched high atop 1600 Pennsylvania Avenue back in Washington—even the hundreds of poised pale figures, lining the tops of the Colonnades and the facade of the Basilica itself—Christ, eleven of his apostles, and Popes and Saints of centuries past, gazing upon the square in horror—lit in vibrant tones of gold.

Had DiBianco's mind not been clouded with stress and confusion, he might have stopped to appreciate its splendor—if only for a moment. Instead he was hustled toward the entrance of the basilica; Crystal grabbed his hand, trying to keep his strides equal with hers; equal with Camillin's; equal with the man, a man who's identity was still a mystery—a man whose bull-legged strides and Texas belt-buckle seemed oddly out of place—even more out of place than DiBianco found himself.

She yanked him harder, "We're supposed to meet Father Fredrick in the basilica—"

"Father Who?" DiBianco asked, his ears obviously playing wild tricks on him.

"The Vatican Secretary of State," she explained.

DiBianco couldn't believe what he was hearing. *It can't be.* "Father Fredrick?" He said again. He had to be sure he heard right.

"He's likely waiting for us right now." She hurried him along faster, trying to keep up with Camillin, who was nearly at the crest of the stairs. "Please, Michael, we must hurry."

109

11:05 PM

He had heard right. Father Fredrick was the Vatican Secretary of State. The man they were about to meet. A man likely involved with The Pulse and the murder of his parents.

DiBianco glanced at the army of agents, gathered at the foot of the Grand Staircase, awaiting further orders. DiBianco never imagined that God's Army would come equipped with black suits, dark shades, and bright red neckties.

The events of the last week had DiBianco utterly exhausted; however, the events of the last sixteen hours had him ready to keel over at any moment. He prayed for strength; the fate of the world rested on him solving this boggling mystery—at the very least, his own life depended on it.

His mind turned to his adoptive father, Father Fredrick, and what Savanna had said on the plane. *I just can't believe that he would...* But he did believe. And something in his soul suddenly told him they were after the wrong man. DiBianco broke Crystal's grip and sprinted up the remaining few steps. "Stop!" he shouted. "It's not him!"

Camillin stopped, his shoes skidding on the wet stone; his face startled by DiBianco's outcry.

"It's not the Chamberlain!

110

11:06 PM

The Sistine Chapel filled fast. Every cardinal in the world—a hundred and sixty-five of the world's holiest men—were there, and concern began to settle in. No one understood; why now? Why so late? They had received orders from the Chamberlain to gather at first light, which was commonplace. This was strangely unexpected.

The College—suited in common dress: black cassocks with red piping and buttons, red sash, pectoral cross on a chain, and a red zucchetto—began to wonder if they should ditch the black cassocks for the red ones. Then the doors slammed shut and the room fell silent.

Father Fredrick skimmed along the earth-colored carpet—a dark mat laced with swirly white lines and dizzying patterns—through the doors of *The Screen,* a seven-foot-tall decorative barrier, spanning the center of the room, separating the Chapel's entrance from the ornate Altar Wall.

Stepping onto a large platform at the base of the altar, Father Fredrick gazed at the massive mural of Michelangelo's *The Last Judgment*—Jesus Christ, the Judge, compels the damned with his left hand while lifting the saved with his right. Surrounding Christ are the planets, the sun, and the saints. The flamboyant monstrosity of a mural looked more like a festive orgy, than a religious symbol. In fact the entire Chapel reeked of blaspheme according to Father Fredrick's interpretation of Christian literature. It was no wonder so many Priests had lost faith in The Church.

Father Fredrick lowered his gaze toward a monument of the crucified Christ perched on the Altar, then turned toward a brightly lit Sistine Chapel. Spreading his hands he spoke, loud and clear to the College below. "We are gathered on this night to embrace changes—changes, which are about to transpire both within our world, and within our very walls."

"Changes?" One cardinal questioned.

"Patience, my brothers; soon, you will understand."

111

11:07 PM

Camillin yanked DiBianco under the massive portico—its vaulted ceiling, towering columns, and five masterfully crafted doorways, made this entrance the most grand DiBianco had ever seen. Pulling him behind a column, Camillin brought his head in close to DiBianco's.

"What do you mean it's not him?" he said.

"I know it sounds crazy," DiBianco started, unsure how Camillin would react to what he was about to say. The Vatican Secretary of State was, after all, Camillin's friend. "There's someone else."

"Who?"

"Someone with the power to make things happen in the Vatican. A man who could have easily been responsible for those calls and emails to the DoL and had made it look like someone else. A person I thought I knew, until today."

"Mike?" Camillin's face grew concerned.

"How well do you know your friend?" DiBianco said.

"Friend?"

"Father Fredrick," he explained.

Immediately Camillin's eyes lit ablaze, it was a look not easily read. Was it anger? Concern? Whatever it was, it was like a light had gone off in Camillin's head. "Father Fredrick is not my friend." Camillin paused, seeming to collect his thoughts. "He's my father."

DiBianco looked on in amazement.

"My *real* father. My dad."

A weight like a lead brick fell into the pit of his stomach. He didn't know what to say next. How could this be? How could he have not known? "He's my father, too," DiBianco finally said.

Camillin's chin hit the floor as all the blood drained from his face gathering somewhere in the back of his throat.

112

11:08 PM

"Not blood, of course," DiBianco explained, "he adopted me when I was twelve—"

"That was you?" Camillin said, almost laughing. "The little red headed kid with the book. What was that—"

"The Mysteries of Science," he said.

"Ah, yes ... of course, *The Mysteries of—*"

"Camillin." DiBianco was dead serious. It didn't matter who the man was, or how close he was to Camillin's heart. "Father Fredrick is our man. I know it to be true. He's the one who—"

"What are you two lovebirds chattin' about?" the man with the Texas belt-buckle said, peering into the shadow of the column.

"Fuller!" Camillin snapped. "You scared the shit out of me."

Where have I heard that before? he thought.

"So, what are you doing?" Fuller asked again.

"Looks like the Chamberlain's not our guy."

"Oh *really.*" Fuller's voice sank into a pit of sarcasm. "What changed your mind?"

As Camillin explained, DiBianco's attention was drawn toward one of the five doorways. It was something he never expected to see on a Holy Basilica. The panels were plastered with haunting scenes of death. There was the instantly recognizable crucifixion, but then there were other murders; hangings, stabbings, stonings, unthinkable torment against life.

"Are you out of your mind?" Fuller said. "Father Fredrick is the head of the Vatican. The Pope is dead and every cardinal is here to elect a replacement, and you think he's..."

Just then, a terrifying thought occurred to DiBianco. *The cardinals.* Every vital church leader was in the Vatican. Every one of them. All it would take is one carefully placed bomb to take out every last one of them, bringing a very sudden and gruesome end to the Catholic Church.

It all made perfect sense. It was terrifyingly perfect. The Descendants not only planned to wreak havoc on the world, by destroying its technologically advanced infrastructure, killing billions, but they were going to destroy the Church and form a new governing body in it's place.

"Camillin!" DiBianco snapped, yanking his arm. "We've gotta stop The Pulse!"

Camillin looked confused. "Of course!" He stared at

Fuller, who simply shrugged, then back at DiBianco who quickly turned shades of red.

"They're going to blow up the Sistine Chapel!"

113

11:09 PM

Much to DiBianco's surprise, Saint Peter's Basilica was empty. One of the five massive doors, the one just right of center, had been left open—the bronze panels on that door depicted the seven sacraments. The basilica was bright, but the silence was deafening. They expected to see Father Fredrick, but there was no one—no one at all.

Camillin gazed at Fuller, who was peering into the bowels of the vaulted corridor, like he was expecting someone.

Walking in, DiBianco's shoes clicked off the gleaming marble, echoing through the space like rolling thunder through a wide open field. He had never witnessed such a spectacle. Sure, he'd researched the Vatican with all its rich history and stunning architecture; but all the pictures in the world hadn't done the real thing any justice.

Apart from the building, with its gold-lined archways, frescoed walls and ceilings, intricate carvings and stonework, and breathtaking palace-like decor, it was the eclectic collection of priceless artifacts and holy relics that truly stood out.

To his right was Michelangelo's *Pietà*—a glorious marble statue of Mary cradling her dead son, Jesus, moments after being lowered from the cross. DiBianco recalled stories about how this sculpture was vandalized by some idiot with an axe back in the seventies; ever since, this marvelous work has spent its days and nights behind several inches of bulletproof plexiglass.

To his left he caught glimpse of the Baptistery Chapel; but it was the sight of a monumental canopy—*Saint Peter's Baldacchino*—directly ahead, that grabbed his eye and held it for a long moment. A towering bronze monument, which sprung four intricately crafted legs lined in gold-leaf accents, down to the papal altar and the holy relics of Saint Peter.

The basilica was like a hand crafted cave, with offshoots to the right and to the left of the main corridor. Each of these vaulted cubbies housed a virtual museum of religious artifacts, monuments, and sculptures.

Like the rest of the Basilica, the floor was stunning. At DiBianco's feet was a red disc, framed in white, gold, and grey motif. Though this artifact shone with the rest of the basilica, there was something oddly unique about it— something about the very spot on which DiBianco stood that had tingles chasing goosebumps up his back.

"That porphyry disc," Camillin started, snapping DiBianco from his gaze, "was taken from the original basilica, centuries ago." Camillin's eyes grew wide. "You're standing on the very spot Charlemagne was crowned emperor of Rome."

114

11:10 PM

The irony was so intense that DiBianco's heart sank in his chest; for it was at *that* very point that Newton predicted *The Roman Catholic Church* had fallen into apostasy. From that day forward—the day Pope Leo III crowned Charlemagne—there would be 1,260 years of corruption, sickness, even murder amongst the church's most faithful.

"Hey!" The sudden shout startled DiBianco out of his daze. In an instant, Fuller was running, deep into the heart of Saint Peter's Basilica.

115

11:11 PM

"Where are you going?" Camillin said.

"Come on," Fuller fired, "I know where Father Fredrick is!"

Without hesitation Crystal and Camillin took off, DiBianco followed. *Man, those bull-legged trunks can move,* he thought. Swiftly as DiBianco was moving—his strides such that it made his breathing labor and his heart jackhammer—he couldn't help but notice the stunning work of centuries past.

The Monument of Pope Leo XII stole his eye; it depicted the pope imparting a blessing during the Jubilee of 1825. DiBianco recalled studying Pope LEO XII for a class project back in '96. DiBianco prayed he'd be able to stop The Pulse and regain order in *The Church* before it was too late; but time was ticking, only minutes remaining.

"It's hard to believe this place is little more than a glorified cemetery," Crystal said. She was absolutely right. Under every altar—and there were many—rested the body. There were hundreds surrounding them, and filling the earth beneath.

DiBianco was stricken with more chills. "Where are we going?"

"The Confessio," Fuller finally replied.

"Saint Peter's Tomb?" Camillin asked. "Why?"

Camillin didn't slow, but DiBianco senses something was wrong, and he would soon learn just how right he was.

116

11:13 PM

Agent Fuller ran up to a circular, waste-high marble banister, surrounded in rich decorative rails, rimmed with what appeared to be a hundred brass fixtures with flickering flames, creeping up from behind the banister like vines—DiBianco knew they were eternal flames, forever keeping God's light on the tomb of Saint Peter—and jump, vanishing into the void beyond.

"What the—" DiBianco stared in amazement.

"That's the Confessio," Camillin said, running toward a brass gate at the center of the banister. "Don't jump; there's stairs on the other side; you'll brake your legs."

DiBianco sensed a weighting feeling of entrapment and backed off, watching Camillin pull the gate open and rush in, Crystal following behind.

There was a scuffle.

DiBianco retreated, slipping into the Gregorian Chapel—the cubby they passed moments before. He caught his breath and peeked around the corner, back toward the Confessio.

At first he saw nothing; then he spotted the top of a black hood; moments later there was shouting—it was a familiar voice that seemed to leap out of a not so distant past.

117

11:14 PM

In the heat of the moment Crystal reached for Camillin's transmitter, the one he kept attached to his hip and pressed the call button—she had to get through to the agents outside—but without hesitation Fuller kicked it. It fell to the marble steps with a shattering crash. The larger of the three hooded figures swooped it up and crushed it in his bare hand.

"What are you doing?" she cried.

"Shut up!" the massive man in the black mask shouted. He was middle-eastern, of this, she was sure. The voice reminded her of—

"Afridi?"

The man pulled the hood from his head and gazed at Crystal with vengeful eyes.

Crystal's face went pale. "What's going on?"

"I thought I told you to shut up!" Afridi shouted, then reeled back his arm and slammed his cast against the side of her head. "Get down stairs. Now!"

Camillin was speechless and with rifles at their backs, neither one of them hesitated to move.

"Get on the floor!" Afridi shouted. *"DO IT!"*

They did.

Crystal hadn't noticed that DiBianco wasn't with them,

her focus was drawn solely toward the dark hooded figures.

"Nothing's gonna get in our way," Fuller demanded. "It's been too long in the making, and in minutes the world will see how perfect we are."

Crystal couldn't believe what she was hearing. She had little doubt about Afridi, but Fuller... He was one of the *good guys*. She had been so sure.

"Don't think for a second you have a chance," Fuller started. "Our power goes all the way to the top, all over the world. Why do you think the leaders of your governments couldn't care less about *the people* anymore?"

It was then she realized how deep the infiltration had gone. She thought she had discovered a lot while undercover, but in the grand scheme of things, she had barely skimmed the surface. The DoL had woven themselves into every layer of society. There was no way to stop it. For the first time in her life, she felt defeated.

Afridi, Fuller, The Chamberlain, The Secretary of State. Crystal was sure, Fuller was speaking the truth. It explained so much; it made sense out of the sudden level of corruption in the world. The Descendants had won a long time ago; this was simply the icing on the cake.

118

DiBianco glanced at his wristwatch.
11:15 PM

He had to do something, and fast. There was no doubt the Descendants of Lucifer were planing to blow up the Sistine

Chapel. Getting there would be his only chance of stopping The Pulse, or at the very least, save the cardinals. He had to let them know about the Descendants, about their plans; he needed to break the news that Father Fredrick was likely involved in the plot—perhaps even the mastermind. *The Antichrist,* he thought.

But how could he get there without being spotted? He clenched his eyes shut and tried to bring up maps and floorplans of the basilica and surrounding areas. He spent plenty of time researching Vatican City and had seem many floorplans, not just of the basilica, but the Apostolic Palaces, including the Sistine Chapel.

He struggled to get a clear map in his head. Time seemed to pass faster now. He had to move. Opening his eyes he spotted a door. Across the isle from where he stood, still within the archway, out of sight of the Confessio, was the Monument to Pope Gregory XVI.

DiBianco ran toward the monument—toward the doorway, silently praying it would lead somewhere, somewhere close to where he needed to be—anywhere was better than where he was.

The monument depicted Pope Gregory XVI—the last monk elected Pope—seated on a throne in the act of blessing. His thrown rested on a base that rose over a sarcophagus. Above the sarcophagus was a bas-relief depicting a scene referring to the propagation of the Faith, assiduously supported by Pope Gregory XVI with the institution of the Catholic Missions.

But it was the door alone that interested DiBianco at the moment. He pushed it, and surprisingly it opened with ease. On the other side was a sight that instantly brought a mental map to his mind. For he now stood in the Blessed Sacrament Chapel. The Sistine Chapel was just feet away.

He glanced up at a banner seemingly carved into the marble. *Only those who wish to pray may enter.*

119

11:16 PM

DiBianco knew where he needed to be, and now he knew how to get there. He only hoped the access would be clear, for it led straight into the Papal Apartments. He could now see the route in his mind. Just outside this room was a corridor, with a stairway passage leading up into the Papal Apartments built by Pope Sistus V during his service, but there was also a direct route to the Sistine Chapel. He was just yards away.

DiBianco ran toward the door to the left of the altar, passed several rows of pews and swiftly heaved the doors; they didn't budge. He tried again; throwing himself into the doors with all his might; they still wouldn't budge. After a moment of panting, he dropped his hands and retreated, gazing ominously at the impenetrable obstacle that stood before him. He had little doubt it'd be locked; but he had to try.

DiBianco knelt at the altar and prayed. It occurred to him, he ought to have prayed before charging at the door. After all, *only those who wish to pray may enter,* that's what the sign above the archway read. To DiBianco, the choice of topics was simple. He had to get to the Sistine Chapel; he needed to tell the cardinals what was happening, bring an end to it; at the very least get them as far away from the Chapel as possible.

DiBianco clasped his hands tightly and closed his eyes; he prayed from the soul; prayed from the heart; for the first time in his life he felt the spirit touch him; and he wiped the tears from his cheeks. It touched him again, this time stronger, bringing him to his feet in a hurry, nearly knocking the Chamberlain to the ground.

120

11:17 PM

The Chamberlain looked much younger than he had in photographs.

"I heard a ruckus in here," the Chamberlain said. "Are you all right?"

DiBianco glanced at the Chamberlain who showed genuine concern; something DiBianco didn't think killers did. Then he glanced at the door which led out to the Apostolic Palaces—it was open, two Swiss Guards stood in the opening.

He must've come in while I was praying, he thought.

DiBianco glared at the Chamberlain.

"Is something wrong?" the Chamberlain said.

DiBianco wasn't sure how to react. The Chamberlain's attitude was strange, in that, it wasn't strange at all. He was acting like everything was normal. If Camillin was right, then the Chamberlain had to be the mastermind behind the whole damn thing, he was cool, like a Mafia hit-man.

"Perhaps we should talk about it?" he said, wrapping his arm around DiBianco's shoulders and guiding him toward the open door—toward the Sistine Chapel.

121

11:18 PM

DiBianco had to let the cardinals know about The Pulse, and stop it, if that was even possible, otherwise none of this would make any difference; however, if the Chamberlain was the mastermind like Camillin had thought, the last thing DiBianco could risk, was letting him know he knew.

"What brings you here so late?" he asked. "You do realize this area is not open to the public at this hour?" The Chamberlain quickened his strides and led DiBianco out of Saint Peter's Basilica, into the corridor. The guards closed and locked door, then surrounded them, methodically guiding them down a short corridor toward the Sistine Chapel, far closer than DiBianco had imagined.

"Wait," DiBianco said, almost in a panic, grabbing the Chamberlain's cassock.

The guards instantly reacted, grabbing DiBianco by the arms, yanking him away.

The Chamberlain waved them off; they released DiBianco, but stayed close.

"What is it, Brother?" he said.

DiBianco sensed sincerity in the Chamberlain's eyes, a real warmth that no evil man could emit; then the words spurted out of DiBianco's mouth like a well-tap bursting from the icy cold. "You're in extreme danger," he said. "There's an evil in this place I can't begin to explain—"

The Chamberlain eyes grew impatient.

DiBianco knew right away that he was babbling and that it was getting him nowhere fast. "I'm with the FBI..."

The Chamberlain pushed the doors to the Sistine Chapel open, then waved to the Guards who instantly grappled DiBianco, lifting him clear from the floor.

"Wait," he pleaded, "you have to listen..."

With a nod, the Guards hauled him away.

"I'm with the FBI," he said again. "There's a bomb..." But it was too late, the Chapel doors slammed shut.

122

11:19 PM

Father Fredrick lowered his hands, pointing toward the door as it opened. The cardinals turned and gazed at the man striding into the room.

Father Fredrick looked dismayed. "Nice of you to join us," he said. "A bit late, aren't we?"

"Why are we here?" the Chamberlain said.

"Patience, soon you will know."

The door swung wide and everyone spun, freezing stiff at the ghostly sight. Silence fell upon the Sistine Chapel. Death itself had entered the room, the door slamming shut behind him.

123

11:20 PM

"You don't understand," DiBianco pleaded, the Swiss Guards violently hustling him—his feet barely touching the floor—down a long frescoed corridor. A set of bronze doors loomed ahead. DiBianco knew where they led; into Saint Peter's Square, far away from where he needed to be, away from being able to stop The Pulse.

"There's a bomb in the Sistine Chapel," he cried. "You have to save the cardinals!" It was a last ditch effort, which had no affect. The bronze doors came up swiftly and in the bat of an eye the bitter rain stabbed his face yet again and he tumbled down the stone steps, landing hard in Saint Peter's Square.

124

11:21 PM

Pope Seises XVI strode toward the pulpit, the cardinals gasping as he blew past. Even stranger than the fact that he was dead, was the fact he had suffered with Parkinson's disease for the last twelve years of his life; he practically lived in a wheelchair.

The cardinals stood stunned. Many cried.

"It's a miracle," one shouted.

Was it possible? Had the Supreme Pontiff risen, like Christ himself had risen? The Chamberlain thought of the man whom he took for crazy, and had escorted out of the building. *The FBI*, he thought. *Something is certainly not right here.* He suddenly regretted throwing the stranger out.

125

11:22 PM

Pope Seises XVI was a tall man, the Chamberlain had never noticed his height before, he had always been hunched over, in extreme pain; now he stood like a soldier. *Could it be true,* he thought. *Could he have risen?*

At nearly six-foot-five—and adding another three feet for the pulpit—the Pope towered above the cardinals, who were now sprawled on the chapel floor beneath him.

"The time has come," he announced, his voice commanding like it hadn't been in years.

At once, a group of cardinals rose from the floor and gathered behind the Holy Father. The remaining cardinals stirred in confusion. The room, which had been silent, was now overrun with bickering and mumbling.

A dozen elders now flanked the Holy Father in a stance unlike that of holy men.

126

11:22 PM

"Where is he?" Afridi shouted, ramming his cast into the side of Crystal's head.

Why the hell doesn't he slam that thing into Camillin's head, she thought. She was dizzy; she wasn't sure how much more abuse she could take; besides she hadn't a clue *where* he was. He had been right beside them, moments before storming the Confessio; she could only hope he was well on his way to stopping The Pulse.

"You," Fuller said, pointing at one of the hooded figures. "As much as the thought of you screwing things up any further sickens me, you're the only one able to get close enough." Fuller shook his head, doubtful of his decision. "Get those frickin' robes off and get out of here!"

Swiftly and nervously, the woman pried off her hood and the black outer layer of clothing and straightened out her hair.

"Find him, and for *your* sake, stop him."

The woman's long brown hair, short skirt, cut just above the knees, and white blouse were more than just familiar to Crystal.

"Savanna?" she said. "I thought—"

"You're so lost kid," Savanna said, then ran up the stairs and out of the Confessio, her high heals clicking loudly off the marble floor, quickly fading into a dull echo.

127

11:23 PM

Time was up. It was over. DiBianco lay motionless, face down on the wet brick of Saint Peter's Square, gazing at a slick black tire, inches from his face—it belonged to one of the dozens of limos which had raced into Saint Peter's what felt like hours ago—but certainly only minutes.

The agents, he thought.

Like a tidal-wave, the remembrance struck him. *There's a hundred armed men at the foot of the Grand Staircase waiting for orders to move.* The Swiss Guards hadn't ended his chances of stopping The Pulse, they had unwittingly increased his odds.

DiBianco leapt to his feet, glanced over the parked limos toward the basilica and saw that, indeed, the men in the black suits, dark shades, and bright red neckties were still there. He ran toward them, full speed; faster than he had ever run in his life. He didn't look at his wristwatch; he didn't want to know; he saw real hope, gathered at the foot of the Holy Basilica, and he was going to use it to the fullest level possible.

From where DiBianco had fallen to where the agents gathered was nearly two hundred feet, but the adrenaline suddenly pumping through his veins made his strides longer and faster; and within seconds he was upon them.

But the agents heard his approach, swiftly from the rear,

and instantly reacted with pistols drawn and a sudden blow to DiBianco's head.

DiBianco fell, his vision blurred; then darkness.

128

11:24 PM

Pope Seises XVI took a deep breath and grinned. His body was old, the same man the Chamberlain had watched deteriorate over the last decade, however, he seemed unaffected by his disease; and his demeanor had changed. It was *not* the same man, not the man the Chamberlain had grown to love and treasure. The spirit of the Lord was stripped from the Sistine Chapel, replaced by something else, something cold ... something evil.

"This day has been decades in the making," the Pope proclaimed.

The Chamberlain stood baffled, along side a hundred-plus cardinals, who's fear was no less than his own. He needed to stand ground for his brothers, for his church. He needed to replace the fear in their hearts with a force far greater than fear, or *any* evil—the spirit of the Lord. But the darkness was so great; it crushed his soul and churned his stomach, throwing his mind into utter turmoil.

"This makes no sense," the Chamberlain said, stepping into the center of the chapel, the cardinals staying behind.

"It makes perfect sense," the Pope fired. "I have waited longer than you can imagine—longer than you've been alive—for this day to come."

"What day *is* this, Your Holiness?" The Chamberlain called the man *Your Holiness* out of instinct. He felt his skin crawl as he spoke the words; he was the furthest thing from holy.

The Pope fell silent, cocked his head slightly, and grinned. It was a sick, lustful smirk. His chin poked the air like a hungry beast salivating over fresh meat; his eyes bled with sinful delight. "This is the day, we prepare for the Second Coming!"

The cardinals reeled in astonishment at the bold statement; the sudden commotion from behind startled the Chamberlain, yet not enough to tear his gaze from the Pope, who looked ready to pounce at any moment.

"Everything is about to change," the Pope declared. "Soon, our King will reclaim his thrown, his people, his church."

More chatter flared from behind. The Chamberlain could sense the fear in the room wane, overrun with something else, fury perhaps. Whatever it was, he knew something was happening—something outside of his control.

129

11:25 PM

"The time has come for us to put an end to *he* who has twisted the minds of those who ought be followers of our Lord, our King—he who has restricted the growth of our people. I would not expect you to understand," the Pope said. "I chose not to bring you into the fold for many reasons, but perhaps the most vital was security. It was your unyielding faith in 'God'—your God—that drove you out. You," he shouted, pointing at the Chamberlain, "are a lunatic, along with the rest of you! You wouldn't understand, even if you could."

"I *do* understand," the Chamberlain snapped. "You're a fake. An impostor. A lie." The Chamberlain's attention was yanked away from the Pope by the appearance of black and red cassocks on either side of him. The cardinals now flanked him, the power of Christ flooding his veins.

The Pope flicked his hands and the dozen elders standing at his sides leapt off the pulpit, their face's dark, evil, their grins wide with vengeance. Within seconds, before the Chamberlain had a chance to absorb what was happening, a dozen cardinals were tossed to the floor—their necks snapped—blood spurting from their mouths.

The elders danced like demons around the Lord's cardinals—their speed, swift; their objective, clear. For the first time in the history of The Church, standing in the sanctity of the Sistine Chapel, the Lord's cardinals had to do something they had never dreamt would ever come to pass. They must fight for their lives.

130

11:26 PM

An earth-shattering explosion rocked the Boston skyline.

Flames tore through the Hancock Plaza, shattering windows, sending choking debris and people raining from the upper floors—souls jumping to a death, surely less torturous than the one they'd face inside.

The smoke was thick, and getting heavier by the second. *How did this happen? Why?* It didn't matter anymore. All that mattered was finding a way out. But the smoke was too thick and his lungs started to—

"Michael?" a woman shouted. DiBianco couldn't move, nor could he see. He welcomed the feeling, happy to no longer be escaping the inferno.

Murmuring filled his head—filling the darkness. None of the chatter made sense, but he could tell there were many voices—many men, chatting about something important; something he wasn't supposed to hear, but desperately needed to know.

"Michael?" the voice said again. It was a soft voice, one that brought comfort, though he struggled to place it. He tried to ask, *who are you? What's happening?* But no sound left his lips.

The chatter grew louder and DiBianco felt himself being lifted into a sitting position.

"Come on, Mike," the voice said, "please, wake up."

Suddenly, there was a flash of light. Arcs of light flickered in his mind ... another vision.

A stack of old papers, messy handwriting plastered every page. *The Newton Papers*, he thought. The room was dark, lit only by the scant light of a flickering flame. Beside the papers was a small black box, the size of a CD jewel case—but a perfect cube. In the top was a small square hole.

Then blackness.

Another flash.

The room reappeared, only the flame was now dying; beside it was a shimmering object, he couldn't make it out, the flame was fading fast—

"Hey!" a male voice fired, sending his heart into trepidation and his eyes jetting wide open.

131

11:27 PM

DiBianco jumped to his feet and gazed around at the virtual army of men dressed in black suits and bright red neckties then steered his gaze toward the only person who stood totally out of place. Against the sea of black masculinity, she looked absolutely stunning. She seemed so pleased to see him that it pushed all the doubt about her into the back of his mind—if only for a moment—but the moment wouldn't' last.

"Savanna, what are you doing here?" He said.

"I'm here to help."

"Bullshit!" He shouted, then glanced around at the army of agents. "She's one of them!"

An agent, who had been standing beside Savanna, moved toward DiBianco and looked straight in his eyes, "If not for her, you'd be dead."

DiBianco glanced at her, then back at the agent.

"Camillin was captured," DiBianco explained, "I managed to get away, but they fell right into a trap. I think Fuller led them into it on purpose."

"We know," the agent said. "Your friend explained everything, that's why we need you to come with us."

DiBianco sensed another trap and gazed at Savanna. "Why would you tell them?"

"I'm sorry," she said. "I'm sorry for not being honest with you. Mostly, I am sorry for ever getting involved with Afridi, and his group—"

"His group?"

"There's no time to explain," she said. "We must go. The Master is the only one who can stop The Pulse—"

"I don't believe you," DiBianco said. "Why are you suddenly on our side?"

"There's no time!" she shouted.

"We can't trust her!"

"Things aren't happening the way they were supposed to," she explained, in an impatient tone. "The Master has gathered the cardinals into the Sistine Chapel—"

"Yes, I know," DiBianco interrupted. "He plans to kill them using The Pulse."

"You don't understand," she cried. "When The Master found that the Newton Prophesies were wrong ... that the DoL's plans were not going to follow the course the founding Master had predicted, drastic changes were made. Changes we simply cannot allow to happen!"

DiBianco was shaken.

What Prophesies?

He tried to visualize every Newton manuscript he had ever read—tried to recall anything about a prophecy outside of the prediction of the end of days, 2060, he knew that one, and the page he read in the taxi on the way to the airport certainly seemed prolific, but—

Then it occurred to him.

They think Isaac Newton's their founding Master.

132

11:28 PM

DiBianco knew it couldn't be; Newton was a staunch believer in God, even Christ, though it did make a certain amount of sense. It did explain why the DoL had stolen the Newton Papers and why they attacked The Church—Newton had denounced the teachings of The Church countless times, even wrote about his findings on the apostate church in page after page of his manuscripts—however Newton was not a follower of Lucifer; he wrote of his belief in God.

"Michael," Savanna cried, "he's going to destroy everything."

DiBianco stood bewildered. "What about the gathering? I thought the DoL were gathering in the Holy Land?"

"Like I said, everything is different now. The Pulse is gonna set off a network of bombs laced throughout the city." Savanna paused, looking more serious than DiBianco had ever seen her look before. "Vatican City, Michael. The crazy son-of-a-bitch is going to kill every last one of us!"

DiBianco knew she was serious; not just serious, but right. This was so much bigger than he had ever thought. Every time he felt he was getting close to the answers... *BANG!* ...another wrench in the gears.

Whether she was redeemable or not seemed irrelevant at this point. She was afraid for her life, and that was reason enough to believe her. "Follow me," he said, "I know where they are."

133

11:29 PM

The spirit in the Sistine Chapel was anything but reverent, but it was clear to the Chamberlain that the Lord's spirit had returned and it had given extreme strength to the concourse of elders who had unwittingly raged battle against the spirit of the devil with their bare hands.

As if directed by a higher power, the cardinals charged at the circling demon-like men.

Though outnumbered, these men were quick and agile. They dodged many of the cardinals, grabbing them by the head as they flew by, snapping their necks with a quick twist. Killing came so effortlessly for the followers of evil. Nonetheless, the dark men were quickly overrun by the cardinals. They huddled around the men, kicking, punching, crying, "Lord, forgive us!"

The Chamberlain ran toward the Pope who made for the door. "Stop!" he shouted, running, trying to catch up. He grabbed the Pope by the shoulder and spun him around. The Pope skillfully increased the momentum of the spin and the Chamberlain felt a searing pain in his stomach.

Pope Seises XVI glared at him with bold eyes, sneered, and pulled the blade from his gut.

The Chamberlain reached for his stomach; his hands filled with blood.

"How dare you touch me," the Pope snapped, then

turned to leave.

The Chamberlain's knees grew weak; his head began to spin.

A large number of cardinals ran out from behind the Chamberlain and jumped onto the Pope hurling him to the ground. The Pope let out a loud, inhuman howl. It would be the last sound the Chamberlain would ever hear.

134

11:30 PM

DiBianco led Savanna and the procession of agents through the bronze doors on top of the steps of the Colonnades, leading into the Constantine Wing, and into the same long frescoed corridor the Swiss Guards had escorted him through moments earlier. They hustled through the entry and filled the corridor with the brash hubbub of heavy footsteps.

Up ahead, DiBianco saw the guards who had tossed him out gaze at him, their bladed staffs ready, as if they could take on a hundred armed men. DiBianco knew they would, if they had to.

A violent crash shook the building. The guards spun at the sound; the doors beside them flailed open, sending a mass of bodies barging out, pilling on top of them; one of the men stopped outside the doors—his cassock twisted, his face smeared with blood—gazed at DiBianco and the army of agents, then ran, disappearing into the blackness.

135

11:31 PM

Beneath the onslaught of black cassocks and red sashes, amidst the rainbow of flailing Swiss Guard attire and silver plate armor, was an elderly man. DiBianco gazed at the scene. *There's no way,* he thought. *He's supposed to be dead.* But the longer he stared the more sure he became. It was the Pope.

Panic filled his soul and, like spoken by an angel—or perhaps God himself—a voice filled his head. Speaking softly, yet bold, strong, deep, comforting; it spoke a short and simple phrase; rather, a number. *Six-sixteen.*

In an instant the message was clear. It's him, he knew. He couldn't believe the pieces hadn't come together sooner. But how was he to know? Pope Seises XVI was supposed to be dead.

136

11:31 PM

DiBianco remembered the first time he had heard the Pope's name; it was long before the man called Seises had ever seen the papal office. It was the fifth grade, one of his earliest memories.

His math teacher, Ms De'Soto, he recalled, was rambling off a slew of numbers in Spanish, when all of a sudden nothing made sense; it was like she had switched to another language all together. "What are you saying?" he asked.

She explained, "I'm speaking one through ten in Spanish."

Young DiBianco was confused. "I know my numbers," he said, "and that aint them."

Ms De'Soto glared at young Michael, "Isn't," she said. "Don't let me hear you say that God-awful word again."

Michael apologized, but she hadn't answered his question. "What was that?" He asked again, but she said nothing. He never was able to forget about Ms De'Soto—her wavy brown hair and chocolate eyes—he also, oddly enough, never forgot the lesson she had taught him that day. It didn't seem important then, but now it seemed almost deliberate, like it was meant to be. She had walked to the chalkboard and wrote out a series of words in large white letters: *unos, doses, treses, cuatros, cincos, seises, sietes, ochos, nueves, diezes.* "They are numbers," she explained, "in their plural form. It's a great vocal exercise. You should try it."

Seises, he thought. *Plural form of six.* DiBianco couldn't believe how obvious it had been, yet somehow, it never dawned on him. Seises, or seis, equals six and XVI equals sixteen. 616. Or one could simply deduce that Seises alone could mean 666. In either case it clearly implied the same thing. Pope Seises XVI was the man behind the DoL; the man who could stop The Pulse; the Antichrist himself.

"Wait," DiBianco pleaded. *"STOP!"*

137

11:32 PM

The Pope fought with the strength of twenty men. DiBianco watched the cardinals fall to the man's relentless wrath—one cardinal howled in pain as he was thrown to the floor—blood gushing from his neck. Another fell like a rock, a blood-gushing hole gaping in the temple.

The cardinals kicked and punched and cried, praying for the strength to end the raging beast from killing them all.

The two Swiss Guards managed to finagle their way out of the pile and crawl off toward the wall and perch themselves against a wall, watching the madness unfold before their bewildered eyes. DiBianco knew there was nothing they could do—Christ, there were over a hundred armed men standing behind him who could do little more than watch the events come to an ugly end.

The cardinals stormed out of the Sistine Chapel, a heroic attempt to subdue Seises. But Seises had the upper hand, he had a weapon—a long dagger-like blade. One after another, the cardinals fell. The stench in the corridor grew rancid. DiBianco's stomach started to dry-heave.

DiBianco and Savanna were shoved aside. One of the agents plowed through and fired two quick rounds into the mayhem. The sound was deafening; before DiBianco knew what was happening his hearing was dead; then came the droning buzz—a sound that made his mind numb and his skin crawl. In the enclosed space, it felt more like a bomb, than a pistol.

The first shot struck a cardinal in the side of the head, sending him skyward; the second struck the Pope in the chest. The crowd of cardinals scattered like roaches, leaving the Pope bleeding to death on the floor of the corridor.

138

11:33 PM

Father Fredrick bolted through the door leading into the Blessed Sacrament Chapel and ran toward the Confessio. Fuller was supposed to retain DiBianco there; obviously something had gone terribly wrong.

Father Fredrick was not about to let their plans falter. At all costs he had to be sure that everything stayed the course. The fate of the future depended on it. His life, in comparison, was purely dispensable; and he was prepared to shed his own blood to assure divine victory.

139

11:34 PM

DiBianco ran toward Seises and took him in his arms. "Where is it?" he shouted. "Tell me, now!"

Seises gazed at DiBianco with sad eyes. "You?"

DiBianco saw a tear form. "How do we stop it?"

Seises frowned. "You?" he cried. "Why?"

"What the hell are you talking about?" DiBianco screamed, loosing his patience, ready to drive his fist deep into the hole in the old man's chest. "How do I stop The Pulse?"

The cardinals looked squeamish.

The Pope laughed, then hacked up more blood. "You can't. It's much too late for th—" the Pope's words were cut off by more hacking, sprays of blood flailed through he air.

"You're the Pope," he cried. "Known for preforming so many Christlike acts. You've healed the sick, freed the slaved, blessed the weak, and strengthened the poor. I *know* you can stop this ... I beg you!"

The Pope's face was serious, yet saddened. "You were to lead our people. Why didn't you—" Just then he started to seize; his body became rigid, and his hands shook with ferocity.

"No!" DiBianco shouted. "You must tell me!"

As if programed—perhaps from decades of going through the motions—Seises crossed himself and clutched his crucifix, raising it off his chest. "Go," his voice was weak. "Son of White." Then he fell, limp, his final breath blew rancid across DiBianco's nose.

"*No!*" DiBianco gazed at Savanna, confused and dismayed, then at the cardinals who stood in shock over what had happened.

"What's The Pulse?" a cardinal asked.

"There's no time," DiBianco said. "In less than thirty minutes this entire city will be destroyed; the church will perish, along with everyone in it." DiBianco was stricken with a feeling of helplessness, he didn't know what else to do. How could God allow such madness to take over his church—his world? "We must search his room," DiBianco said.

"Should we evacuate?" A cardinal asked.

"Did you hear a word I said?" DiBianco shouted. "There's no time! We must search the Pope's room ... now!"

"Room, Sir?" a cardinal said. "Which one?"

"All of them!" DiBianco was astonished at the reluctancy of the cardinals.

"My brother, there are over one-thousand rooms in the Apostolic Palaces," a cardinal said. "Two hundred of them are used for papal apartments, including a private chapel, a kitchen and sleeping quarters for the Pope's nuns and staff."

DiBianco's heart sank. *A thousand rooms?* There was no way they could search them all, no matter how many people they had. "We need to search his private quarters."

140

11:35 PM

"There are sixteen rooms in the Pope's apartment," one cardinal said, "eight of them private, only the Pope and his assistants may enter."

"Where are they?" DiBianco asked. "The Pope's assistants."

The cardinals grew silent. The impact of what had happened must have been settling in. A few cardinals vomited at the sight of the Pope's blood-drenched body and without warning several others ran into the shadows; soon the corridor ignited with the sound of weeping and vomiting. One cardinal pointed into the Sistine Chapel. The Chamberlain lay face down, mere feet from the door, a thick pool of blood soaking through his upper torso.

"Where are the keys?" Savanna said.

"What keys?" A cardinal replied.

"The keys to the Pope's private quarters?"

"There are no keys, Miss; well, none like you might think."

"What do you mean?" DiBianco asked.

The cardinal glanced at the dead Pope and raised a pointed finger, "His thumb..."

Of course, DiBianco thought. Gazing at the Popes hand, focusing on his thumb, laying in a pool of blood on the floor—the knife used to kill so many of the Lord's faithful cardinals inches away—DiBianco knew exactly what the cardinal was trying to say. *The Pope's thumb is the key.*

DiBianco crouched down beside the Pope and out of respect for the church, crossed himself.

"No," the cardinal cried, obviously struck by what DiBianco was about to do.

"Do you have a better idea?" DiBianco said. "Any of you?"

The cardinals shook their heads in disgust and took a step back allowing DiBianco to grab the bloodsoaked knife in one hand, and the Pope's right hand in the other.

141

11:36 PM

The cardinals retreated into the Sistine Chapel, fell to their knees, and began to pray. The floor was sodden with death—its once earthy tone, now painted in smears of blood. Only a few dozen men remained, and no one knew for sure if they were on the same team. A few of the cardinals began to care for their fallen brothers, blessing them, removing their sashes, shrouding their faces from the darkness that stole them away.

In the corridor, DiBianco dropped the bloody knife to the floor and approached one of the cardinals, discreetly shoving their passkey to the Pope's private quarters into his pants pocket.

"You," DiBianco said, "what's your name?"

The man looked shaken, "Father Driscoll."

"Come with me, Father."

"Where?"

"You're taking us to the Pope's private quarters."

"But—"

"There's no time for buts, Father. We're going to be dead before you know it, if you don't lead the way, now," DiBianco reminded him. "Trust me, Father, you'll be blessed for this." DiBianco felt strange saying such things to a cardinal, but he was compelled to say it, and he did.

Father Driscoll looked like he had something to say, argue the point further perhaps, but then he stormed off.

DiBianco was stunned, unsure of the cardinal's reaction.

Father Driscoll stopped and turned. "Are you coming, or not?"

Without hesitation, DiBianco grabbed Savanna by the forearm and followed Father Driscoll. The heavy tromping of hundreds of thick healed souls hustling behind him assured DiBianco there was plenty of backup, in case things got ugly, and they surely would.

142

11:37 PM

Two agents rushed ahead and gained on Father Driscoll; they drew their weapons and flanked the Father. DiBianco could tell none of the agents here planned to die in a blaze of DoL glory. If anyone was going to die tonight, it would be them—the Descendants of Lucifer.

Father Driscoll led them out of the corridor, into a grand, well lit space—the floors, walls, even the ceilings, coated in brilliantly painted marble; it was the anteroom of anterooms and it led to one of the most impressive staircases DiBianco had ever seen. They climbed the dozens of spiraling steps to the mouth of the Papal Apartments where two Swiss Guards stood with bladed staffs drawn.

He wondered how it was possible for the Pope to climb such a staircase in his perceived condition. He quickly asserted that there must be a papal elevator; he wished the Father had led them that way; his legs were at their ends, his thighs were burning.

DiBianco had always envisioned the Apostolic Palace to be a phenomenal place—a grand monument of holiness—but actually being there sent a chill down his spine that numbed his soul and slowed his pace.

The staircase was lined in priceless treasures—paintings, carvings, tapestries by masters of lifetimes past. Knowing he was walking on holy ground, amongst countless holy relics, was surreal enough, knowing it was all going to be a thing of the past in the next few minutes filled DiBianco with panic, and his head throbbed with pain as his vision started to blur. His hand instinctively reached for the railing, but there wasn't one there.

DiBianco was falling.

143

11:38 PM

In a sudden flash, all light turned black. A small box and a stack of old papers appeared on a wooden desk, lit only by a flickering flame—*an oil lamp,* DiBianco thought—it's amber flame so hot, it licked his face like a hungry dragon. However, impressive as the flame was, the room, and everything around it, fell into a pitch-black void.

DiBianco felt something hit the back of his head and in an instant the box and papers disappeared. However, the flame remained; its warmth somewhat weaker now; and there was something else, something shimmering in the dying light, something unseen before. He tried to focus on the object, but the light was dying quickly—

"Michael," Savanna shouted, sending DiBianco's eyes bolting open wide. "Snap out of it, there's no time for stupid panic attacks."

DiBianco knew it wasn't a panic attack; something—or someone—was trying to tell him something, and he was listening; DiBianco knew what it was they were looking for. All he needed now, was to find where in the palace it was.

144

11:39 PM

The Swiss Guards, stationed just outside the Papal Apartments at the top of the stairs, stood aside watching Father Driscoll approach. One of them nodded, while the other opened the doors.

That's odd, DiBianco thought. There's no way the Swiss Guards would just let a brigade of armed men storm into the Papal Apartments. DiBianco gazed at the Father. What was it about this priest that had the Swiss Guards stepping aside like well trained guard dogs?

Father Driscoll led them into the reception area where they fanned into rows. DiBianco climbed upon a stone table at the center of the room and directed the agents to circle around him.

DiBianco couldn't believe how many men could fit into the room; sure it was large, but DiBianco was doubtful it was intended to house a hundred men. The room filled quickly, many men were shoved into nearby hallways, some stood outside with the guards.

"We have next to no time and over a hundred rooms that must be searched," DiBianco started. "We're looking for a small black box, the size of a small jewelry box. It's likely perched on a dark wooded desk next to a stack of old papers. I need you to split into teams. Search every room swiftly."

"What do we do if we find something?" an agent said.

The question took DiBianco by surprise, he hadn't thought of that. He spotted something on the agent's belt.

"Do you all have one of those," he said, pointing at the small transmitter.

"Sure," the agent replied. Without further ado, the agent removed the transmitter from his belt and tossed it to DiBianco. "We'll call you the moment we find the box."

"Perfect," DiBianco said. "The Father and I are going to search the Pope's private quarters, I need a handful of you to accompany us—"

"Absolutely not!" the cardinal interrupted.

"What?" DiBianco said, shocked at the Father's reaction. "You must understand the magnitude of the situation—"

"I certainly do, however I cannot allow those sacred quarters to be ransacked or defiled in any way."

"We must search!" DiBianco declared.

"I will do it myself," said the Father.

"No," DiBianco said, "I'm coming."

Father Driscoll took a deep breath, obviously about to loose his temper, then smiled—if only an uncomfortable grin—and motioned for DiBianco to follow.

DiBianco gazed oddly at the Father, but then lunged off the table into the crowd and squeezed his way through. Then it occurred to him. *Father Driscoll.* Without thinking of the consequences he approached the Father and blurted—

"Wasn't there a Father Driscoll assassinated in Cambridge Massachusetts last week?"

The Father froze in his tracks.

145

11:40 PM

Father Driscoll's face dropped with disapproval. "It's been two weeks." He led DiBianco out of the reception room, down a hall toward the Pope's work area.

Then Savanna appeared out of the crowd. "I'm coming, too."

Father Driscoll looked furious, but forced another crocked smile and turned away. "He was my brother," he continued, "a bit of a rebellious type, I'm afraid; didn't know how to obey orders, but nothing he did deserved what he got."

The three of them walked briskly into the Pope's working room. DiBianco glanced around for the box, but nothing looked right. It wasn't there.

The Father led them down another hallway, this one much longer than the first. Even the common areas of the Palace were adorned with the most spectacular decor.

"You know the FBI has linked your brother in some way with the group responsible for The Pulse." DiBianco knew the moment he started, he was digging a hole he had no time to dig out of. He needed to shut up, but Father Driscoll wasn't about to let him.

146

11:41 PM

They entered a room where three goblin tapestries adorned the walls. Savanna looked unimpressed; but DiBianco was. However, there was no box. DiBianco knew they weren't going to find it until they got into the Pope's private quarters.

"We had many differences," the Father said, "but we both believed in God, this I know. He was not a member of the Descendants."

They entered a wide open space, a great hall—the Pope's private chapel—a space grand enough to appease a congregation of the overachieved, this however, was for the Pope alone.

The floor in the thrown room was covered with a priceless Spanish carpet. Behind the thrown room was the Anicamera Segreta, the outer chamber of the Pope's private office. A member of the Swiss Guard stood at the entrance, nodding at the Father as they entered.

"I never said he was a member," DiBianco said. *I never mentioned the Descendants of Lucifer either*, he thought, suddenly uncertain about the Father's motives. "In fact," DiBianco continued, "I believe the Descendants have been assassinating those who perhaps knew too much and were about to let the cat out of the bag, so to speak."

Father Driscoll led them into an office, which to DiBianco looked more like a rec-hall. It had seating for

242 † Keith Katsikas

dozens of people, a massive wooden conference table, which looked oddly small at the center of the room, and hundreds of books, new and old lined the walls. Hanging from the center of the room was the most extravagant chandelier DiBianco had ever seen.

Situated on the corner of the palace, the Pope's private office was a room with a view, offering a spectacular view of Rome. DiBianco gazed out the window at an endless carpet of light, illuminating courtyards, streets, and homes in a thick golden glow. It was hard to imagine how much devastation one crazy group could cause. They had to find that box; looking at the Pope's desk, he realized, it wasn't there either.

"What could my brother have possibly known about *this?*" the Father continued; his voice beginning to heat up. "I have spent a lifetime in the service of this church. The last twenty years alone, I have spent personally assisting the last two Popes—"

"Wait," DiBianco interrupted. "I thought the Chamberlain was the Pope's assistant?"

"The Holy Father has two personal assistants. If anyone should have known about this, it's me." Father Driscoll was becoming irate. DiBianco had never sensed such anger come from a holy man. "I knew nothing of it," he said. "I can't believe what's happening here. What in the name of God is going on?"

"The end of the world is what's going on," DiBianco said. "If we don't find that damn box and disarm The Pulse, God's church is history and billions of people are going to die."

Father Driscoll fell silent. His eyes hit the floor then returned to DiBianco. "I know where it is."

147

11:42 PM

With incredible speed Father Driscoll led them up a narrow, spiral staircase into a small room where the Father placed his thumb into a tiny hole—a scanner, hidden within the frame of the steel door. DiBianco would have never guessed that the thumb scanner was there.

DiBianco placed his hand over his pocket and gazed sharply at the Father. *You just watched me cut the damn guy's thumb off.*

There was a click; a bolt released; the door popped ajar, the Father pulled it open wide. "Come on, follow me."

DiBianco's heart jackhammered. Not only were they in the most sacred place on earth, but there was something definitely not right about the man guiding them.

Father Driscoll led them through a twisted labyrinth of scantily decorated rooms, large and small, not what DiBianco expected to see in the Pope's private quarters. Quickly they approached a small door—simple, white, with golden raised panels. The father grabbed the brass knob and pushed it open. The room was dark. DiBianco's mind flooded with horrifying images.

Skyscrapers exploding into giant mushroom clouds, filling the sky with darkness, casting a rain of soot over the land; warheads fired in every direction; nuclear power plants burst into flames, melting into the ground, the deafening sound of sirens blasted throughout neighborhoods, warning of the impending doom.

Total devastation.

Total annihilation.

There, on the desk, just beyond the door, was an amber flame, next to it, a stack of old papers, and a tiny black box.

They were there.

148

11:43 PM

It was a perfect, symmetrical cube, exactly like his vision. DiBianco ran his fingers along the square hole at the top. *A key hole,* he thought. "Is there any more light than this?"

"That's all there is," the Father said, pointing at the flickering flame. "This is a very special room," he explained, "and that's a very special flame."

DiBianco pulled open the drawers to the desk and searched everywhere for a key. He had no idea what it would look like, he only knew it would have a square head. Suddenly the door closed and the room went black.

Father Driscoll spoke, only in the dark, his voice was different. Deeper. Stronger. Powerful.

"Everything happens for a reason," the voice said. "Nothing is accidental." He paused. "Do you believe in fate?"

149

11:44 PM

"You're supposed to be here," the Father said, "but, you cannot stop what is meant to be."

"What?" Savanna cried.

DiBianco turned toward her shrill voice.

"Why'd you bring us here," DiBianco said, "if not to stop it?"

"I brought you here, so you could not stop it."

"What are you talking about? This is the box, the device that can stop The Pulse ... is it not?"

"It is," the Father replied.

"Then help me," he shouted, "help me stop it, Goddamn you!"

"Is that the way to speak to a Priest?" the voice said, as it began to circle. DiBianco watched the silhouette pass through the flame. "Your bloodline has led you down a path you cannot change. Do you even know why you're here, Michael?"

DiBianco didn't have a clue what to say. *What the hell is this guy talking about?*

"You will never find the answers you seek without first understanding the key."

The key, DiBianco thought. Something about that simple phrase struck him and plunged his consciousness into a not so distant memory.

"Go ... Son of White," the Pope said. DiBianco gazed at the dying man, at his shaking hands, and the

cross held tightly in his grasp.

The room went black. The flame reappeared; it was fading; next to it was an object, shimmering in the dying light, only this time it was clear.

In a sudden surge of inspiration, DiBianco stormed toward the door, yanked it open, and ran down the hall.

"Wait!" Savanna shouted, struggling to catch up. "Where are you going?"

DiBianco didn't answer. He had to get back to the Sistine Chapel ... and fast.

150

11:45 PM

A massive bang rattled the basilica and like that, the lights were dead. A tiny LED blinked red on a transmitter attached to Afridi's belt. Afridi's eyes adjusted quickly to the glow of Saint Peter's Tomb and the glow of ninety-nine eternal flames rimming the Confessio. It was more than enough light to keep watch on their captives.

"Yes," Afridi said into his transmitter.

"We have a problem," the voice crackled.

"Sir?"

"It's DiBianco." The voice paused. "He knows about the key. He's on his way to retrieve it now."

"The key alone won't stop The Pulse; you know that."

"No matter," the voice snapped. "Stop him!" The airwaves fell silent. "And Afridi."

"Yes, Sir."

"He is of no use to us any longer."

"No!" Crystal shouted. "You can't!" She leapt to her feet and whaled her tied hands against Afridi's chest.

Afridi swung his arm, smashing his cast against the side of her head for the third time.

She instantly fell limp to the floor.

151

11:48 PM

The Sistine Chapel was dark, lit only by small candles carried by cardinals as they crept about the somber space. Out of a-hundred-and-sixty-five men, fewer than sixty had survived. The traitorous attacks against God, by the very soul called to stand in his place, had the once confident College of Cardinals questioning everything; but still they picked up the pieces, all the while aware, the end was coming ... and coming soon.

DiBianco stood in the door—a broken passageway to a once glorified chapel—and watched the broken men cover their fallen brothers with blood drenched cassocks. DiBianco took in a deep breath, raised a candle to his wristwatch and froze.

Ten minutes!

He shifted his gaze toward the Pope's dead body, still lying in the pitch-black corridor, untouched, unshrouded. DiBianco figured, the Pope's betrayal had bitten so deeply— his act, so heinous—that the cardinals where not about to look at the man, much less attend to his body.

DiBianco had no choice. He needed the key and

something far more powerful than himself had taken control, he could feel it. DiBianco crouched down beside the frigid, greying corpse, rested the candle on his chest, and grabbed the golden crucifix that the Pope had latched onto seconds before death. He pride it from his fingers; they held on with great strength—it was like he was still protecting the key, even in death. He yanked harder. The candle fell over. The crucifix finally broke free. DiBianco grabbed the candle and pulled the cross from the Pope's neck—its gold chain snapped effortlessly, falling to pieces on the floor.

DiBianco tucked the cross into his waistband and ran back toward the staircase. "Come on!"

Savanna tried to keep up, but DiBianco was pumped, running fast. She could barely see with just the light of her candle.

They were going to make it. He had the key. Nothing could stop them. Suddenly, he rammed into something, knocking him backwards, landing hard on the stone floor. The candle smashed into pieces and the flame extinguished.

A blinding light flooded his eyes.

"Get up!" Afridi shouted, driving the barrel of his rifle into the top of DiBianco's head, his finger squeezing the trigger. "Get to your feet, now!"

152

11:50 PM

"I could have sworn you were sent to stop him," Afridi shouted, glaring at Savanna, "not hold his Goddamn hand."

From behind him crept Crystal and Camillin; they were

hustled along by a short man in a black jumpsuit with a hooded mask, an automatic rifle aimed at their heads.

Savanna grabbed DiBianco, squeezing the blood from his forearm.

Afridi grabbed Crystal—still dazed from several blows to the head—and Camillin and threw them toward DiBianco. Fuller and Father Fredrick appeared from the darkness and fanned out along side the assassin, blocking the way upstairs. Afridi stepped in front of his men—his human road block—and glared at DiBianco.

"It's over," he said, very calm, very certain.

Savanna glanced at the dark assassin. It was a strange, quick glare that made DiBianco curious.

"What makes you so sure?" DiBianco said.

Afridi said nothing.

He took aim at DiBianco's chest.

There was a click.

In a flash of brilliant white, time came to a standstill; from the corner of his eye, he watched Savanna leap from his side, throwing herself in front of him, spinning, her eyes locking on his as the impact of the shot shook him. A stream of blood sprayed from her mouth, striking DiBianco's face. He watched in horror as Savanna's back arched and she wailed in pain.

Then she fell, blood pooling around her head.

"NO!" DiBianco cried.

There was another click.

"Such a pity," Afridi said.

Another gunshot ripped through the air.

153

11:51 PM

DiBianco clutched at his chest, knowing it was over, knowing he was dead. He looked down. There was blood, but not his own.

He gazed up. *What just happened?*

Afridi stood motionless, rifle still aimed at his head, eyes locked on his. Suddenly blood gushed from a hole in Afridi's chest and he fell like a rock.

Fuller spun, shining his flashlight on the dark assassin. "My God, what have you done?"

The assassin took aim at Fuller.

Fuller tried to react, but it was too late. There was a click. Then another. The rifle was empty. Fuller charged at the assassin, throwing every bit of his three-hundred pounds into the tiny man. But the assassin moved quickly, taking the barrel of the rifle in his hands and swinging hard. The butt of the gun struck Fuller in the side of the head with such force, it nearly lifted him off his feet and sent him tumbling into the corner, collapsing to the floor, blood pooling at his head.

Father Fredrick, seeing the relentlessness of the dark assassin's ferocity, fell to his knees, pleading for his life. "I'm a Priest, for Christ's sake," he cried, "a man of God ... I beg you ... spare me!"

The assassin turned his attention away from the cowering priest and gazed at DiBianco. The priest crawled into the darkness and disappeared.

DiBianco was shocked. *What just happened?*

Several cardinals stormed out of the Sistine Chapel quickly filling the hall with the glow of flickering candlelight.

The assassin lowered his rifle, letting it crash to the floor and stood in silence.

"Who are you?" DiBianco said.

The assassin said not a word.

DiBianco looked bewildered at the man and asked again. "Who are you?"

Then the assassin lifted his hands and peeled the hood from his head and face and gazed at DiBianco with shimmering eyes.

All the blood instantly drained from DiBianco's face and his heart froze like a block of ice in his chest. *How is it possible?* "You're dead." DiBianco had seen the sky erupt with his very own eyes, steeling him away in a thunderous flash of amber and blue fireworks. DiBianco's heart swelled and his face grew flush. The death of Savanna almost seemed to fade into the past and a smile invaded his face.

"Come on," Clinton shouted, glaring at his watch, "it's 11:53 ... what are you waiting for?"

154

11:53 PM

In the Papal Apartments, the agents begun to gather in the reception area. The mood was somber. Their luck, poor. Finding anything became nearly impossible with the lights out. And it was impossible to escape before midnight. Many made cellphone calls to family, a final message of love before the end.

A transmitter crackled to life and agent Smith pulled it near. "Agent Smith... Are you there?"

"Sir?" the Agent said, sounding surprised. "We've searched every room. We found nothing matching the box you described."

"Agent Smith," DiBianco said, taking a deep breath, "I've found the box, along with the key to operate it."

Every agent in the room erupted in cheers. The room was so loud that Agent Smith couldn't hear what DiBianco was trying to say on the transmitter.

155

11:54 PM

"Agent Smith?" DiBianco shouted into the transmitter. DiBianco ran up the staircase, Clinton, Crystal, and Camillin following close behind, all with the bright flashlights they grabbed from Afridi's team. "Can you hear me? Make sure the coast is clear. I need to get to the Pope's quarters in less than five minutes. Please confirm!"

The noise coming from the tiny speaker was a horrible static; distorted; DiBianco suspected that the battery had died in the agent's transmitter.

"Damn it," DiBianco said, clipping the transmitter to his belt. "We should have taken Afridi's gun. I have a feeling we're going to need it."

"It's all right, Michael," Crystal replied, "I have total faith in you."

It was then, things seemed to be forced into perspective for DiBianco. If he failed to stop The Pulse, billions of people would die, including them, and the Lord's church would be destroyed.

It was a responsibility he did not want to have—but he knew he would have to perform; and as they say, *failure is not an option.*

156

11:55 PM

DiBianco realized fast that Agent Smith had not heard his message. Agents with lights brighter than theirs bolted down the staircase at full throttle. The looks on their faces were that of pure delight. DiBianco knew then, the message had been misunderstood; DiBianco tucked in close to the wall, and let the herd pour down the stairs. Most of the men didn't notice they were there; the ones who had, didn't seem to care, they just kept running—obviously ecstatic to be alive.

Soon after the dust settled, DiBianco finished the hike up the steps and the four of them ran into the reception area. Perhaps, in a way, the miscommunication worked out for the best. There was no one there to slow them down. DiBianco hoped they didn't find a reason to need them.

"How pray-tell can you be here?" DiBianco yelled at Clinton as he led them through the maze of rooms leading toward the Papal Staircase. "You were dead!" DiBianco's tone was that of delight, mixed with anger, mixed with anxiety.

Clinton explained that he dived off the London Eye

seconds before the explosion. "Somehow I managed to make it to shore with only an injured leg." Clinton explained that the freezing water must have helped slow the bleeding. "Have I ever told you how much I believe in fate?"

"I do believe you've mentioned it, once or twice," he said with a smirk.

"This entire day has been like, some higher power has been guiding me. Know what I mean?"

DiBianco nodded. He most certainly did.

157

11:56 PM

DiBianco led them into the Pope's private chapel. *So far so good*, he thought, *no guards.*

"My God," Crystal said. "Even in the dark this place is nicer than anything I've ever seen."

"There was no way I was going to abandon you guys," Clinton continued. "So I wrapped my leg, thankfully, it was just a surface wound, and hitched a ride to the airport where I meet up with Pete—you know, my friend with the Cessna?"

Clinton explained that outside the hanger, where his friend parked his plane, they had noticed loose papers strewn about the tarmac. It was a huge mess that took several minutes to clean, a few of the sheets found themselves stuck to the plane's windshield. "Talk about fate," Clinton said. "I couldn't believe it. They were the very sheets we printed at Afridi's apartment."

"That's... That's really something," DiBianco said. He was

starting to believe; he could believe almost anything after the last week. Fate was becoming less and less of a stretch.

"And the kicker," Clinton said. "Along with the printouts was a strange piece of paper. It was like nothing I've ever seen before." Clinton pulled the folded piece of paper from his pocket. "This is what led me here. This is how I found you."

158

11:57 PM

It was the Newton Paper—the one DiBianco had read in the taxi on the way to Heathrow.

"Fate," Clinton said.

DiBianco nodded, then took them around a corner, and up the narrow spiral staircase. He was really starting to think so. "There is one thing really nagging me, however."

"What's that?"

"How in the world did you end up in Afridi's hands; and why in God's name were you holding Camillin and Crystal at gunpoint?"

Clinton hesitated a second, seeming to analyze the question, then spoke. "Fate." He smiled. "You can't make this stuff up." He explained that after arriving at the *Leonardo Da Vinci* airport he found Savanna; she was loading something into the back of a limo; she had told him that the DoL had changed their plans—something about the prophecy being wrong and the Son of White not being who they thought he was. "She told me they were going to destroy everything, even the Holy Land. And she wanted no part in it. It was then we planned the whole thing," he said. "She brought me to Afridi. Told him I was a skilled assassin from England, one of them ... a DoL ... Can you imagine that?"

He explained that Afridi had given him strict orders to stick close to Savanna and accompany them on their mission in the Vatican. "Well, here I am," he said. "Fate. In the flesh. But that's far from all there is. You're not gonna believe what else I discovered—*Christ,*" he said, the realization finally gripping him. "I can't believe Savanna's dead."

"Me neither," Crystal said.

DiBianco gazed at Crystal with sad eyes. "What in the world would have drove her to take a bullet for me? I understand she loved me, I loved her too, but..." Reaching the top of the stairs DiBianco fished the stiff, greying, thumb from his pocket and shoved it into the scanner hole in the frame of the door. Nothing happened. "What the—"

"I know why she did it," Clinton declared.

"Hold that thought," DiBianco interrupted, not even hearing him. He yanked the thumb from the scanner and massaged it in his fingers, blowing hot air in to his hands as he rubbed. "Why isn't this working?" He stuck it back.

Nothing.

"There's something about your family," Clinton started, "something I bet you haven't even thought about; something you will never believe."

DiBianco began to panic. His pulse raced and his forehead dripped of sweat. "Why won't this freakin' thing work?" he cried, seeing the end coming fast, and no other way inside to stop it.

"Let me see that," Agent Camillin said, swiping the severed digit from DiBianco's trembling hands. Camillin took the thumb, massaged it into a bent position, like a hook, then stuck it back into the scanner. A second later there was a click.

DiBianco grabbed the heavy door and pulled it open, then ran into the Pope's private quarters at full throttle, leading his followers through the small labyrinth of rooms, finally ending at a simple white door, adorned with raised gold panels.

"Mike, *wait!*" Clinton said. "There's something about your past—about your parents—that I think you really need to know about."

But DiBianco didn't wait. He knew exactly what Clinton was about to say. His parents were not killed in an avalanche, they were murdered by the Descendants of Lucifer. He didn't need to hear it again. He turned the knob, and opened the door.

Inside, Father Driscoll stood, a small pistol taking dead aim at DiBianco's head. "I can't let you do it."

There was a click.

159

11:58 PM

DiBianco dove behind the desk.

The pistol fired.

The amber light flickered.

There was a rustle of paper.

Then the sudden scuffle of feet.

The Newton Papers rained down over the room, over him; but there was something else. His right cheek was wet, it burned, an agonizing pain that penetrated to the bone.

DiBianco lurched from behind the desk, briskly wiping the searing liquid from his face with the sleeves of his shirt.

The room seemed darker.

Camillin and Clinton must have charged into the room the moment the pistol fired; they had subdued the Father. Clinton stood over the cowering Priest, the small pistol perched in his hands, aimed at the Father's head. Crystal stood in the doorway, gazing at DiBianco, panic filling her shimmering blue eyes.

"You've been shot!"

DiBianco panicked, then realized what she was looking at. The light was fading quickly, it was easy to misconceive. "No," he said, "it's fine. The fuel from the eternal flame spilled onto my face. The shot must have pierced the canister. Hurts like a son-of-a-bitch, but I'll be fine." He paused. "Does it really look that bad?"

"My goodness," she said, "you're gonna need some serious counsel after this."

"If there is an *after this,*" Agent Camillin reminded. "Come on, stop that Goddamn thing!"

160

11:59 PM

DiBianco grabbed the crucifix from his waistband and placed the butt of the shaft into the hole at the top of the box.

Instantly, the box split in two; the top raised, allowing a thin drawer to slide out.

A keypad, DiBianco knew.

As it extended, the keypad lit like a cellphone. A bright red display flashed rapidly descending digits—

56 ... 55 ... 54 ...

"Shit!" DiBianco shouted. "What's the code?"

52 ... 51 ...

DiBianco's pulse raced, possibly, he thought, for the last time. He glared at Father Driscoll, who glared back. DiBianco's breathing labored. *"Not now!"* he pleaded. *Please, God!* "What's the code?" he shouted at the Father. "Tell me, you son-of-a-bitch!"

The priest grinned, his teeth shone black in the dimming glow. "I haven't a clue, really" he said. "However, I do know something ... something you may find rather interestin—"

BANG! BANG!

The shots happened quickly and felt like an explosion in the confines of the tiny room. The sound of the priest's lifeless body striking the floor seemed almost lost in the numbness following the blasts.

"Wo-holy shit!" DiBianco cried, gazing at Clinton in bewilderment. "What the hell did you do *that* for?"

But instead of answering, Clinton turned the gun on DiBianco. "I've learned so much in the last few hours," he started. "More than you could ever imagine."

"I don't understand," DiBianco said, then glanced at the dwindling countdown.

46 ... 45 ...

"I've always been somehow driven by fate," Clinton continued, "and the truth that has been made known to me this day has brought clarity to my life ... a clarity I've never even dreamed possible."

"Peter..." DiBianco's voice was weak, stricken with shock and despair; he struggled to find words. Something about his meeting up with Peter Clinton felt purposeful, almost divine.

There was an instant bond. "I trusted you like a brother."

Clinton's face softened for a moment. "I suppose, in a way, we are like brothers, Michael; or should I say, Son of White?"

"Excuse me?"

"I should have known it would eventually come to this," Clinton said sadly. "You mapped it all out so clearly in your book, *God Science.* Only none of it's really a theory at all, is it, Michael? It's all fact. I know that now."

DiBianco was speechless. If ever there was a point in the last sixteen hours where he felt totally and utterly bewildered, it was now.

Clinton glared at DiBianco with incredulous eyes, "How could you write such things, Michael?" For an instant, DiBianco thought he saw a tear form in Clinton's eye, but then it was gone. "The gospel writers were brutally murdered keeping the secret you so thoughtlessly revealed to the world."

"What's he talking about?" Crystal demanded.

DiBianco didn't know what to say. Nothing made sense, except the fact that in a matter of seconds, they'd all become a kind of human stucco. He gazed at the keypad ... at the countdown which almost seemed to be speeding up:

39 ... 38 ...

The theories in his books were not always his own. Many had been around for years, centuries, even millenniums. His primary focus in *God Science,* was to shine a floodlight on a centuries-old theory, claiming a connection between Jesus Christ, the Prieuré de Sion (or Priory of Sion), and its prestigious members (including none-other than the scientific genius and Grand Master himself, Isaac Newton).

His book had also brought fresh light on the theory that the authors of the early gospels—Matthew, Mark, Luke, and John—had doctored their *own* accounts of the Lord Jesus, in an attempt to keep secret the fact that Christ had a family, a child even, a boy, born shortly after his death. Many of his apostles would later die protecting that sacred truth.

DiBianco gazed at Crystal, then back at Clinton and the small pistol still aimed at his head. "He speaks of a belief held by those closest to God that the heir to the throne of Christ would one day reveal himself, spawning the Second Coming."

Clinton smirked. "And?"

"This heir will be a man, born of this earth; a man whose blood is that of Christ." DiBianco's heart sank in his chest as panic rushed in. "My God ... You think *you're* the heir to the throne of Christ?"

"No!" Clinton snapped. "I believe you are."

DiBianco's face went pale. Every piece of the puzzle came rushing together in one massive implosion. He knew it was true; somehow, he had always known; it was always there, caressing the surface of his consciousness, waiting for the chance to burst out.

"I, on the other hand," Clinton injected. "have been sent to make sure you don't stop the Descendant's plan to reclaim what's rightfully theirs."

"And what the hell is that?" Crystal shouted.

Clinton glared at DiBianco, who clearly already knew the answer. "The same thing he wants!" Clinton paused, then cocked the pistol's hammer. "The throne of Christ."

There was a click.

But no blast.

DiBianco gaped at the blinking keypad.

19 ... 18 ...

He closed his eyes, crossed his chest, and let the spirit take control. Instantly, the numbers came to him; and without a thought he punched them in:

2 ... 0 ... 6 ...

"No!" Clinton shouted as he lunged over the desk,

nocking the keypad to the floor. The flashing red digits still descending:

12 ... 11 ...

Clinton grabbed DiBianco's throat and hurled him across the pitch-black room, both of them slamming into a bookcase, sending books and artifacts through the air, smashing under their feet.

"Stop it!" Crystal screamed, as she and Camillin charged toward Clinton.

Clinton and DiBianco were on the floor. Clinton's hands around DiBianco's throat. DiBianco couldn't breathe. His head was pounding with such ferocity, it felt as though it would explode.

DiBianco bucked and jetted his body up and down, trying everything and anything to release the massive grip on his neck, if only for a second. He was certain he was going to die. But then, miraculously, the grip was gone. So was Clinton. And the breath that followed was one of the most glorious he had ever taken.

As his eyes adjusted to the darkening room and the crazy commotion filling it, DiBianco came to the conclusion that Agent Camillin and Crystal had somehow knocked Clinton off him, and were now attempting to wrestle him to submission.

Quickly regaining his senses, DiBianco crawled across the floor—covered in leaking lamp oil, books, and broken glass—to where the keypad now laid, flashing rapidly descending numbers:

06 ... 05 ...

Without hesitation he punched in the final digit, *0* ... and gazed at the panel, just to be sure:

2 0 6 0

He knew in his heart, it was right.

The sound of melee—flying fists, grunts and scowls,

wreaking havoc upon wrestling prey—and the unmistakable screeching of female screams filled the tiny room.

DiBianco tried to block it out.

He hit enter.

In an instant, the flashing red display turned green. The countdown stopped at ...*01*. DiBianco dropped the keypad to the floor and froze. The brass lamp lay sideways on the floor next to him, it's eternal flame still spitting out flickering spasms of amber; beside it, the golden cruciform key, shimmered slightly in the lamp's dying glow.

161

By the time DiBianco walked out the giant bronze doors, exiting the Constantine Wing of the Basilica, Saint Peter's Square was overrun with media. Vans, trucks, and satellite equipment packed the square like a carnival, broadcasting the thrilling events live around the world.

The media had been close, DiBianco knew that, the College of Cardinals had been scheduled to meet in the morning to begin papal election proceedings; however, DiBianco couldn't imagine how the night's events could have reached the media so quickly.

As DiBianco started down the steps leading to Saint Peter's Square, Camillin hurried out—Crystal close behind— hustling a roughed and cuffed Peter Clinton into the fast mounting crowd.

Cameras flooded DiBianco's face as the plethora of journalist flocked the exiting group. *"Is it true the Pope was behind the assassination of the United States Republican*

Nominee?" one man shouted. *"Did The Church steal the Newton Manuscripts?"* another said. *"Is Pope Seises XVI truly alive? ... Is it true he is the Antichrist?"* another asked. *"Are you going to write about this in your next book?"* ... *"Did the College kill the Pope?"* ... *"Was the FBI involved in the DoL's plot?"*

How could they possibly know this stuff? DiBianco thought, unable to believe how quickly it had all happened. *Someone had to have set this up.*

Something is wrong.

DiBianco was gazing at the ocean of reporters piling into the square; when Clinton's face broke through the crowd right in front of him.

Gazing into DiBianco's eyes, then into a camera, Clinton said, "The Catholic Church is evil. It must be stopped!" It wasn't Peter Clinton. At least not the Peter Clinton he had met that morning—

DiBianco couldn't believe it had only been a day. They had only just met that morning, yet he knew, he was not the same man. Something was different. Something in his eyes ... in his soul.

Camillin yanked Clinton away from the cameras. That only served to grab the media's attention even more. All cameras turned their focus on the crazed man, spreading dirt about the Church.

"You have me all wrong," Clinton pleaded. "I'm not what you think." His eyes were dark, oily slicks. Wide. Crazed. Most people call these eyes, *shinning* eyes. It was like a demon had taken possession of his body. He turned to DiBianco, now several feet off, drifting farther away with each passing second. "You haven't seen the last of me." Not a shadow of doubt loomed in his voice. He focused intently at DiBianco. Making sure DiBianco heard his voice. "Did you forget something, Michael?"

DiBianco gazed at Clinton with sudden terror. Had he forgotten something? He had stopped The Pulse. The immediate danger was over. What could he possibly be talking about?

"Father Fredrick," Clinton started. "Did you forget your own adoptive father? You'll never guess what he's done."

Back in the Constantine wing, just outside the Sistine Chapel. Clinton had killed Afridi and Fuller. Father Fredrick knelt on the floor, pleading for his life. Clinton let him go. He quickly disappeared into the darkness of Saint Peter's Basilica.

"What does he have to do with any of this? The Pulse is disarmed ... It's over, Peter!"

DiBianco could barely see Clinton's face now, the crowd was thick and Agent Camillin was hustling his arrestee toward an idling Limo. But as dense as the crowd was, and as far off as Clinton's face had drifted, DiBianco managed to spot a glimpse at *that* look. It was an evil glare that would forever become etched into his mind by the massive explosion which swiftly swallowed Saint Peter's Square.

162

A flash of light—a blinding glare that had DiBianco throwing his hands in front of his face—filled Saint Peter's Square. A split-second later, a thunderous blast lifted him from his feet. For a moment, it was like being on that mountain, watching his parents devoured by the avalanche. It all happened so quickly, yet took forever to end.

The weight of the bodies crushing him was enough to cause panic in the strongest man. Yet to DiBianco, it was unbearable. He couldn't breathe. He had to get out of there, and now! He was suffocating.

But the heat.

He heaved the limp weight off him and crawled out of the blackness into the searing heat which engulfed the square. The mass ocean of reporters and spectators which had been crowding into the square, had all been plowed down by the blast. He knew it was their flesh, their bodies and equipment, which had saved his life. It was a bitter sweet moment. Gazing at the mounds of burning flesh and blazing vehicles, DiBianco had little doubt that many had perished in a blink of an eye.

DiBianco turned and faced the basilica and felt his chest tighten with despair.

Saint Peter.

Flames and black smoke billowed out of blistering holes in Michelangelo's glorious dome. It was at that moment he knew what had happened. *Father Fredrick,* he thought. *The son-of-a-bitch planted a bomb in the Confessio ... in Saint Peter's tomb!*

DiBianco stood in shock, gaping at the blazing remains of a once blessed church, filled with countless numbers of the worlds most holy relics, a weighting shiver of defeat suddenly took hold. The ground began to move. People digging themselves out of the grisly remains, slithering about the death fields like one might imagine survivors of 9-11, digging their way out of the debris after the death clouds had settled.

A sudden squeal of tires pierced the rolling thunder of the crackly inferno. A black limo sped off, striking dozens of confused souls as it roared out of Saint Peter's Square.

It was Clinton. DiBianco knew it.

He was slipping away.

"Camillin!" he shouted. "Crystal!"

There was no answer.

EPILOGUE

Two years later.

"What's the difference between the end of the world and the date Isaac Newton predicted?" Michael DiBianco grinned, gazing out over his packed classroom. His was one of the largest classes at Harvard, everyone wanted to enroll in DiBianco's *God Science* course, but few—unfortunately—ever had the chance.

After the debris at Divinity School had cleared and the damage was assessed, previous plans to merge the schools were expedited, and within eighteen months, the universities became one.

Clinton was never heard from again. His body never found in the rubble of Saint Peter's, and Agent Camillin couldn't seem to remember a damn thing that happened before, or after, the blast. DiBianco knew it had been Clinton, squealing off in that limo. Agent Camillin retired shortly after returning home from Rome and very swiftly relocated his entire life to Las Vegas. Isn't it strange, how quickly people can change?

DiBianco opened his monstrosity of a leather-bound bible—the one he had bought shortly after discovering that everything from his class at Divinity had been turned to a kind of concrete puree—and flipped to *Daniel 12* and read, *"How long shall it be to the end of these wonders?"* He knew, the answer to that question, was not an easy one to swallow. Even now, two years later, DiBianco struggled to make sense of everything that happened. And of his future, and the future of the world.

"What does it mean: *a time, times, and a half of time?"* DiBianco asked his class.

It took all of his first year back home to realize the magnitude of what the Descendants had achieved, how close they had gotten to succeeding at the greatest act of terror ever conceived; infiltrating nearly every government around the globe, as well as religious organizations, The Church being only one of hundreds, setting in motion a series of events that took over fifty years to execute.

It was nearly perfect.

After writing about the experience in his first internationally acclaimed bestseller, *The DoL Network*, he began to realize the implications of it all. Of course he tried to downplay The Church's involvement, but that's precisely the type of thing the media thrived on—the slightest grain of dirt often materialized into a raging mudslide, and that's precisely what had happened.

The Church bounced back, however, like it has countless times in it's questionable past. To DiBianco, God was the glue that held everything together, without Him everything just falls apart. It's not possible for God to go away, not without taking the entire world along with Him.

Even the remains of Saint Peter were miraculously unscathed by the blast. It was a clear sign that God was still in control. However the holy structure surrounding the apostle's tomb would take decades to rebuild. Countless relics were lost.

"Professor," a young woman said. She was attractive. Her

crystal blue eyes and radiant smile reminded him of Crystal, perhaps the only great thing to have happened as a result of the Descendants. Readjustment to married life had not been a smooth one; however, the last year had brought some of the happiest moments in his life. He now had a writing companion worthy of his attention and a wife whose faith in Christ was oftentimes stronger than his own—although, *that* was slowly changing. She was the glue that held *his* world together. His own personal Goddess in an otherwise bleak reality.

"Professor?" The young woman said again, snapping him from his daze. "I've read your latest book, *The DoL Network,* as I'm sure we all have, yet there's something that just keeps nagging me."

"Sure," he replied, "what is it?"

"Why? ... Why do you want more? Why are you still here, searching, teaching, longing?"

DiBianco grew silent, taking a long moment to ponder the question. The class was eager to know, it was, after all, a good question, and DiBianco knew it.

DiBianco stepped up to the podium and gazed into the eyes of his class, his voice falling into solemn grace. "I'm going to tell you something that very few people know, something I've only just discovered in the last few months."

"What is it?" a young man said, the suspense obviously getting the best of him.

"As you all know, Pope's take on a new name once elected, leaving their birth name behind." He started pacing the room, wearing away the tiles along the front of the class. "Can anyone tell me what Pope Seises XVI's birth name was?" Many hands shot up at once.

DiBianco pointed to a girl in the third row.

"Agosto Bianco," she said.

"Son of White," he explained. "That's what Pope Seises

XVI had said to me before he died."

Son of White.

"What's the point, Professor?"

"In Italian, *Bianco* quite literally means *White.*"

A few members of the class reacted with a gasp, but just as many nodded in agreement.

"But that's not all," DiBianco said. "What may not be so clear is that *Di* literally means *Son of.*"

Now the class's eyes lit ablaze with comprehension.

DiBianco means Son of White.

DiBianco knew that the implications were just as dark as they were enlightening, not to mention incredibly controversial, and there was still a great deal of research to be done before even he could make sense of it all. Waving his hand in a shooing motion, obviously unsettled by the fact that he just announced that he was the Pope's—*the Antichrist's*—son, he sternly stated, "I'm not going to answer any more questions in this regard. I'm sorry. I should not have mentioned this."

Having great respect and admiration for Professor DiBianco, the class settled quickly. They did not want to upset him, no matter how intrigued they were.

"I'm sure I'll have plenty to say about this one day. For now, I only intended to give a reason ... a reason why." And for the last several months it truly was the reason. Had it not been for Crystal's cohorts of biblical scholar friends he would likely have moved on. But the theory they had whipped up to explain the event that unfolded, only served to draw him in even deeper.

† † †

Isaac Newton had predicted many things: The end of days, The location of the true Holy Land, Even that the heir to the throne of Christ would one day reveal himself. DiBianco had a difficult time absorbing the thought that this *heir* could actually be *him*.

His newly founded scholar friends—most being longtime friends of his new sweetheart and wife, Crystal—had explained that, though obscure, there was a list of names tracing back to the time of Christ that many felt were linked directly to Jesus.

His direct bloodline.

One of those names was DiBianco.

Son of White

So being a DiBianco could very literally be interpreted as being an actual son of Christ, several times removed, of course.

Newton had prophesied that the *Son of White* would enter into the Holy Land on his own accord and would lead a great army of darkness into battle against the supreme infidel. The Descendants believed this *Son of White* was to none-other than Michael DiBianco. Agosto knew that the Holy Bloodline ran through his veins.

The blood of Christ.

Aqosto believed that Michael—his son—was the one who would spawn the second coming. Michael DiBianco was the heir to the throne of Christ. He would undoubtably live to fulfill the Master's prophesy.

However, Michael could never fulfill such a prophesy if he remained in the care and influence of the Bianco family. The prophecy was clear. *He would come of his own accord.* Michael had to leave the family. But Agosto must be sure that his plans would not falter. Michael must return. For it is him and him alone that can stop the second coming of Christ. He sent his son to America, where he was adopted by Agosto's most trusted servant, Father Fredrick.

Agosto had hired the best surgeons in the land to have a device—a nano-processor—implanted in Michael's brain, a nearly invisible chip that would manipulate his deepest memories. But he couldn't stop there; he needed to be sure the prophesy would be fulfilled. The chip would also plant messages over time that would ultimately guide him home.

† † †

In the end, it was Michael who had led an army of blackness into battle—one hundred agents in black suits, dark shades, and bright red neckties. It was a victorious battle against the powers of Lucifer, and his attempt to thwart his brother's second coming by altering the will of the soul of whom God selected to fulfill his plan. In Michael DiBianco's mind, Newton's name had been cleared. He hadn't predicted the fall of Christianity; he had predicted the fall of Lucifer.

Michael returned his eyes to the page and silently read a verse from Daniel; a verse he had read countless times, but now it rang with a new truth that had just now become clear:

Daniel 12: And at that time shall Michael stand up, the great prince which standeth for the children of thy people: and there shall be a time of trouble, such as never was since there was a nation even to that same time: and at that time thy people shall be delivered, every one that shall be found written in the book. And many of them that sleep in the dust of the earth shall awake, some to everlasting life, and some to shame and everlasting contempt.

"Mr. DiBianco," a female voice said from afar, shaking him from his dreamlike daze. "Are you okay?"

Michael shook his head, the massive bible weighing heavy in his left arm, and wiped a collection of moisture rimming his right eye. "Yes," he said. "Life has a strange way of stealing you away at times." He gazed into his bible, found another relevant passage to read and continued his lesson.

AUTHOR'S NOTE

This is a work of fiction inspired by a BBC Documentary about the Heresies of Isaac Newton. Apart from the facts we know today about this Scientific Genius, (mentioned in the following section) the views and theories presented in this work are fiction and are not intended to be introduced to the public in any other light or fashion.

There are several highly public persona mentioned in this novel. Though they are real people, anything they have said within the pages of this novel have been made up by me.

Parts of this story are so dark that I feel the need to clarify that much of the thoughts expressed in this novel were merely made up by my mind as it tackled the dark, often depressing task of imagining what motives may be going through the mind of a deep-rooted satanic terrorist.

I find it necessary to make clear that I am a devout Christian who has a strong testimony of the divinity of Christ, and of the Holy Trinity, consisting of: Our Father in Heaven (God), His Son (Jesus Christ), and the Holy Ghost (Holy Spirit).

I want to thank you for reading this novel. The extensive research I did while working on it was exciting and enlightening. Though I had the basic plot mapped out from day one, every twist and turn in the journey took me by surprise; I hope it treats you with the same thrill.

I often hear writers say that their best work seem to appear out of thin air. The words spill onto paper in a matter of days, and reading it back almost feels like reading someone else's work, someone else's masterpiece. I have finally experienced that feeling. I hope you will enjoy reading *The Newton Prophesies*, as much as I enjoyed writing it.

If there's one thing I enjoy even more than writing, it's reading comments from readers of my work. I look forward to hearing from you all.

Thank You,
Keith Katsikas
Nov. 1, 2008

THE FACTS

All technologies written about in this novel are based in documented fact and either currently exist, or likely will in the very near future.

✝ ✝ ✝

This novel was inspired by facts discovered in the last several years about Isaac Newton. The following is background explaining some of those facts:

It wasn't a secret that Isaac Newton believed Science and God couldn't be separated—that they are the same. He believed that every fact found in science does nothing less than bring one closer to God.

Newton had another belief—one that he took to the grave. Only recently have we discovered (through his endless stacks of parched papers) that he believed God was a uniquely powerful being, and though Jesus was indeed his son, he was not God's equal. As an Arian, a follower of the 4th century priest Artius, Newton believed The (Roman Catholic) Church was breaking God's first commandment, Thou shalt have no other Gods before me, in worshiping the Godhead—the Holy Trinity. Though death was unlikely for his belief, Newton knew he would most likely live out the remainder of his days in prison if he voiced it.

Newton was also secretly obsessed with calculating the date

of the second coming of Christ. Studying the Holy Bible for nearly 50 years, writing in the area of 4,500 pages, desiring to know of the actual date, the very year of the End of Days, the end of the world as we know it, the dawning of Christ's thousand years of rule over man in the flesh—The Millennium.

Late in life—presumably on his deathbed—Newton scribbled down a small passage along with the numbers 2060. His years of work on the subject, journalized in those endless stacks of hand scribbled papers, explain precisely how he arrived at this alarmingly close date.

In Summary:
* Newton determined that The [Roman Catholic] Church fell into complete apostasy in the year 800 A.D. with the total conquest of the 3 Kings.

* He also determined, through tireless study of the chapters of Daniel (among others), that the end of man's rein would come 1260 years after such apostasy.

Adding these dates gave Newton his answer.

References:

Book of Daniel
(King James Version ~ New Testament ~ 23 pages)

The following was taken from an official statement by:

Stephen D. Snobelen
Associate Professor
History of Science and Technology

University of King's College
Halifax, Nova Scotia
B3H 2A1 Canada

Reprinted from **www.isaac-newton.org** *with permission.*

The logic of Newton's apocalyptic calculations

Newton, like many historicist prophetic commentators of his age, believed that the prophetic time periods 1260, 1290, 1335 and 2300 days actually represent 1260, 1290, 1335 and 2300 years using the "day-for-a-year principle".

For Newton these time periods (especially the 1260 years) represent the time span of the apostasy of the Church (for Newton this means the Trinitarian Church, chiefly the Catholics). Thus, he looked in history for the likely date when the apostasy formally began (one sign of this for him was the date when the papal church obtained temporal power). From there it was a simple matter of adding the time period to the beginning date...

The prophetic time periods

• *The time period 1260 days appears in Daniel 7:25 (as "a time and times and the dividing of time" [=a year, two years and a half year]), Daniel 12:7 (as "a time, times, and a half" [=a year, two years and a half year]), Revelation 11:3 (1260 days), Revelation 12:6 (1260 days) and Revelation 13:5 (42 months)*
  • *The time period 1290 days appears in Daniel 12:11.*
  • *The time period 1335 days appears in Daniel 12:12.*
  • *The time period 2300 days occurs in Daniel 8:14.*

How did Newton arrive at the date 2060?

This did not involve the use of anything as complicated as calculus, which he invented, but rather simple arithmetic that could be performed by a child. Beginning in the 1670s and continuing to the end of his life in 1727, Newton considered several commencement dates for the formal institution of the apostate, imperial Church. Earlier commencement dates include 607 and 609 A.D. As Newton grew older, he pushed the time of the end further and further into the future. In Yahuda MS 7 Newton twice gives 800 A.D. for the beginning of "the Pope's supremacy". The year 800 is a significant one in history, as it is the year Charlemagne was crowned emperor of Rome in the west by Pope Leo III at St. Peter's in Rome. Since Newton believed that the 1260 years corresponded to the duration of the corruption of the Church, he added 1260 to 800 A.D. and arrived at the date 2060 for the "fall of Babylon" or cessation of the apostate Church. It seems that Newton believed the fall could perhaps begin somewhat before the end of the 1260-year period and continue for a short time afterward. Whatever the precise chronology, Newton believed that sometime shortly after the fall of the corrupt (Trinitarian, Catholic) Church, Christ would return and set up a 1000-year Kingdom of God on earth. On page 144 of his Observations (1733), Newton cited Daniel 7:26-27 as evidence of this:

But the judgment shall sit, and they shall take away his dominion to consume and to destroy it unto the end. And the kingdom and dominion, and the greatness of the kingdom under the whole heaven, shall be given to the people of the saints of the most High, whose kingdom is an everlasting kingdom, and all dominions shall serve and obey him.

Newton espoused a premillenarian eschatology and thus held that Christ would return to earth to establish the Millennium.

Keith Katsikas is a loving husband and father of six who loves writing nearly as much as he enjoys watching his children grow and his beautiful wife smile.

Keith resides in New Hampshire, where he works as the Creative Director and Production Manager for a medical diagnostics and pharmaceutical resources company. Keith loves spending time with his family and is blessed with the ability to sharpen and fulfill his lifelong passion for writing and publishing.

Keith has been the President and CEO of several corporations throughout his 22 years of entrepreneurial enterprise and is currently the President and CEO of *TopShelf Indie Authors & Books, LLC,* owner of the *TopShelf Publishing* Imprint.